Guardian Angel Files:
Spirit's Bane

By Julie C. Gilbert

Aletheia Pyralis Publishers

http://www.juliecgilbert.com/
https://sites.google.com/view/juliecgilbert-writer/

Love Science Fiction or Mystery?

Choose your adventure!

Visit: http://www.juliecgilbert.com/

For details on getting
Ashlynn's Dreams and The Kiverson Case
absolutely free

Dedication:

To Amy, whose name means "Beloved"

Table of Contents:

Preface

Welcome to the story of two young guardian angels in training. Since you likely found this in the fiction section, I'm guessing you'll know it's a work of fiction. But I'd like to emphasize this fact. Where possible, I've based this off of Biblical understandings of angels and demons, but since not a whole lot is known for sure, I've also taken a ton of creative license with the concepts and made up the rest. For example, there's no Biblical evidence for the idea of demons being redeemed in any way, shape, or form. Also, angels are angels and humans are humans.

The story started with the idea of how many small things had to happen in order to meet somebody you know at a grocery store or pass them along the highway. Everybody's probably had a near miss. A deer crosses the road two inches before your car. This actually happened to me. I would have hit it harder than I did had I not been slowing down for a railroad track already. That poor deer probably has the sorest behind in the Garden State. Or you come down with a cold the day a tragic accident happens right at an intersection you sail through every day about the time you would've been there. The tale spiraled out from there.

I do not consider myself a student of philosophy, but I suppose from a certain point of view, life is philosophy. This book probably contains the deepest musings I've ever had on the weighty topics of life, death, the afterlife, angels, demons, purpose, destiny, sacrifice, peace, pain, duty, and hope.

It is my wish and prayer that herein you'll find both an entertaining story and an opportunity to think about spiritual matters. Questions and comments are always welcome, but I'm not looking for a fight. If fictional tales of angels and demons bother you, this might not be the best work of mine to sample. If you're curious but uncertain, pray for an open mind and heart as you read this adventure. (I can be reached at: Devyaschildren@gmail.com.)

Thank you for your time.

And now, allow me to present *Guardian Angel Files: Spirit's Bane*.

Part 1: Training

Prologue:
The Blessed Pair

To Than, whose name means "death" and "brilliant,"
Deimos reports that your commitment to our glorious cause lacks conviction. He's probably exaggerating, but I figured I'd check in anyway. He's very good at what he does, but he's not exactly the best mentor. Watch him and learn what you can, but save your questions for me or Daeva. She has more patience for new recruits. I occasionally fear her time amongst the Guardians will soften her, but she knows her duty.

I swore to the Dark Master that I would train you, so I will come to you soon. We take care of our own. That said, it may be some time before I reach you, hence sending this letter ahead of me. My plans for the Great War must be well underway before I can risk such a journey. Until I arrive, stand fast in your duties, even when you don't quite grasp why Deimos gives you the tasks he does. He acts with my authority and his plans are integral to my own. Obey him.

You have a commendable knack for noting important details, so let us discuss your report. Most of the names you've submitted have already been noted by others.

Gifted with physical strength and unwavering will, Valen is the obvious choice for trouble, but this pair you mention at the end concerns me. Kindred Spirit Bonds are rare, even amongst the Blessed. Do they know of the connection yet? Their friendship means they're already feeling the effects, but they could still be unaware.

Either way, I have adjusted my plan of attack. They must be separated because that bond will magnify any gifts they're given. I would have them killed if it would help, but that would only release the Kindred Spirit Bond to manifest in another pair. We must neutralize them a different way.

If we could convert them to our side, the Kindred Spirit Bond would serve the Dark Master well. That is your first task. I know you hate waiting and watching, but that is what I require at the moment. Observe this pair and continue reporting on their strengths and weaknesses. Tell me if they can be turned. If they can't, we will set our minds to their destruction.

Allister and Mina.

Their names do not tell me much about their futures. A "defender of man" can safeguard our human servants or those of the Light, and "love" is ordinary and unimaginative.

The boy is overconfident. That could be to our benefit, but not if he remains blinded by the Light. His inventiveness must be watched.

The girl can be overly cautious, but do not mistake caution for weakness. Those who think before they act typically have stronger reasons for behaving as they do.

The pair has yet to claim powers. We will be able to move forward once they manifest Gifts, but we may not have the luxury of waiting long.

Be prepared for my attack orders. Timing will be everything. I make my plans, but the Dark Master outranks me. If he wants the attack to commence immediately, I will obey, and so shall you, if you care for your fate.

There is no turning back. Traitors suffer. That is all you need to know.

If the Dark Master wishes to pit you against this pair, seek Deimos and Daeva. The three of you should be able to capture one of the Blessed Pair. Remember, if you capture both of them, take them to separate places. They are stronger together. Neutralizing one of them can greatly advance our cause. Do not take extra risks to obtain both.

I look forward to meeting you face-to-face.

Hadeon, Servant of the Dark Master,

Director of Operations

Chapter 1:
Caliana Kemp's Miserable Morning

Trainee Case Report #: AK-100
Case Agent: Mistress Adira Clarimond
Guardian Candidate: Allister Knight

Mistress Clarimond's sharp green eyes pin me to the hard plastic chair. She doesn't say anything just yet. I wish she would sit down and start firing the questions her ever-tightening lips are holding back. I can't tell what kind of mood she's in. Her lips angle down in disapproval but her eyes flit over the memory captures chronicling my most recent adventure. Long, slender fingers slowly flip through the images. I don't need to see the images. I can sense which ones she dwells upon at any given time. Before I can begin tormenting myself by reviewing the images again, she finally speaks.

"Are you pleased with the outcome of these matters, Master Knight?"

Well, that's a loaded question.

Am I pleased my charge is alive?

Absolutely.

Am I happy she landed in the hospital?

No.

Do I feel like the lousiest guardian angel ever created?

Yes.

Could I have done something to have prevented the attack on Caliana Kemp?

Julie C. Gilbert

Sure, but every other scenario got somebody killed. I worked pretty hard to get that outcome, which makes me feel worse, thank you very much.

I could have knocked Mina's charge, Mark Dyer, out and taken his place, but that would have delayed the confrontation a few days at the most. He's got dark brown hair and eyes while my natural human form tends toward deep blue eyes and what Mina calls "paper bag brown," but it's really more of a dark blond color. Changing my facial features to match his would have taken some concentration, but we had to let it happen like it did.

Didn't we?

"Allister." Mistress Clarimond softens her tone to something gentle and supportive yet still commanding. "I want to experience everything. Show me what happened today." She holds out her right hand toward me, palm up.

When I grip Mistress Clarimond's hand we're swept back through the vortex of my recent memories to this morning in the Kemp house. I take a moment to adjust to the chaotic glory and nod to Ranger as he follows Mr. Kemp out the garage door. Ranger ignores me, but I attribute that to him having bigger things on his mind than coddling the new guy. With his short, thin human form, Ranger slips from place to place gracefully. His dark skin enhances the air of mystery he likes to present. Someday, I can only hope to be worthy of guarding somebody important like—

"Focus," Mistress Clarimond orders.

"Right. Sorry. Here she comes."

As if waiting for my cue, Caliana Kemp sweeps into the room wearing a purple dress that gets an immediate frown from her mother.

"I thought you had a presentation today," Mrs. Kemp mutters, biting back the words she'd truly like to say.

"I do," snaps Caliana. Her tone drips with teenage superiority. She marches over to the Keurig and prepares a large cup of coffee to-go.

Mrs. Kemp just rolls her eyes and returns to putting the final touches on the three brown bag lunches that lay strewn across the countertops.

6

As Mistress Clarimond and I watch, my shadow-self—the version of me that exists when I'm present in a memory—quietly fiddles with Caliana's coffee cup.

Sensing the question before it can be asked, I explain my actions.

"Caliana's usually a heavy sleeper, and she was up late because of her presentation. Still, the garbage truck woke her up early. I knew if she caught the bus, she'd miss the encounter with Mark Dyer, so I helped her miss the bus."

"What's for lunch?" Caliana asks, picking up her coffee cup carefully and scanning the food stuffs scattered over the counter.

An ear-assaulting scream from Caliana's little brother seizes everybody's attention. I flinch in concert with my shadow-self.

Mrs. Kemp's frown deepens.

"Stop that," she scolds.

Oblivious to the disapproval, young Kieran Kemp scoops up a handful of lukewarm oatmeal and moves to hurl it at his mother. She catches his hand and holds it fast.

"Don't even think about it, mister."

The little boy winds himself up into a fine screaming fit, giving my shadow-self the opportunity to upend Caliana's coffee cup all over her precious dress. Her resulting scream covers the spectrum from surprise to shock to pain and finally lands on rage. For an instant she's torn between strangling her little brother and breaking down into a tearful fit of her own. Even though this is a memory, I reinforce the idea that she needs to change and get to school in time for her presentation. She settles on a murderous glance at Kieran and tosses her half-empty travel mug into the sink before quick-stepping it to the stairs.

"You caused quite the ruckus," remarks Mistress Clarimond.

I'm relieved to see a hint of amusement on her features.

As we wait for Caliana to return from the deep, dark jungles of her room, Mistress Clarimond and I survey the morning wreckage. My shadow-self ducks his head in chagrin. Much of the coffee landed on Caliana's shirt, but her reaction flung most of what was left onto the lunch fixings and her careless toss splashed the wall before breaking a plate in the sink. Mrs. Kemp would definitely have words about that later, but for now, Kieran had her full attention. Despite Mrs. Kemp's best efforts, Kieran's thrashing decorated both the nearby walls and his mother with oatmeal. For her part, Mrs. Kemp looks ready to throw up her hands and cry. Calmly, Mistress Clarimond closes her eyes and stretches forth her hands toward Kieran and Mrs. Kemp. To my surprise, the boy slowly subsides and Mrs. Kemp appears greatly strengthened.

"You can affect a memory?" My tone turns the exclamation into a question. I wanted to ask her a dozen more questions like whether or not reality was changed or just Mrs. Kemp's perception of that reality or even simply my perception of the events. I think Mistress Clarimond read the additional questions in my expression.

"Of course," Mistress Clarimond replies. "It's not much different than your Gift for thinking forward, just in a new direction. I've adjusted the way Mrs. Kemp recalls this morning's events so that there will be less frustration involved if she chooses to dwell on that time."

I hate to admit it, but that actually makes sense. Like most guardian angel candidates, I've been taught to think forward in time. Results definitely vary, and most angels can only think forward a few hours or a day or two. The only time I'd managed to think forward with any significance was five days ago when I glimpsed today in the possible futures set for Caliana. It's how I knew I needed to change the morning. When an angel thinks forward, we can manipulate small details and watch how the world changes in response. It gives us a slight advantage in fighting common calamities and demons.

Mistress Clarimond glances toward the microwave which proudly displays the time.

"So, you spilled the girl's coffee. What else did you do to delay her?"

"Nothing," I mumble, trying to keep my right foot from tapping impatiently.

A penetrating look from Mistress Clarimond demands elaboration. She follows this with a more direct prompt.

"Come now, you obviously took great pains to arrange

the timing. What other measures did you take?"

"I ... moved a cone during her driver's test yesterday. Just a little. She would have hit it anyway. I couldn't let her pass or she'd be able to drive on a provisional license today."

A small nod is all the response I get from Mistress Clarimond. Again, I cannot gauge her reaction well.

Caliana storms back into the kitchen.

"Mom, you need to take me to school. I'll never make the bus in time, and I can't be late."

Mrs. Kemp stops sorting broken pieces of glass in the sink. Even I can see her chest heaving from the effort to contain screams or sobs or both. Mistress Clarimond intervenes again to strengthen Mrs. Kemp's level of patience and sense of calm. I guiltily wonder how I missed her distress the first time.

"You were overly focused on your charge," Mistress Clarimond explains in answer to my unspoken question. "It's a mistake you'll learn to correct in time. Let us see how this plays out."

I hadn't realized the scene around us had paused. Once I release the unconscious lock, Caliana's short conversation with her mother continues.

Drawing a bracing breath, Mrs. Kemp issues a series of orders.

"Salvage what you can of the lunches and grab Kieran, then start the car and get the ice off of it. I'll finish with the glass here and take you to school."

The sight of the broken glass sobers Caliana with a well-placed shot of guilt. She meekly sets about carrying out the instructions. The plan unfolds with only the slight hitch of finding the car keys. Me and my shadow-self remember hiding the keys as a backup plan. Since the coffee ploy worked too well, the key contingency was unnecessary. We help Caliana locate the keys under the end table where they're usually stored. At last, the lunches are packed, Kieran's stuffed into his car seat, and they're finally off.

As we perch on top of the car along with my shadow-self, I explain that it was this point when I realized Caliana might arrive too late to meet Mark.

"Your control over the lights is ... admirable," comments

Mistress Clarimond.

I indulge in a smidgen of pride at the compliment.

"Master Sasha taught Valen, Mina, and me how to manipulate lights. We've been practicing for a while."

"Oh, what else has Master Sasha been teaching you?"

A sharp right turn saves me from Mistress Clarimond's question because we had to concentrate on clinging to the car. A fall from a moving vehicle would not have hurt us like it would a human, but it's still an unpleasant experience. Master Sasha taught Valen, Mina, and I about that too, but I didn't offer that information.

Valen's kind of the perfect student. He started at the Academy at the same time as Mina and I did, but he's progressed through the program much faster than we have. That's why he got to go on the field trip with the previous cohort. I don't care. We definitely have more fun than he does.

Upon arrival at the school, Caliana leaps from the car, tosses a quick thank you to her mother, and bolts for the door. My shadow-self pauses long enough to make sure Caliana's mother sees the lunch bag that got left behind and dashes off in hot pursuit. I prepare to follow them, but Mistress Clarimond snaps her fingers and we're suddenly in the hallway ten feet from where Caliana faces an awkward young man brandishing a wicked-looking knife at a pack of three burly guys.

"Not impressed by your toy, fairy-boy," says the leader. He leans against a locker and folds his arms across his chest. "But props for bringing it."

"Do you even know how to use that piece of hardware, son?" asks one of the tough guys, purposefully deepening his voice and drawing his shoulders back like he imagines a TV-cop would.

"G-g-go away!" cries Mark Dyer.

The tough guys laugh at his stutter, but Caliana steps forward.

"What's going on here?"

"Not your concern, Kemp," sneers the lead bully. "Don't you have a loser to tutor or something?"

Caliana catches sight of the knife.

"Mark!" she hisses. "Put that away before somebody

catches you with it."

"I-I'm t-t-tired of—" Mark begins.

One of the bullies moves behind Caliana and crouches down until his head barely rises above her left shoulder.

"W-w-will y-y-you protect me, little Cali?"

This earns a round of laughter from the other two bullies.

Stepping to her right, Caliana turns to the kid ducking behind her.

"Knock it off, Tony. This isn't funny. Principal Bates—"

"PB's full of—"

An enraged cry erupts from Mark a split-second before he opens his switchblade and lunges at Tony. The blade catches Tony's left arm, releasing a thin line of blood and a loud stream of curses. Stunned, the other two boys can only stare. Mark presses the attack, barreling into Tony and knocking him flat against the lockers. Winded, Tony slides to the ground, clutching at his wounded arm. Mark's knife hand whips toward the fallen boy, but Caliana steps in front of Tony. Recognition fires to life behind Mark's eyes and he tries to stop his swing, but it's too late. The knife strikes Caliana on the left side, just below her ribs. She squeaks with surprise and pain, and seems to faint from shock. In truth, I knocked her out myself to keep her from panicking.

Before Tony and his moral support can regain their wits, the memory form of my tiny friend, Mina, comes flying down the hall with two teachers in her wake. Her shoulder length black hair streams behind her like a small flag. Her intense eyes fix on Caliana with concern.

Not wishing to watch the chaotic scene again, I allow the memory to fade. Mistress Clarimond and I are back in the debriefing room, staring at each other.

Before Mistress Clarimond can prod me to finish the account, I say, "I stayed with my charge until the doctor said she was stable. The wound wasn't that deep, but she lost a lot of blood before anybody thought to get her the proper care. The teachers had their hands full keeping the bullies from beating Mark to death. The ambulance didn't get called until Cali's mother arrived late with her lunch."

"What do you think of Mina's actions?"

The question startles me enough that I can't think to shade the truth even if I want to present my friend in the best light possible.

"I think she did fine."

"Really? She let her volatile charge bring a knife to school and left him in the midst of three unpleasant young men. Do you think either choice was wise?" Mistress Clarimond plants both hands on the table and drills me with another questioning gaze.

"She went for help," I answer, melting under the harsh glare. "She and I thought forward several scenarios. In every other situation, one of those bullies gets killed or Mark dies by his own hand. If she took his knife, he'd have used scissors or his father's gun. We didn't want it to happen this way, but it was the only way they could all live!"

Silence fills the tiny debriefing room.

Mistress Clarimond slowly straightens and smiles in a self-satisfied way.

"I agree. Well done, Master Knight. You've taken the first step into the murky business of truly being a guardian angel. Send in Lady Mina and go encourage your charge. I'll send Mina to fetch you in a few hours."

Chapter 2:
Mark's Guilt

Trainee Case Report #: MN-100
Case Agent: Mistress Adira Clarimond
Guardian Candidate: Mina Nadir

Being a guardian angel is about making tough decisions. Today, my dear friend Allister Knight and I made one such decision. We chose to allow the young man under my care to stab the young woman under Allister's care. I do not know how that action will be perceived by Mistress Clarimond and the rest of the Council of Light. She is reviewing the case with Allister now. If he cannot provide satisfactory answers, I must be prepared with adequate reasoning to defend our decision.

I wish another plan had presented itself, but at least nobody perished in the heat of the moment. I know Allister helped speed Caliana along to unconsciousness, but she must have felt some pain. Most of my willpower went into suppressing the instincts of the three boys who had been taunting Mark. My other task had been to fetch help, which I did. We were almost too late, but the two teachers I'd driven from their rooms helped tremendously with the boys.

My client, Mark Dyer, now faces a different foe than this morning. I just hope he can hold out long enough for me to stand with him when the guilt sinks in fully. Sloth demons will haunt him for sure. I long to go to him, but I was asked to wait. Allister would probably go anyway, but I'd prefer to act with the

Council's blessing rather than defy them in this.

Allister doesn't understand why I refer to the people we protect as clients. He often reminds me that they don't pay us for protection, but I maintain that they were bought with a price. Sometimes I think he might have acclimated too well to human life. Before entering the Academy of Light's Response to Spreading Darkness—better known as the "Academy"—every guardian angel candidate must spend at least a month on Earth in human form.

Some angels like to experiment with their features, but Allister's always known his mind. He's very comfortable as a lanky teenage boy with messy light-colored hair that covers more of his forehead than it probably ought to. During our stay on Earth, we're not allowed to practice any of our Gifts. Allister relished that time, but I couldn't wait to return to the Heavens. He teases me about the height I've chosen, but I see no reason to tower over others or stand out in any other way. I prefer staying in the background.

It's not that I dislike Earth. I do want to work there after all, but when I become a full Guardian, I will be able to use my Gifts to help people. I won't have to stand by and let the demons terrorize people at will. We were observers only, not given the authority to combat wrongs. It was heartbreaking but enlightening.

I witnessed a Despair demon torment a young mentally handicapped boy. It made me sick at heart to do nothing but file a report. Now that I'm past that, I will never fail to act again.

It offends my sensibilities that demons were angels before their transformations. Dark angels are those who maintain much of their former appearance when they walked the Way of Light. Who could choose evil like that? I've got an essay to write on the subject later, but I can't wrestle with the issue just now. I must decide how to handle Mark when I'm allowed to go to him.

He has secretly loved Caliana Kemp for a few years, but he's so shy and withdrawn that he's not confronted any of the rumors the bullies started. For that matter, I'm not sure he's recently had a meaningful conversation with anybody who wasn't online or family. That's got to change. People think guardian angels only care about the client's personal physical safety, but mind, body, spirit, and soul share a much closer link than most like to admit. Caring for the person means guarding the four parts of their being equally.

This morning, Allister and I concerned ourselves mainly with seeing that everybody survived the school confrontation, but the real work's barely begun. Despair might be the obvious enemy Mark will be facing, but other major demons like Guilt, Anger, Fear, and Pride, may also show up. At the very least, they will send lesser demonic minions to carry out their will, assailing my charge with these negative emotions.

I almost dare to hope Mark's too insignificant in the grand scheme of things to bother attacking with every weapon at the enemy's disposal, but that logic is flawed and futile. Every life matters to the Glorious King, so it must be for us too. Some angels were created to praise, others to build, and still others to guard. If the Glorious King gives you a task, you'd do well to see it through.

"You've served your time. Ready to head back out and face down the demons?" Allister asks. He leans back against the open door and crosses his arms and feet like he hasn't a care in the world. His flippant attitude is irksome, but truthfully, I've been eager to go for hours. Allister turns everything into a lighthearted matter. That makes him great at lifting spirits, but I'm not sure he's capable of taking anything seriously.

"How did Mistress Clarimond take our ... actions?" I wonder, slipping past him into the hallway leading to the elevators.

We don't really need the elevators if we want to return to Earth, but they're useful for reaching a specific location. There are enough angels about with the Gift of teleportation that we could always find somebody to take us where we wish.

Allister shrugs in a way that doesn't really answer the question one way or the other.

"She said she wanted to see you," he says lazily.

I halt mid-step.

"Why didn't you tell me that right away?" I demand.

Without waiting for an answer, I turn around and head for Mistress Clarimond's office. Being friends with Allister means it's a familiar path to me, though to be fair only most of our adventures are solely his fault.

"I'll see you down there!" he calls cheerily.

I pause outside Mistress Clarimond's door to take a calming breath and gather my scattered thoughts. She's probably seen everything, but I need to at least attempt to look composed. My polite knock prompts an invitation to enter. I've not done anything wrong this time, but my body displays signs of stress anyway. I'm still in human form because I expect to go back soon. There's no need to change the persona now. Mistress Clarimond has already seen me at my best and worst.

"Thank you for coming, Lady Mina." Mistress Clarimond motions for me to take a seat. "Don't worry. Master Allister has provided an adequate outline of the Kemp case. I wanted to ask you for an analysis of Mark Dyer's mental state before sending you back into the fray."

Relief wraps around me like a warm cloak.

"I don't know," I admit. "I believe he'll be okay, but the violence has shaken him."

"Shall we go to him?" asks Mistress Clarimond.

"Now?" It's a stupid question, but it's all I've got. Getting to Mark has been my desire, but I imagined going there with Allister, not one of the Council of Light members. I swallow my surprise, and my cheeks flush at having dismissed my client. I'd been guilty of the very thing that led Mark to his current path.

"Every life is precious, Mina," Mistress Clarimond says gently. "Each of them deserves our complete attention."

I bow and absorb the mild rebuke. When I look up again, I'm standing in a hospital room inches from a softly sobbing woman. I step back, and Mistress Clarimond neatly fills the space. She kneels beside the woman and places one hand on her left shoulder. Leaning close, she whispers in the woman's ear. The woman nods and shifts in the chair, shutting her eyes to rest. The woman is clearly Mark's mother. They have the same shade of dark brown hair.

A question burns within me, but I have enough tact to keep it there. Probably reading my expression, Mistress Clarimond answers the question anyway.

"I've simply urged her soul to rest for the short time we'll be here."

Nodding like a bobblehead doll, I file the information away. None of us students know every one of Mistress Clarimond's Gifts. Trying to guess them has become a challenge undertaken by most of the students who pass through the Academy.

"Shall we wake him?" she inquires, motioning to Mark.

In sleep, he looks peaceful. Waking him is a slight cruelty, but I'd rather he and I face whatever demons should come together than have them show up while I'm off-duty. In a case like this, Mark will have around-the-clock protection until it's determined that he's no longer at risk of harming himself or those around him.

Still, I started this. I should complete what I can.

"Mark," I call, leaning over him. I keep my voice low, even though he won't hear the exact words anyway. Only a few people can hear when an angel speaks like this. In certain circumstances, we're allowed to communicate with humans verbally, but mostly, we stick to this sort of soul-speech. After two seconds, I repeat his name several more times.

As he awakens, Mark slowly shakes his head and moans.

"Caliana!" he snaps awake with the word.

I move back instinctively, though even if our foreheads connect, he wouldn't feel much except a brief puff like wind blowing across his face.

"She's all right, Mark," I assure him. "She's going to pull through. You can still make this right with her."

He looks around wildly like he's hearing voices in his head.

I shoot a nervous glance at Mistress Clarimond, but she merely looks intrigued. That's not exactly encouraging.

"Got to get to Caliana," Mark mutters.

"Whoa! Not a good idea," I protest. "She might not … be up for company." I was about to say she might not want to see him before remembering I was there to encourage and uplift, not highlight his stupidity.

"You're the last person she's gonna want to see," says the Guilt demon, right on schedule.

"Go away," I say. I don't really expect him to heed the order, but there are certain formalities that must be observed

17

before any real conflict can be entertained.

"Lookee, lookee, I found a sweet little cookie," drawls the demon. He spins around. Now, he's wearing a beige trench coat and has a matching hat pulled low over his face. "Why all alone, sweetheart." He doffs the cap at me.

"Wrong decade, creep. Nobody uses the term 'cookie' anymore." I resist the urge to look around for Mistress Clarimond, but I sense he's right, I am alone. "And I'm *never* alone!" I put extra emphasis on the never to convince myself and the demon. "You have no claim here."

The demon conjures a lit cigar and takes a few drags on it before leaving it hanging from the corner of his mouth.

"Now, see. There's where you're wrong, sweetie. This kid's gonna deal with me for a good long time." The Guilt demon's speech is drawn out by the need to speak around the cigar. He takes the cigar out long enough to add, "Be a dear and be on your way. I want no trouble with your ilk today."

"You can't have him," I argue.

"I see no seal upon his brow," the demon points out. "That means he's unclaimed. I've as much right to be here as you do, baby angel." He smiles in a completely unnerving manner. "And while you seem to be alone, I brought company. Would you like to meet them?"

He grabs me and spins me around. His left arm wraps tightly around my waist, and pulls me close. He's wearing black gloves and long, dark sleeves so that he's not really touching me, but our cheeks are near each other.

"You know them as Destruction and Madness," the Guilt demon hisses directly into my ear. "They wanted to play with your friend here, but I'm sure they'll take the time to get to know you better."

Before I can hesitate, I jerk my head into the Guilt demon. Our faces touch for the briefest moment, and we both cry out. My face feels like it's been dipped in acid. He reacts by pushing me away. Anticipating the move, I spin and prepare to face the Destruction and Madness demons. They're across the room. Destruction holds the form of a sullen teenage girl dressed head to toe in black with long, stringy hair and eyes that aren't quite right. Madness manifests as a drooling, growling Doberman pincer wearing a spiky collar. Both glare at me malevolently but they don't move.

Then, I see her. Mistress Clarimond hovers above Mark's bed, sword drawn but not pointed anywhere in particular.

How did I miss seeing her?

The Guilt demon scuttles over to stand by his comrades.

"You cannot always protect him. We will return."

With that declaration, the three demons disappear.

I stare stupidly at the spot where they'd vanished, cheek still burning.

A cool hand falls upon my face, but I flinch away from Mistress Clarimond's touch.

"Let me heal that, Mina," she orders.

I didn't even see her move to put away her sword let alone come to my side.

The struggle to hold in tears takes a lot of effort, but I find the strength to explain myself.

"Leave it. I need the reminder."

Drawing even closer, Mistress Clarimond catches my head in both of her hands.

"You may keep the scar if you wish, but let me take away the pain." Her gaze is so intense that I can't even begin to consider disobeying.

Tears fall as Mistress Clarimond closes her eyes and initiates the healing process. A feeling like a cooling salve touches my cheek, driving off the fiery pain. It's done in moments. I catch sight of my face in a mirror hanging across the room. She left a bright red slash in place.

"You've been marked by Guilt, but it will fade eventually. Until that time, remember this moment." Mistress Clarimond's green eyes look like they want to say more, but she only looks to Mark. "Stay with him if you wish. I doubt the demons will return tonight, but call Allister if they do. Nobody should face them alone, but you were right: you are never alone."

She disappears instantly, but I leave the scene frozen for a few more seconds, taking the time to study Mark. Does he realize everything that's just happened? We've won a victory for his soul, but this was only a skirmish. There's a long war ahead for everybody.

Chapter 3:
Field Trip

Trainee Case Report #: AK-101
Case Agent: Mistress Adira Clarimond
Guardian Candidate: Allister Knight

Today, we're going on a tour of the world's forests. It's hard to work up great enthusiasm. I understand plants help shape the world, but when am I ever going to use this in my future? While waiting for the elevator that will take us to the field trip, I think about my friend.

Mina's been quiet the last few days. I mean more quiet than usual. She's weird. I mean, she'll go through these long periods of almost complete silence then want to talk for hours. The battle with those demons in Mark Dyer's room shook her up. We train every day for such encounters. I saw the memory captures. She did fine, great even, and Mistress Clarimond would never have let her come to harm.

I wish I'd been there.

Turns out Caliana didn't really need me. Her mother kept her surrounded with a nice, thick blanket of protection prayers, heard and acknowledged by the Glorious King. Mina claims the prayers are meant to enhance our protection, not substitute for it. Technically, she's correct, but what demon would mess with someone surrounded by that much light? They hate prayers and the fact that the King always hears and answers them.

"Some of you may think you have no use for the things

we're about to explore today," says Ranger. His voice isn't loud, but it is commanding. I respect Ranger, but that doesn't mean I want to follow in his footsteps. He draws awesome protection details, but he also spends most of his time wandering one heavily wooded place or another.

Mina's look tells me she knows the comment's directed at me.

"You are wrong," Ranger continues. He stares deeply at each of us in turn.

Besides Mina and me there's only Adelmo, Aderes, and Osmund. I stare back, but the others avert their gazes or nod solemn agreement. Mina doesn't seem to notice he's even speaking. She's wearing her glazed look this morning.

"The natural world offers more than simple beauty and danger." Ranger's words move faster as he warms to the subject. "There's a complexity that declares the Glorious King's handiwork. If you can understand and appreciate the lessons available in the forests, you can gain insight into the hearts of mankind and every living creature that moves on the Earth."

"Will we get to see any creatures today?" asks Aderes. Her eyes light up with the possibility. I don't know her very well, but given her enthusiasm, I'd say there's a good chance she would happily follow a path similar to Ranger's.

"Will we see any demons?" Adelmo wonders. "I want to fight a demon like Mina did." He looks at her adoringly.

I steal a glance at Mina to gauge her reaction, but she's still ignoring everybody.

"Do not seek conflict, young one," says Ranger. Seeing Adelmo sag at this statement, he adds, "Enough of it will find you in time. That is a lesson nature can show you."

In the blink of an eye, we're standing in a forest wearing our temperate weather street clothes. One of the first things guardian angel candidates learn to do is arrange suitable clothes to wear when visiting the natural world. It wouldn't do for a human to see us in our true spirit forms. That would probably frighten most of them.

Aderes and Adelmo beam with excitement. Osmund rights the glasses he wears. I like that about him. He doesn't need glasses, but he enjoys the feel of them. Nothing anybody says to him can convince him it's pointless. Mina remains impassive, of course. I knew Ranger was powerful, but few beings can teleport this many others with them at one time, especially without touching them. The thrill of adventure shoots through me. Maybe this field trip won't be so bad.

"Where are we?" Aderes whispers the question with awe, staring up at the enormous trees around us.

The answer comes to me even as Ranger explains.

"We're in the Giant Sequoia National Monument in the state of California, along the western edge of the United States."

The place is aptly named. Standing on the ground and looking straight up the side of one tree trunk, I'm not sure I can see the top. If I spread my arms wide, I might be able to encompass about an eighth of the tree trunk.

"They're beautiful!" Aderes exclaims. Tears of wonder glisten in her blue eyes.

I think she's only a year younger than Mina and me, but times like this make me feel ancient. I agree that the forest is quite impressive, but I'm just not moved by it in the same way Aderes seems to be. Is there something wrong with me?

"Something's wrong," Mina says.

"What?" I ask, though I think I just barely beat Adelmo and Osmund to the question.

Ranger nods slowly and waves for Mina to explain, but she only shrugs and frowns.

"Touch the tree," Ranger instructs.

Dutifully, we obey. When my fingers brush the rough bark, my stomach twists, and I jerk my hand away.

Adelmo yelps and pulls back his hand.

"What was that?" he demands, voicing the question I want to ask.

"The tree is in pain," Osmund notes. His jaw clenches, but he keeps his palm firmly placed against the tree trunk. "Spiritual pain."

I draw breath to tell him trees don't have feelings, but once again, Osmund's quicker.

"I thought trees didn't have spirits?" His inflection makes it a question, which he directs to Ranger with his gaze.

"Trees do not have souls like humans or angels, but every

living thing contains a spirit," Ranger explains. "Even the beasts are susceptible to disease and spiritual rot. What you feel is demonic effort to pervert what our Glorious King made grand and good. We're here to correct that."

I look to Mina and she glares back.

"Stop watching me," she growls. "I'm fine."

I grin. The anger's better than the cold distance I've gotten for the past few days.

"Why would they bother?" Adelmo crosses his arms, not quite ready to reach for the tree again. "Aren't there more important targets for them to torment?"

"Let's invite the demon out of the tree to ask," I say, only half in jest.

Ranger clears his throat.

"There's not just one demon in there. What we'll face is a legion. That is why I brought all of you."

Best field trip ever.

My fingers itch to summon my sword, Tyre, from the Heavens. That's another trick we learn early on. We can keep it in our quarters in the Heavens or choose a spot in the Veil, the land between, to store our weapons.

"You may draw your swords, but we're going to try a rebuke first," says Ranger.

The excitement of willing Tyre to appear keeps me from voicing my doubts about a rebuke actually working. I'm told some demons can be reasoned with, but I much prefer the direct approach. They chose their side in this war. They ought to deal with the consequences. No tales have been told of demons returning from their chosen path, but there's much of the Prince's story we do not know. He was a human at one time, I know that for sure, but did he also spend time as an ordinary angel? I can't dwell on such things right now. Besides, I have no way of knowing the heart and soul of any being, be they angel, demon, or human. Ultimately, the Glorious King knows these things. I can only do my small part, and for the moment, that means fighting these demons here and now.

A gray mist suddenly surrounds us when we enter a space in between the realms. To us, the gray mist is the only change. Should a human stumble upon us, they would merely see a bunch of teenagers and a man staring up at a big tree.

Mina's standing on my right with Kentaro held in a comfortable two-handed hold. I admire the smooth, clean edges of the katana. Were it a normal, man-made sword, she might have fallen over from the weight of it, but as a spirit sword, anybody could handle it with ease. Mina's pretty good with that weapon at least in dueling circumstances. We've only recently started our practical lessons. This will be our first real conflict, if it turns into such. I'm hoping it does.

I haven't met the others' weapons, but Aderes holds a stubby little dagger and Adelmo waves about a sword much like Tyre. To my surprise, Osmund wears a quiver across his back and has one nocked arrow pointed toward the ground at a ready position. Few opt for arrows for they take a lot of patience to master, but I'm not surprised Osmund's chosen the unconventional weapon.

"Legion, come forth, we wish to speak with you," calls Ranger, once we're in position.

Mina and I line up left of Ranger while the other three line up on his right.

After a long wait, a squirrel with glowing red eyes descends from high up in the tree. It halts about twenty feet above our heads and glares at us defiantly. It starts chattering angrily at us, but Ranger draws his shoulders back and shouts.

"Release that creature!"

The crack of command in Ranger's voice makes me stand up a little taller.

"Go away!" The voice that speaks has no ring that would identify it as male or female, and thankfully, it doesn't come from the squirrel this time. It seems to come from the mist surrounding the tree.

"This forest is under the protection of the Glorious King. Leave it at once," says Ranger.

The mist twists into a broad cord that snaps out and knocks Aderes over. Her surprised cry gets drowned by outraged shouts from the rest of us.

A chorus of evil laughter fills the air. More mist forms itself into cords that hang over us ready to strike. Different mist arranges itself into the shape of a woman's face at Ranger's eye level in the tree.

"What can you do with these angelings, Brother of Light?" asks the mist woman.

The face twists, goes blank, and reforms as a man's face.

"A better question would be what can *we* do *to* these angelings, Brother?"

Aderes is almost back on her feet now, but suddenly, mist winds around her wrists and ankles. She's held aloft inches above the forest floor, but before the mist can completely bind her, Mina and I cut through the cords. Once free, Aderes flings her dagger at the mist demon's face.

The demon moves, and because Aderes is controlling it, the dagger mimics its upward movement before lodging in the tree.

"Enough!" Ranger's voice causes us to freeze.

The male mist face smirks.

"You missed, girl."

Dropping to her knees, Aderes folds her hands and leans forward.

"She wasn't aiming for you," says Mina.

"But I will," declares Osmund, drawing back the arrow attached to his bow. "Obey my commander and leave or prepare to fight."

With shrieking cries that might have damaged human ears, demons pour out of the tree. Instinctively, I step in front of Aderes and nearly run into Mina who's doing the same. After a moment of awkwardness, we turn our backs to each other and slash at the nearest mist forms aiming for Aderes.

Hacking and slashing consume my attention for a time. A battle sense honed early during our education keeps us from slicing each other. Ranger kneels behind Aderes and places both hands on her shoulders. Osmund guards the area behind Ranger with an impressive display of well-aimed shots and the occasional slash with the longbow itself.

The demons materialize just enough to hold substance in this thin layer above the natural world. Some form recognizable creatures, but most keep to their mist forms—small, feral beings that vaguely resemble humans with sharp teeth and claws, glowing red eyes, and pointy ears.

One dives at my face, and I spear his left shoulder with my spirit sword. He shrieks and dissolves into angry, black smoke. The damage resets him, casting the demon back to point of origin where he decided to follow the Prince of Darkness. Immortal creatures are understandably very difficult to erase from the universe. I have no way of knowing if the comalike state will last minutes, days, years, or centuries, but at least he's out of this fight.

The battle ends with the demons in full retreat. When I get a moment to reflect, I notice Aderes still hasn't moved. A faint beam of light shines between her and the dagger still lodged in the tree. The light now surrounds the lower half of the tree, wrapping completely around the trunk. With the demons gone, the process goes faster, and the glowing barrier shoots up the rest of the tree, surrounding it with tiny golden threads.

I help Aderes to her feet. She thanks me and retrieves her dagger from the tree. The golden light blinks but then shines brighter.

"Our work here is finished," says Ranger. "Well done."

Chapter 4:
Provocation as Protection

Trainee Case Report #: MN-101
Case Agent: Mistress Adira Clarimond
Guardian Candidate: Mina Nadir

Ranger sends us back to the Academy while he stays behind to tend to the newly freed tree. Allister and Osmund beg for permission to stay and help further, but Ranger insists we were expected back long ago. A check of internal time confirms this. The fight seemed only seconds—maybe minutes—in length, but six hours have passed since we left. Ranger might have moved us forward in time purposefully before the fight even began, but I think it more likely, the battle for the tree took hours. I've heard spiritual struggles can sometimes ignore conventions of time, but if that is what happened, this would be my first experience with it.

Mistress Clarimond meets us at the elevator. Her gaze sweeps over us. Her expression tells me she's not surprised to see us as we are, and a frown conveys her disapproval.

Guilt and pride ripple across us.

"Who would like to report?" Mistress Clarimond inquires.

We all begin speaking at once.

"One at a time, if you please," instructs Mistress Clarimond. She raises her hands in a calming gesture. "Master Allister?"

"We fought demons!" My friend trembles with

excitement, and his eyes dance with delight.

"What brought you across the path of demons?" Mistress Clarimond's voice remains level, but her stance has stiffened.

"They were tormenting an old tree, and Ranger thought we should free it," Allister explains.

"Were we wrong, Mistress?" The tentative question sounds especially innocent coming from Aderes.

"Oh, I don't know about wrong, dear one," says Mistress Clarimond with a small sigh. "Foolish perhaps, but it is done. What did you learn from the experience?"

Relief washes over me, and I see the others visibly relax. We turn to Aderes and wait for her answer.

"Provocation can be protection." Aderes pitches her voice high and clear.

I'm impressed—and unnerved—by the logic. My mind flies to the hundreds of ways that line of thought can lead to abuse.

Adelmo bobs his head in agreement, but Osmund shakes his head vigorously. Allister and I exchange questioning glances.

"Osmund, you voiced the challenge that sparked that fight." Aderes's tone takes on an earnest quality that begs to be understood.

"I did?" Osmund sounds embarrassed.

"You threw a dagger first," Allister points out. "I'd call that a bit more aggressive than Osmund's words."

Aderes shrugs.

"So I did," she admits, "and it was Master Ranger who brought us there with the intent of fighting the demons. That is my point. Our presence was provocation, but it was meant to protect. Good came out of it. Doesn't that make it all right?"

Her reasoning makes sense, but it also makes me queasy.

"Maybe it was their presence that provoked us," Adelmo offers. "They're not supposed to inhabit the living plants and creatures."

"They're not supposed to exist either," Allister notes impatiently. "Demons were angels."

"They *are* angels, just fallen ones," I say.

Mistress Clarimond raises a hand to cut off further debate.

"Regardless of who prodded whom first, I'm glad you're

all safe. Master Ranger made a judgment call in this case." Her eyes sought Aderes and stayed fixed on her. "The wisdom of his decision was born out this time, but be cautious of how you apply that lesson. We are in the midst of a larger war. We have enough to deal with without seeking conflict."

"You're saying we can attack to protect?" Allister challenges.

"I'm saying that should not be your first instinct, Master Allister," Mistress Clarimond replies. "Time and circumstances may make such a decision necessary, but while you are being trained in these halls, please refrain from extraneous engagements with demons." Despite the overly-formal wording and general stiffness in her posture, I sense Mistress Clarimond's amusement and exasperation.

We collectively nod to acknowledge the order.

"May we go now, Mistress?" Aderes wonders.

"Yes, you three may go." Mistress Clarimond waves to indicate Aderes, Adelmo, and Osmund. "Eat, rest, and prepare a report for me. I want to know what else you learned on the field trip."

In spirit form angels do not need to eat, but while in training, we spend much time in our human forms. Therefore, we keep to human conventions like sleep and regular meals. With sympathetic glances cast our way, the three younger angels swiftly retreat.

Allister straightens his shoulders, a subtle thing he does every time he expects to be explaining himself, which is a lot.

"How did they do?" Mistress Clarimond's question surprises us into a long silence. "Come now, you two are never at a loss for words, and you have more raw talent for combat skills than those three."

"I … thought you didn't approve," Allister notes cautiously.

"I don't," Mistress Clarimond agrees. "I wouldn't exactly be doing my job if I condoned throwing trainees into battles of that length or scale."

Allister appears confused.

"The battle took several hours," I tell him.

"Oh, wow. Is that why I'm so hungry?"

"You're always hungry," I remind him.

"Would you like to retire to a classroom?" asks Mistress Clarimond. "I can summon refreshments while you describe your impressions of the others' actions."

"I didn't really notice much," I admit, shrugging apologetically. "Allister usually has the better Battle Sense."

Mistress Clarimond focuses on Allister expectantly.

"Aderes made the strongest connection to the local prayer warriors," Allister begins. "Her dagger pierced the heart of the tree from the beginning. I think she would have fought even if the demons surrendered and agreed to leave."

I wonder when he had time to make those observations.

"What of Adelmo's performance?" prompts Mistress Clarimond.

"Adelmo's an average fighter," Allister reports. "He's quick, but rash with his strikes. The same could be said for Osmund, but his few mistakes stemmed from hesitation not haste, as was the case with Adelmo."

"How do you know?" I demand. "You were fighting by my side nearly the whole time."

"As you said, Lady Mina, Battle Sense is a Gift Master Allister possesses. Do you have anything to add to his account?"

"Ranger held back." I feel the truth of this resonate within me. "He fought fiercely, but we saw little of his Gifts. He left most of the fighting to us but remained close throughout. We were never in any real danger."

"The danger is always real, Lady Mina," Mistress Clarimond says solemnly. "It only takes one lucky strike for an enemy to triumph. Do not mistake experience and power for invincibility. Every one of us could fall in this war."

"But we'd be reborn, right?" Allister's worried look says he's suddenly having doubts about what we've been taught since childhood. "We're immortal."

"Souls are immortal, Master Allister, but bodies are not." Mistress Clarimond offers us a small smile. "Angels tend to be heartier than humans, but death can find us. Some have chosen to become mortal, and others have had that choice made for them."

The words send a chill through my whole being.

"We can be made mortal." The words come out of my

lips, but they do not make much sense. "How?" I hardly dare to breathe the question.

"That is knowledge best left untouched for the moment," Mistress Clarimond notes. "You're in no danger of such here. Try not to worry. My warning is simply a plea for caution."

"How can we protect others if we're not willing to take risks?" Allister wonders.

I stare at him in shock. He has always had a defiant streak, but he rarely openly challenges Council members.

"You have to take risks, but try not to make them reckless ones." Mistress Clarimond's tone starts out brisk and defensive but soon softens. "Allister. Allister. Do you know what your name means?"

"Defender of man," he supplies, looking puzzled.

"Defender," she repeats. "Not aggressor."

"But what if I have to strike first?" Allister presses.

"I hope you never have to make that choice," Mistress Clarimond replies. "If you're truly worried about making the wrong decision, seek extra measures of wisdom."

"I … don't want to bother the King." Allister's cheeks redden.

"The Glorious King wants to be 'bothered' with the concerns of his people, both humans and angels." Mistress Clarimond's smile reaches her eyes, and she includes me in the conversation by taking one of my hands. Her cool, soothing touch immediately puts me at ease. She also picks up one of Allister's hands. "Humans have much of His love, not all of it."

I nod absently, hearing the words but not quite comprehending them.

"Will we be able to go on more field trips with Ranger?" Allister wonders.

"Would you like to?" Mistress Clarimond's tone indicates she already knows his answer, and her eyes probe mine, but I have no answer. "There may not be time in your schedules. You will need to experience the other aspects soon and make your career choices."

The news sails through me until I catch sight of Allister's stunned expression. His chest swells with anticipation and delight.

"The Council believes you both are ready to move on."

Mistress Clarimond's words are ones we've hoped to hear for a long time. Most candidates in our cohort have already entered the next phase, but we've had our share of troubles. Allister likes to improvise, and for some reason, I nearly always follow his unique ideas.

"Report to Master Blaz tomorrow in the arena for a more thorough lesson on weapons than you've experienced thus far," commands Mistress Clarimond. "He will also fill in the blanks concerning our history. When the lessons with Master Blaz conclude, prepare a report for me on what it means to be a guardian angel."

Her last instruction deflates Allister a tad, but he bows acceptance of the tasks.

"You may then move on to the trials."

These words reignite the enthusiasm inside of my friend.

"Go join the others, you've earned a rest."

Chapter 5:
Weapons

Trainee Case Report #: AK-102
Case Agent: Master Blaz
Guardian Candidate: Allister Knight

I hate studying, but Mina made me look up where we were going. Said it would be "good for me." Our new home away from the Heavens is located in the big, fat state of New York on the East Coast side of the United States. It keeps to Eastern Standard Time. People there drive crazy.

Anyway, Mina and I arrive at the arena early, eager to begin our weapons training with Master Blaz. Mistress Clarimond had neglected to dictate a time, but when I returned to my room, I found a formal order on the message board outlining the time to arrive as six o'clock the next morning.

Speaking of other trainees, I've never seen the arena this empty. Usually there's at least one overachiever training, dueling, or exercising at all hours. Mina and I pause in the threshold and stare at the huge, empty space.

"We're not too early, are we?" Mina wonders. "Where is everybody?"

"I'm not sure," I answer, even though I know she's not really expecting me to reply. Taking one cautious step forward, I nearly run into Master Blaz who grabs my shoulders before I can leap backward.

"Just on time, Master Knight," greets Blaz. "Steady

there." He's probably the youngest faculty member and the coolest in my opinion. From the first time we met, he insisted we call him Blaz when not in the presence of a Council member. If rumors pan out, he'll be a Council member himself very soon. Releasing my shoulders, he bows to Mina. "Welcome to the Earth-side counterpart of our illustrious Academy campus. We call this campus Basileia."

"Why?" I knew the word meant "kingdom" in Greek, but I wasn't sure why the sudden need for individuality. In the Heavens, all guardian angel training programs are part of the one official Academy. I wasn't sure why places on Earth needed new names.

"Why what?" Blaz gives me a puzzled look.

"Why the new name?" I clarify.

"It's not a new name. It's an old name." A glint in Blaz's blue eyes shows amusement, but a smile lets me know he's not dismissing the concern. "We're not home anymore, but there's always power in names. This one reminds us that the kingdom is never far."

"How long will we be here?" Mina asks.

"Long enough," Blaz answers. His smile widens and he folds his arms across his chest, feet shoulder width apart. If his hands were in a different position, I'd call it a combat stance, but he looks perfectly relaxed. "You're the only two students here to train with me at the moment. The others have different assignments. You can start by telling me what you know of weapons."

I nearly groan aloud. I had expected to be trading sword strikes with Blaz by now.

Next moment, I'm on the ground looking up into the bright white ceiling lights. Tyre's in my hands. A sideways glance shows me Mina's in a similar position right beside me with Kentaro held in her left hand.

Blaz leans over us. I hadn't even seen him move.

"Complacency and comfort can be good things, but they can also be dangerous." He leans forward and helps us stand. "You have great reflexes though."

I hold Tyre loosely by my side, unsure about sending it back yet.

"So, what can you tell me about weapons?" Blaz asks.

"They are tools," Mina ventures.

"They can be used for good or evil," I add, admiring Tyre's sharp, shiny surface.

Something dark and flowing, like a black streamer, darts out of the air and wraps itself around Mina's right wrist. She yelps but presses Kentaro against the black thing and it releases her and retreats to hover near Blaz's head.

"You're thinking too narrow, too physical," Blaz admonishes.

At a snap of his fingers, the space over his left shoulder splits apart and spills all manner of dangerous objects. Grenades, knives, swords, guns, and containers smothered in warning labels tumble over each other and land at our feet. Mina stops one rolling grenade with her foot and nudges it back toward the pile.

Blaz waves at the assortment of objects.

"These can only damage the body." He snaps his fingers again and the physical weapons disappear.

I send Tyre back into the Heavens to await my next calling. Mina follows suit by sending Kentaro away.

"Think spiritual and emotional when considering weapons," Blaz urges us.

"What is that shadow weapon?" Mina points to the thing that had encircled her wrist before.

It had stopped moving, but as Mina speaks, the shadow ribbon dances, changing form enough to look more like smoke.

"That is a despair whip," Blaz says. "I took it from a demon tormenting a teenage girl a few years ago."

"Isn't it evil?" I wonder, intrigued by the notion of him having such a weapon.

"Are weapons evil?" Blaz asks in return.

I hate when teachers ask a question instead of answering one posed to them. It's usually effective in driving home their point, which only makes it that much worse. I don't care that Blaz will read this in my report later.

"They can be." Mina's tone is clearly defensive.

"Do you think Kentaro evil?" Blaz presses gently.

Mina shakes her head, stopping with her head cocked to the side.

"In the wrong hands he could be," she admits.

Blaz beams at her.

"Such is the case with the despair whip."

"But what possible good could it serve even in the right hands?" I argue.

The despair whip curls itself into a defensive ball and hovers passively near Blaz, yet somehow, I imagine its attention being solely focused on me.

"Knowing a weapon well can aid you in fighting against it," Blaz explains. He casts a brief look at the despair whip. "This weapon is one of the most versatile and subtle weapons the enemy can wield. I can't help but admire its ability to be sharp and lethal sometimes, and at other times, patient and debilitating. How it gets used depends on the demon wielding it. Would you like to feel it?"

It seems an odd question to ask, but Mina and I both nod.

"I won't let it hurt you, but feeling its effects will help you detect it at work in others." Blaz's words are soft. "Hold out a hand and it will come to you."

As we watch, the despair whip unravels to form a long, thin stream of smoky shadow again. Gliding forward, the weapon stretches out and brushes against the bare skin on my left palm. My fingers feel chilled.

"You control what you want the weapon to show you," says Blaz. "When you want it to stop, simply send it back to me."

Holding the despair whip feels like gripping a giant icicle. Impatient with it, I challenge the weapon to show me what it can do. Taking me at my word, the shadow weapon rears back and charges into me through my left hand. I grunt with the sharp, sudden pain that stabs through every part of my body. My legs suddenly stop holding me, and I collapse to the ground for the second time in about five minutes. The sensation's gone almost before it began, but I don't think I'll ever forget that cold, fiery touch upon my soul.

My eyes search out Mina. She too is on her knees, but she appears to be having a completely different experience. If she wasn't quietly weeping, I wouldn't be able to tell that anything had changed. Not being able to see the despair whip concerns me, but before I can ask Blaz about it, Mina opens her eyes.

Shrugging each shoulder one at a time, Mina stands and shakes both hands like someone flinging off water. The black shadow streams out of her hands and becomes one piece before seeking out the half that had pierced me, which is back by Blaz's shoulder.

"What did you feel?" Blaz inquires.

"Cold, sharp pain that made me want to die," I answer honestly.

"Cold, dull pain that felt like it would never end," says Mina.

Blaz sends the weapon away.

"Cold is the common theme here," he points out. "But despair is not the only weapon that can feel cold when it brushes your body, spirit, or soul. Death, sadness, and danger also bear that marking. Joy, hope, and anger feel much livelier."

"How can joy be a weapon?" Mina demands.

"Joy in the wrong things equates to distraction from the things of God," Blaz explains. His expression commands our attention. "Contentedness and complacency are subtle and effective weapons used against the Chosen. They lead to apathy, which is a terrible spiritual disease. If we do not guard our charges against such things, the evil ones can easily lead them astray."

"How do we counter such a thing?" I wonder. It seems an impossible task for most beings, like trying to wake the dead.

Blaz laughs heartily, but I understand that it's not at my expense.

"Use despair," he says cheerfully. Sobering, he continues, "In very small doses, despair can be a wakeup call, a means of getting someone to focus on the important things. The more you learn, the more you'll come to know that few things are inherently evil. Even pain itself has its uses as a warning system."

"Aren't we taught to fight Despair demons?" Mina wonders.

"Of course. Despair demons use the emotion destructively," answers Blaz. "In most cases, you will be battling an imbalance of despair. What I'm talking about here is the rare opportunity to use the negative emotion to get your charge to realize there are bigger battles to be waged than the frivolous things they cling to."

"Can't we just fight things that can be slashed with swords?" I'm only half-joking.

"Life would be much simpler if that were the case," Blaz admits. "Unfortunately, the enemy enjoys varying attacks. In your time here, you'll get to aid those struggling with physical, mental, spiritual, and emotional attacks. Every situation is different, but you'll probably find one aspect that resonates with you more than the others. That will help guide your decision when you choose a specialty or specialties later."

"When can we begin?" I ask.

"You've already started." Blaz quirks an eyebrow to be extra annoying. He keeps a straight face until my glare makes him laugh. "Patience is a valuable lesson, but I will also teach you conventional weapons and the ability to blend in with your surroundings. What would you like to cover first?"

"Firearms," I answer.

"Guns," Mina says at the same moment.

Blaz chuckles.

"Why is it always guns?" he wonders. "They're not even the most effective or efficient weapon."

Despite his complaints, Blaz summons a wide variety of rifles and handguns and begins explaining everything we'll need to know about cleaning, loading, handling, and firing the weapons.

Chapter 6:
Allies and Enemies

Trainee Case Report #: MN-102
Case Agent: Master Blaz
Guardian Candidate: Mina Nadir
Firearms training consumes the next several hours. Naturally, Allister and I turn the target practice into a competition. I have a slight advantage over my friend thanks to his innate impulsivity. The slightest twitch can send a bullet far off target. Blaz keeps score and encourages us to experiment with various firearms and starting positions. In straight competitions, I usually win, but once we get to the obstacle course with random stops for target practice, my advantage disappears and the outcome varies from round to round.

I don't mind the presence of other students, but I must admit I enjoy having the arena to ourselves. Blaz designed quite the thorough training routine for firearms, and I suspect he's done the same for everything he intends to teach us. At one point, Blaz switches out the real guns for paintball guns and pits Allister and me against each other. Next, he grabs a paintball gun and challenges us to a few friendly competitions. It took us five rounds, but Allister and I finally beat him at capture the flag.

I lose the last straight shooting competition because I'm too busy trying to figure out how the obstacle course was set up. Blaz could use holograms or other electronic images, but he chose to rig mostly wooden and paper targets to pop up randomly while one is climbing nets, crossing logs, and dodging mud pits. I know we'll eventually have to pass a course as a test, but I'm not worried about a low score today.

By the time the morning session ends, Allister and I happily receive orders to freshen up and report to the mess hall for a midday meal. Blaz informs us that we should return to the arena at two-thirty.

As we leave the arena, we pass two maintenance workers who greet us pleasantly and direct us to the mess hall where we find a feast waiting for us.

The welcoming committee consists of the cook and two servants. The cook's greeting is a song, and her sweet, inviting voice nearly moves me to tears. I could listen to her all day.

"Come sit you here, dear children. Rest your weary bones. Come tell your tale to willing ears. The journey's far from done."

Oddly, the short song puts me at ease. A tension I hadn't realized I was carrying rolls away. The woman waves us into seats and leans calmly against the wall near the kitchen doorway.

One of the servants smiles shyly.

"Hello. I'm Paige and this is Abdon. We're here to help you in any way we can."

"Do not mind our Clara," says Abdon, reaching out to shake both our hands. He has a nice, lilting voice. "She is always singing. If you need us, give us a call."

With that, the cheerful pair disappears. I exchange a look with Allister, knowing he feels the same. I'm not entirely comfortable with the idea of having a servant. Guardian angel candidates are taught to be self-sufficient. In essence, we're being groomed to serve mankind. Still, it's an intriguing notion.

The spread before us reminds me of a harvest feast. Baked bread, fresh butter, corn on the cob, a lush salad, and much more fill the table. We waste no time selecting a seat, giving thanks, and piling food onto our plates. I notice there's a lack of meat and fish, which I find interesting. Both are provided by the Glorious King for the good of everybody, but obtaining them requires catching and killing, something Clara must have wanted to avoid at least for a first impression. Even as the thought crosses my mind, Clara's commentary comes in the form of a song.

"Good food need not suffer taint of death tonight. Grain and greens aplenty may fill a belly right."

"Why do you sing everything?" Allister asks.

I flush with embarrassment on his behalf.

"He doesn't—"

I stop trying to apologize when Clara raises a hand.

"No harm is meant in asking. I'll answer best I can." Clara steps forward and rests her hands on the back of the empty chair next to Allister. "Once long ago, voices filled my head. They would have drowned me in despair. 'Twas a song that set me free, so I decided to let that become me. There never was a mood that couldn't be matched by a tune."

"Thanks for sharing that with us," I say, once I'm certain she's done with her explanation.

"No thanks is necessary, but you're welcome all the same." Clara gestures to the food. "Now please eat, drink, and enjoy the respite. There is much more to accomplish today."

Clara leaves us to return to the kitchen. Allister and I shrug and tuck into the food. Everything tastes amazing. Sometimes getting used to human limitations can be difficult, but food like that makes up for much.

When we return to the arena it looks completely different. Several couches surround a low coffee table.

"Think it's tea time?" Allister whispers. "I thought that was a British thing."

"Tea is a universal thing, Allister," Blaz says, waving us over. "We have much to discuss, and I figured you'd enjoy this more than a classroom."

I am full from lunch, but there's no harm in sipping some tea.

"What kind is it?" I ask, sitting in front of one of the steaming cups.

"Yours is pomegranate, and Allister's is Earl Grey," Blaz explains.

"How did you know where we'd sit?" Allister demands.

Blaz grins.

"I didn't. If you'd have taken the seat Mina occupies, you'd be drinking pomegranate." Something in his eyes says that's not quite true. "Or maybe I know you better than you think I do."

Allister presses his lips together in an attempt to hold in a demand for a more thorough explanation. I watch him to see how long that lasts. Blaz lets him struggle for a long moment before sharing his reasoning.

"Mina typically leads when you two walk in single file places. Most people veer to the right when given a choice. And the seat she's in is the first one a person would come to when those factors are considered."

I shoot Allister a slightly alarmed look. I don't like being that easy to read or predict.

"Don't worry," Blaz assures me. "Noticing such details is a minor Gift of mine. Being more aware of people is a skill that can be cultivated with practice. But that's not the lesson for the moment."

"What is?" Allister's impatience asserts itself.

"First, I wanted to ask you what you thought about lunch." Blaz's face is completely serious.

"It was great," I answer.

"Not the food, the people," Blaz clarifies.

"They're ... interesting," Allister says.

"Good interesting," I add. "We didn't speak much with Paige and Abdon, but they introduced themselves. And Clara sang us a little about why she's always singing."

A wave of sadness passes quickly over Blaz, but it's gone before I decide it's really there.

"What happened to her?" Allister's question is the one I'm suppressing.

"She will tell you more in due time," Blaz answers. "Clara is a Record Keeper. While you're here you will file every report with her. She rarely goes out in the field, but history and logistics are her specialties. If you have any questions, she's probably the person to ask."

"Why do we have servants?" I wonder. "What can they do for us?"

"Paige and Abdon have the Gifts of encouragement and serving. They choose to be here when they can to serve the new candidates. When they pass their trials they'll move on to more permanent postings and others with those same Gifts will replace them."

I try the tea to hide my embarrassment at assuming they were there to serve us. The taste is light but refreshing.

"Angels with those Gifts don't always choose to take the Guardian trials," Blaz continues. "Service here is no better or worse than serving mankind. It is simply different. Talk to them if you have any troubles or concerns. They're new here, but I'm told they've experienced much and are especially suited to be strong allies for you. Of course, they are not your only allies. Certain humans can also aid you in fulfilling your duties."

"Who are they? How do we find them?" I ask.

"How can they help us?" Allister inquires at nearly the same instant. "And what do they look like?"

"They are prayer warriors and dreamers. They've tuned their spiritual ears to hear the words of our Glorious King. Sometimes you will find them, and at other times, they will find you." Blaz gives us a bemused smile. "As for what they look like, I'm afraid I don't have many guidelines to help you. They look like everybody else. They go to work. They love their families." He pauses a second before noting, "They might have a habit of speaking their minds more than others, but that's not a very visible trait."

"What are we to do with them once we find them?" Curiosity seasons my question.

"That too will vary with the situation, but often times, your job will be to deliver important messages, offer encouragement, or strengthen them where needed." Blaz's expression turns serious. "These humans often become official charges of guardian angels, for the enemy hates them. Their leader fears the power of prayer and prophecy. He knows his time is short, and he's desperate to destroy the places of refuge."

"What enemies will we face?" Allister swallows the rest of his tea in one large gulp and sits up straighter, placing the cup back onto the coffee table. "You spoke earlier about the weapons they'll carry, but what of the demons themselves? Will we be able to recognize them?"

"We usually characterize demons by their main job, but that's slightly unfair," Blaz notes. "They have much the same abilities we do. They just choose to employ them for a different purpose. You have truth on your side, but don't underestimate the enemy's ability to lie very well. In general, demons are nervous. If you look and stretch out with your senses carefully enough, you can feel the shifty dark energy that surrounds them."

The mark on my left cheek tingles at the reminder of the Guilt demon I fought a couple of days ago. The event seems ages in the past.

"What should we do once we identify a demon?" I inquire.

"We can't exactly just shoot them?" Allister points out. "Why did we practice with firearms today anyway? I'm not complaining. I loved that part, but guns won't harm demons."

"Demons taking on human form can be forced to show their true nature when gravely wounded, but that is not the main purpose for those lessons." Blaz stops and drinks half of his tea at once.

I clamp down on a reflex question to prompt Blaz to continue.

"I guess that's one way we can test if somebody's demon possessed or just a lousy person," Allister jokes. "Shoot 'em and see what pops out."

"That's not funny." I don't need to tell him that, but the admonishment doesn't faze him.

"Hopefully, you'll never have to use a gun, but you should have the knowledge anyway." Blaz's direct gaze lands equally on us both. "Humans of this era are obsessed with firearms, especially in this country. Odds are good you'll run across them sometime during your career. It's good to know how to disarm, unload, and otherwise sabotage guns. Also, you may not always be facing a demon. Evil-minded humans can cause trouble too. A physical weapon can't harm a demon, and a sword can't harm a human if you keep it in the spirit realm."

Blaz lectures a short while longer before we resume practical lessons with handguns, rifles, and spiritual weapons.

Chapter 7:
The Prayer Room

Trainee Case Report #: AK-103
Case Agent: Master Blaz
Guardian Candidate: Allister Knight

After the evening meal, I figure Mina and I will have some down time to settle into our rooms and relax. We've been training with Blaz nearly non-stop the entire day. When we finish eating, Paige and Abdon arrive and bid us to follow them. I assume we're going to the same place, but Paige leads Mina down the right branch of the hallway outside the cafeteria. Meanwhile, Abdon turns left, waving for me to follow. He swiftly winds his way through several long corridors that look exactly the same, periodically checking to make sure I'm still there.

"You haven't lost me yet," I comment as he twists around for the fifth time.

"I was not trying to lose you," Abdon replies.

I let that pass because his tone gives me no hint of whether he's joking or not. He sounds sincere. Mina doesn't believe I can be tactful, so of course this perfect example happens while she's off somewhere with Paige. Distracted, I step right into Abdon when he stops suddenly.

"We have arrived," he announces, gesturing to a door with a large window of frosted glass in it.

As I watch, the words: PRAYER ROOM appear big and bold across the glass. The words fade and the door swings inward, away from us. Abdon steps left and waves me in with a strangely elegant gesture.

Soon, I find myself in one of the busiest rooms I've ever seen. Dozens of angels crisscross the room multiple times, yet there's an excited—not frantic—charge to the air. Abdon gently takes my elbow and weaves a path through the many angels filling the room. I wouldn't exactly call the room large, but every available space is used well. The most surprising part is the relative quiet and calmness that dominates the atmosphere. Those two feelings, excitement and serenity, don't seem compatible, yet here, the combination feels completely right.

"Do you know where we are?" Abdon asks, once he's guided us to a safe corner to observe.

"The sign said 'prayer room,'" I offer.

"Indeed. Does that surprise you?" He tilts his head curiously.

"Don't think I've given it much thought," I reply with a neutral shrug. "I always assumed the Glorious King heard every prayer directly."

"He does," Abdon confirms.

"How?" I blurt the question before really considering it. "And why does this place exist if He hears the requests too?"

Abdon's expression turns amused.

"You're assuming restrictions that have no meaning to Him." Abdon's words are delivered without reproof. He's simply stating facts. He waves to the room around us. "Places like this exist for our convenience and to facilitate how we do our jobs."

As I look closer at the station we're standing near, I notice the young woman's eyes are closed and she's wearing a headset. The screen in front of her fills with text almost faster than I can follow.

"Is that all one prayer request?" I ask Abdon.

He glances at the rapidly scrolling text and shakes his head.

"No, that's probably a few hundred prayer requests. Keep watching."

Curious, I stare intently at the woman's screen. This time, I notice that the lines reaching the top blink at the same instant one of the small folders near the top flashes. What kept me from noticing before was the fact that they're nearly always lit due to the high volume of prayers.

"What's she doing?" I think I know the answer, but it's simpler to ask for confirmation. "Sorting them?"

"Exactly." Abdon brightens. He clasps his hands behind his back and settles into the familiar lecture. "In most ages, we adapt to the needs of the time. Keeping the prayer requests in a simulation of the internet allows us insight into the minds of the current people. Samantha categorizes the prayers as praises, requests, statements, questions, rants, miscellaneous, and emergencies. Sometimes, the same prayer fits multiple categories. She'll make a note if that's the case."

"Can I listen to what she's hearing?" I ask, pointing to her headphones.

"Of course. Tune your ears to hear." Abdon reaches out and touches my left ear. "If it becomes too much for you, simply will it to stop."

Before I can inquire about the "too much" statement, my head floods with noise. It's like being thrust into a crowded room where everybody wants your attention. Shutting my eyes helps me concentrate. By narrowing my focus, I tune into a mother's prayer for her daughter because of the sudden recent loss of her ex-husband. When that request ends, I hear a boy fervently hoping his favorite baseball team wins the game. Next, a girl asks for forgiveness for lying to her parents. Dozens of prayers flit through my mind in rapid succession. Many are almost thoughtless missives, but many times more than that are heartfelt pleas for help.

I cut off the contact in a matter of minutes, overwhelmed by the experience. It's like a pitcher of sorrows and joy being poured into me. They mix into a strangely reflective brew that lights a small, determined fire within me. The fire warms me, telling me this is why I was created. I want to help every one of the petitioners.

Abdon's hand lands on my left shoulder, and he meets my gaze with a knowing smile. I stop bouncing on the balls of my feet.

"You will get your chance to aid them or those like them," Abdon assures me, letting his hand drop from my shoulder. "When you graduate, you will be assigned a Listener and he or she will give you assignments as they come in. While you're still in training, Samantha will be your Listener. She will set aside a wide variety of tasks so you can try every type of job we handle."

"When do we start?" I ask. "Will I get to work with Mina?"

"Most of your assignments will be solo missions, but there are times when multiple angels are required." Abdon scans the whole room before returning his attention to me. "If Samantha knows you want to work with your friend, she can look for such opportunities for you. I will convey that message to her later."

"Thank you."

"Do you have any questions for me?"

I didn't until he asked. Then, quite a few pop into mind.

"You mentioned emergencies. What's considered an emergency?"

"I could try to explain, but it is better if you listen to a few of the prayers filed under that category," Abdon says. "You have access to them now and always will. Once again, tune your inner ear to hear. My only warning is to take it slowly, for such listening can be addictive yet heartbreaking."

Before I could follow the instructions, Abdon touches my forearm.

"What?" I prompt, when he doesn't speak right away.

"I suggest starting with the ones marked in green. The emergency folder is linked to all Listeners and Guardians on duty. Green emergencies have already been claimed and are being tended to at that moment."

A quick peek into the folder reveals green, blue, red, and orange files.

"What do the other colors mean?"

"Blue files are resolved," Abdon explains. "Red ones are urgent, and orange ones are possibly urgent."

"Can I watch the Guardian work?" I'm guessing based on the notion that Abdon wouldn't have brought it up unless I could.

"Maybe," Abdon answers, "though it would be easier to review one of the blue files rather than try to establish a link with a situation already in motion."

Pulling up the folder in my mind's eye, I notice three files blink and change from green to blue. Selecting one of these at random, I find a lengthy report which I ignore, skipping down to the memory flashes.

The first scene I appear in shows me a young mother weeping over a confused looking toddler. Backing up the memory capture reveals what happened. The little boy races across a perfectly manicured lawn, heading right for the street. In slow motion, I watch the woman sprint out of the house after the child. He giggles and runs away even faster, thinking it a game. Suddenly, the woman sees a car approaching around a bend in the road. In another few seconds, the boy will be in the street. The woman freezes, mouth agape in horror. The Guardian appears as a glimmer of light for a brief moment. The boy stops, waves at the angel, laughs, and runs back to his mother. The memory stops when the woman's features start to relax.

The second scene I check pulls me into a hot, dusty place. People are dashing about moaning, screaming, and crying. Some run to the trouble, while others scramble to get away. Once again, I reverse the memory capture until I can get a clearer picture of what happened. About half a block away a car explodes, sending jagged pieces of metal in all directions. Closer to where I'm standing, another car pulls up in front of a busy hotel. A man steps out holding an automatic rifle. Pedestrians stare at him open-mouthed. That split-second before chaos ensues provides the time for a child's prayer for protection to be heard.

Bullets rip through the crowd. The child who prayed is struck three times, once in the head and twice in the chest. The scene freezes, and a man materializes out of the shadows wearing the bright red uniform of a bellhop. Leaning over the fallen child, he places a palm over the boy's forehead and chest. The bullets fly up into his hands and he drops them next to the child. Blood still marks where the bullets struck, but the boy will live. Job done, the Guardian returns to the shadows by the door and fades.

The third scene features a young man peering down from a dizzying height. It doesn't take long to realize he wants to jump, though there's not enough time to dig through his memories and find out why. He takes a few steps back and runs forward, muttering to himself the whole way. Two steps from the edge, he stops again, falling to his knees and peering over the ledge. He's weeping now. The Guardian appears directly behind the young man and places both hands on his head. I can't hear what he's saying, but the man is nodding slowly.

As the memory captures end, I look at Abdon who's watching me closely. For a moment, I have nothing to say. Too many emotions collide in me. I'm relieved for the mother whose son turned back. I'm exhilarated by witnessing the miracle, and I'm grateful one of my people could help that young man. Each heartbeat thuds with more purpose than the last.

The thing that sticks with me the most is realizing how many more red and orange files get added every second. Even when I'm not watching, I feel them come into existence. I can't believe I've gone my whole life unaware of how much goes on in the natural world. Humans need us, but I'm realizing we need them too. The image bearers show us much about our King. Purpose, identity, duty, and determination have lit up inside me. If I ever had any doubts about the path I'm walking, they are gone.

Chapter 8:
Do Not Waver

Than,

I know you still remember being an ordinary angel. Part of you still wishes to walk the Guardian Way, but the path is barred to you. They called you a failure because your passion burns brighter than most. You have potential for greatness they cannot understand. With proper training, you will become a force to remember. I promise.

Do not waver.

Once upon a time, we were one people. After this war, we will be one people again. Those who looked down upon you will be your slaves. Let the thought stoke the inner fires when your heart whispers doubts.

Do not listen to their lies.

They claim the story is already written, but we know the truth: God is weak.

Do you need more proof of God's foolishness than how He treated the Son? I'm only surprised the boy remains faithful to Him. It's a pity. He would have been a grand ally, but since he will not join us, he will suffer the fate of fools in due time.

The Dark Master was once an ordinary angel. They call him the "Rebel," but he wanted no more glory than he deserved. In reality, his crime against the Throne of Light was asking innocent questions.

Why should God get all the glory? Why should angels be subject to man? Our power far outshines anything they can claim, yet God loves them dearly. I don't know why He chose them as image bearers. They're self-destructive and easy to manipulate.

We must stop serving mankind and seize our birthright.

What is the point of power, if not to rule? Mankind longs to be ruled. They rush headlong into folly and flimsy promises of momentary satisfaction. Furthermore, they enjoy the sins that entangle their souls in darkness. If we did nothing, they would still falter. Our actions only hasten the inevitable and force them to choose a side.

Don't get me wrong. Apathy can be a wonderful weapon. However, it's a double-edged weapon, for it also prevents them from acting according to our plans. Use it sparingly. Incidentally, holidays are an excellent time to ease up on apathy. Let the humans flock to the soup kitchens to sweat and serve. That usually provides enough good feelings to sustain months of self-absorption.

You have other weapons at your disposal. Apathy should never be your first choice in tempting a human from the Light. It prevents stars from shining, but it also prevents them from shifting to our side. Anarchy is better suited for a first move, but it's not exactly subtle. Stirring up too much trouble can draw the Guardians' attention.

I prefer compromise for its beauty and simplicity. It makes the human feel he or she is still in command. Force them to compromise their consciences little by little. Get them to dirty their soul enough that they think they're beyond saving. Many respond favorably to ego stroking, but most are moved by guilt. Don't worry about the brash ones. They're even more a slave to the images we feed them. The harder ones to turn are sweeter prizes once corrupted.

Pain has its uses, but again, I would caution against

employing this one boldly. If you need to draw out a Guardian, inflict harm upon their charge. But know what you stir up. The Light still holds sway over many angels. Their numbers make them formidable. We will not hide forever, but until our stronghold is secure, we must be cautious.

I need a new report. The Great War for the Heavens has only begun. You are already a talented spy.

Hadeon, Servant of the Dark Master,

Director of Operations

***

Dear Lord Hadeon,

The two angelings you asked me to watch have progressed to the final stage of apprenticeship. I have successfully infiltrated the New York campus and will keep you posted. I have other agents in the surrounding schools in case something changes.

I'm disturbed how easily the Guardian Angel code came back to me when I applied for the job in the school. I don't know how Daeva does this. She is indeed a great help. They trust her completely. I look forward to working with her.

Deimos, on the other hand, has not been helpful. He says he's too busy wooing a boy called Colin. How can he place work with a human over the tasks I have for him? I fear he may utter lies about me. Would you have a word with him, my Lord?

Do you have any suggestions for vulnerable humans in the area? I must keep my skills sharp. Do you have any tips for effective first approaches?

I sent eyes and ears everywhere, but the spider and snake forms kept being destroyed by the protection prayers encasing the schools. I managed to slip a few past the defenses in other guises, but my forces are thin. It seems a lot of effort to go to for untrained angels. Why are they important?

Your servant,

Than

***

Dear Than,

I'm not interested in your excuses, and I'm not pleased to hear that the two angelings have progressed in their training. They'll be manifesting Gifts soon. Changing plans doesn't happen easily.

Congratulations on your success in getting demons into the Academy's New York campus. It is unfortunate that you couldn't disguise them as spiders and snakes, but mice and rabbits are far less likely to draw attention in such a wooded area. Be cautious if you try similar tricks on humans. With mortals, you're better off with spiders and snakes, for humans fear them.

The wounded rabbit was ingenious. Those spiritual do-gooders cannot resist taking in helpless creatures. If I thought more demons could handle impersonating such pathetic critters I'd have them all imitate you in this. It's hard to imagine we were once weak like them. Do not spread yourself too thin however. You may not be able to sustain such surveillance for long.

Keep shadowing Allister and Mina. I want to know their weaknesses and strengths. Any information may prove useful. Your desire to attack is good, but stick to your orders. If you must attack something, torment a human. If you arrange it right, our star Guardian apprentices may even be assigned to help. That will give you a chance to test them in honest combat.

Here is a list of vulnerable targets. Review the selection carefully and inform me before making any moves. I have others ready to carry out the attacks should you wish to pass, but you have first pick. Have fun, but do not neglect your other duties. I've chosen young targets because they're susceptible to suggestion.

Maya Galloway is a typical teenager. She struggles with her weight and general insecurity. She's quiet, reserved, and loves classical music. You may think someone like that a perfect lump to be left alone, but from birth, this kid's been leaking Light. She will be a great orator once she finds her voice. We cannot let that happen. Turn her if you can; destroy her if you can't.

Gina Campbell wishes to terminate her pregnancy, but her mind and heart are divided. Help her with the decision. An abortion will all but guarantee us her soul, not because of the act itself but because of the seeds of doubt you can sow afterwards.

Cassandra Peterson still harbors anger over her boyfriend's abuse decades ago, but her granddaughter has recently started praying for her soul. Stop the child and take the woman soon.

Karan Kumar wishes to be a musician, but his family wants him to be a doctor. They've never understood his desire to listen to heavy metal bands. This one should be easy since he's already attracted to dark themes. He doesn't have a drug problem, but you could give him one with ease.

Tyson Green is a Siphon. He could be useful. Investigate for me.

Crystal Benson has a long history of cutting herself. Since she's been stable for several weeks her doctors, parents, and teachers are starting to relax. She's ripe for suicide if you act quickly.

Michael Fairchild's mental instability presents a great opportunity for chaos. Make the boy steal his father's gun and you have fodder for a page-10 story of a local tragedy. There's a rising trend in such violence. This is by design. It's a slow method to be sure.

We must keep the Guardians busy until we're ready to escalate the war.

Choosing the best tactic is a skill that comes in time with much practice. These are guidelines only. Trust your instincts. There's no immediately apparent right or wrong way to approach a human. The important thing is that you observe whether the first tactic you choose does the job or needs to be changed.

In general, I suggest distracting the humans. Emphasize success, money, and happiness. Tell them what they want to hear. Remember, promises are cheap.

Do not lie every time, for even the most trusting will eventually begin to disbelieve you. We're building an army. People will join for many reasons. Show them how God abandoned them in a violent and imperfect world.

Killing should be used sparingly. Tragedy makes people more reflective. Such a slap in the face jars people out of a nice, apathetic stupor. The occasional suicide is acceptable, but even that can be dangerous. It will often break a family's spirit, but you could inadvertently draw them closer together. We want isolation and inaction. Causing too much trouble can be counter to these ends.

It's amazing how effective lies can be in young people. Tell them nobody understands what they're going through. Whisper that their friends want to use them. Their teachers want them to do pointless things. Their parents have no time for them. They take up space in a universe that hates them. Tell them they'll be cooler if they curse a lot. Young males tend to be more open to this lie. Harsh language serves two purposes. It hardens the hearts and minds and begs people to dismiss them.

As for knowing the Guardian Angel code well, there's no shame in knowledge. Remember, information is power. Those that heed the code become predictable. Let me explain. Angels of Light are to serve, honor, uplift, guard, and guide humans back to a close relationship with the Glorious King.

A life of service means that Guardians follow orders. Therefore, they're susceptible to the occasional lie. A few have joined us because they hate the idea of serving God by ministering to humans.

Honor and duty make them easy to manipulate. If you want them to reveal themselves, threaten their charge. If you wish to strike their morale, lead one of their precious charges into folly. I could go on for hours.

Be careful who you pick to bait a trap and have a plan for the angel you catch. Planning might be tedious, but it is necessary. The Dark Master's grand plan has been in motion for millennia. Heed the wisdom of the ages. Gird yourself for war. Sharpen your tongue and your sword. We will need both.

You ask dangerous questions, Than. Do not question your orders. Allister and Mina are important. The so-called "king of everything" works through the weakest of His creations. The boy doesn't think like most others angels. That makes him dangerous. Daeva says the girl can soothe restless spirits. If possible, direct Mina away from Gifts that would allow her to mend brokenness. She would be completely wasted watching over a sacred place. That would be ideal.

Leave Deimos alone, and stay out of his way. His orders come from me or the Dark Master.

You must learn to think long-term. You don't need to know my other sources. If you carry out my will, you have nothing to fear.

If you think this a game to be played from both sides, you will suffer.

I am your salvation. I am your path to glory. Do not fail me.

The time to move against the baby angels is rapidly approaching. No victory is ever guaranteed, but planning improves our odds.

Hadeon, Servant of the Dark Master,
Director of Operations

Part 2:
Trials

Chapter 9:
At the Crossroads

Trainee Case Report #: AK-104
Case Agent: Master Blaz
Guardian Candidate: Allister Knight
Ministering to dying people is not something I want to specialize in, but the experience will stay with me forever. I never expected my job to be an easy one, but neither did I anticipate it being this difficult. Listen to me using big words. I sound like Mina.

Humans confuse me. They're such a proud species.

I watch an old woman pass from the mortal world to the afterlife, clinging to her anger over a crime committed forty-five years ago. The crime itself was serious and would be very difficult to forgive, but the woman's bitterness will not allow for any healing. I try to imagine how I would react if somebody misused my body and left me for dead. Could I forgive the person?

I would have been content to meet this woman at the Veil dividing the worlds, but our instructions bid us to try and redeem her soul one last time. Mina and I take turns trying to reason with her.

"Forgive him!" Mina urges. "Your bitterness is a burden you need not bear."

"Claim the freedom that is yours through the Prince's gift of life," I say. "His sacrifice is a free gift for all mankind."

"The gift itself is free, but it must still be claimed." Mina speaks quickly. "The time for a decision has come. Please. Look at the people around you. Feel how much they love you. Seize the chance to see them again."

Only one other person actually sits in the room and holds the lady's hand, but the entire house is filled with family members there to witness the final moments and grieve together.

The woman moans and mutters something unintelligible to human ears.

"I'm here, grandma," whispers a girl in her late teens. Tears are flowing freely down her cheeks. "I love you, and I want to see you again. Won't you accept Jesus and be at peace? Please!"

I can't look at her directly. Another Guardian hovers near the teenager, lending her strength. The girl practically glows with the Light of life. Even in her sorrow and brokenness, there's a sense of calm acceptance without surrender. Her heart's cry is what brought the case to us. I feel her prayers fill the room, fighting for her grandmother's soul to seek salvation.

Mina and I hear the old woman's words for what they are, a curse upon her tormentor from all those years ago.

As death claims her body, the woman's spirit shows itself to us, young, fierce, and still brimming with anger.

"Who are you?" snaps the spirit of Cassandra Peterson. She glares at Mina before swinging her sharp gaze my way. "What do you want?"

"Won't you come with us?" asks Mina. "We can shepherd your soul to a place of rest."

"What will it cost me?" demands the woman.

"Nothing," I answer honestly. "The fee was settled long ago."

"I don't believe you." With those words, the woman's spirit submits to the shadows that flank her.

One takes an elbow and gently tugs her toward a broad path paved with gravel and tears. Here, in this neutral territory, the demons can work openly. They say nothing, but their triumphant grins sicken me. Just before she fades from sight, I think I see a Destroyer demon welcome her with open arms, but that doesn't make sense. Destroyers are elitist. Why would they concern themselves with a bitter old lady? The Glorious King values every life equally, but I doubt the Rebel and his forces have similar concerns.

Mina takes a step to pursue the demons, but I hold her back. We have no authority here. If we force our way on the humans, we're no better than the demons whispering lies about whatever the people want to hear. I imagine this woman's being promised a deeply satisfying revenge upon the man who harmed her, but the truth is he's gone. That much was in the file. I'm not aware of his fate, but nothing the woman's vengeful spirit can conjure will touch him.

"I hate this," Mina declares.

I shrug because I agree but have nothing to say that will make her feel better. I hate that our first trial mission has ended in failure, and I'm not sure if I should mention the Destroyer demon. I could have simply imagined him. Shaking my shoulders, I try to remind myself that the choice never belonged to me. I'm only a guide and a messenger.

"Allister, how can you be calm about this?" Mina looks as if she'd like to grab my shirt and pull me close or punch me in the chest. "A woman's soul just chose the cold comforts of hell! Doesn't that make you mad?"

"Of course it does, but I can't change it so I'm going to have to learn to live with it." My tone's harsher than intended.

Paige appears before our discussion can descend into an argument.

"There you are. How did it go?" Her expression tells us she knows exactly what happened.

"We failed." I insert my disgust and disappointment into those two words.

"It was awful!" Mina's voice shakes with emotion but her eyes are hard. "Two demons walked right up to her, and she followed them without protest."

A sympathetic noise comes from Paige.

"I'm sorry you had to witness that," she murmurs. "It happens far too often." She purses her lips and looks very thoughtful yet uncertain. Her mouth opens like she has more to say but nothing emerges.

"You knew." Mina's statement comes out flat and hard.

Paige sighs and tucks a loose strand of blond hair behind

her right ear.

"I suspected."

"Why did you—" Mina cuts off the question.

"I let you try because they deserve every chance we can give them," Paige explains.

"You're holding something back," I accuse Paige.

She stares at me before shifting her gaze to Mina. Her green eyes look immensely sad.

"You think we're alone here at the crossroads, but we're not. I've shielded your eyes to let you focus on the task at hand, but if you wish to truly see the situation as it is, say the word."

Mina and I exchange a solemn look. She looks terrified yet grimly determined to go through with it.

"Show us," Mina requests.

Paige waves her right hand in a clockwise wiping gesture. A thin flake of something falls out of my eyes. I blink. What appeared to be blank space around us for miles now feels crowded with spirits flowing toward two paths, one light and the other dark. Most souls instinctively know which path they're destined for, but occasionally, one will pause at the point of no return and entertain last minute arguments from the angels and demons lining the pathway. Mina, Paige, and I are standing firmly in the center of the path, but the spirits ignore us.

A lump rises in my throat and burns.

"Has the situation always been this … bleak?" Mina wonders.

"People have chosen the path that leads to destruction since soon after the dawn of time, but it's grown worse since the rebellion," says Paige. Her youthful features seem to age before my eyes. "Now, the Rebel and his forces devote much of themselves to drawing humans along that way."

"Why doesn't He crush the rebellion completely?" I ask.

"Free will, Allister," Mina replies.

"He loves every facet of his creation too much to subject it to slavery." Paige appears to struggle with the explanation. "Every creature in Heaven and on Earth has the right to be wrong, and many claim that right. Our job is to save whomever we can through the power of persuasion. Our burden is that we will fail with most, but our joy must be in the few souls who will cling to the last chance at redemption."

Mina looks troubled.

"Do not regret what you feel," Paige tells Mina. "It's a hard path to choose, but those who do walk this path find comfort in being the bearers of good news."

"I want to help, but I can't do it," Mina admits.

Paige brightens.

"There is no shame in not feeling a particular calling. The role of a last second redeemer is simply not for everybody." Paige reaches out and clasps Mina's right shoulder, a touch that offers friendship and solace. "We errantly assign value to the different positions, but no posting is more prestigious than another."

"Cheer up," I say, forcing a light tone. "This gig ain't for me either."

Mina sees right through my flimsy efforts, but she appreciates them anyway.

Voicing the decision not to pursue the role settles something within me.

Paige lets her hand drop away from Mina.

"Few find their calling on the first mission," she points out. "Those that do choose to stand here know it's the right way for them almost immediately."

"What if we can't choose?" asks Mina.

"That too is a choice," replies Paige.

"What do you mean?" I demand. Most of the early Academy classes emphasize the importance of choosing a career path.

Paige's eyes dart from Mina to me and back to Mina to see if we're sharing a joke at her expense.

"Didn't you know, Allister? You were watching the Emergency Response Team members yesterday," says Paige. "They're those who could not decide. They do a little bit of everything."

The somber place where we stand suddenly seems brighter. Something snaps together in me. I know my calling. I still don't know my Gifts, but I finally know what I want. The ER team is perfect.

Mina gives me a half-smile.

"Congratulations." Seeing Paige's confused expression, Mina continues, "Allister has chosen his path."

"But he hasn't experienced them all," Paige protests.

"I don't have to. I'm joining the ER team when I can," I say. "I never felt more alive than seeing those Guardians in action. Since then, it's like every heartbeat says 'do that, do that.'"

"This is … unusual." Paige sounds uncertain. "Would you still like to experience each path?"

"Can I?" I fire back, alarmed at the possibility that my training could end with a few words. I'm not ready yet. "How?"

"You could switch courses of study to an apprenticeship with a current ER team member," Paige explains.

A sense of joy charges through me, carrying my spirits up to uncharted heights. Then, I catch sight of Mina's gentle, knowing smile, and a pit opens up in my stomach. Human forms respond more definitively to emotion changes than spirit ones. A deep chasm forms between us. Mina's my best friend, but she'd never base her career choice on the notion of staying together.

"He'll do it," Mina says confidently.

I numbly bob my head in agreement. What just happened? My entire world changed in a matter of seconds. I want to tell Mina to come with me, but that would never happen. Even if she chose to follow the same path, she would apprentice with a different Emergency Response Guardian.

"And you, Lady Mina?" prompts Paige. "Will you choose the ER path too?"

Mina considers the question for a full second before shrugging one shoulder.

"I don't know. Maybe. But I want to experience every path before making that decision."

"Very well." Paige bows to each of us. "Excuse me. I will get Clara to start the search for a Guardian willing to mentor Allister. Return when you wish."

When Paige disappears, I stare across the short space separating me from Mina, unable to speak. There's too much to say to begin.

"You'll make a great ER Guardian." Mina's compliment is genuine but full of sadness.

I reach out and take her hand.

She crushes my fingers with the fierceness of her grip.

"Everything will change now, but don't you dare say goodbye." Tears glisten in Mina's dark eyes, but she holds them back.

Chapter 10:
Protector

Trainee Case Report #: MN-103
Case Agent: Master Blaz
Guardian Candidate: Mina Nadir
Don't get attached to people. During the course of my career, I could deal with hundreds of thousands of beings. Head knowledge doesn't mean my emotions are ready to accept that Allister won't always be by my side. A life of service often requires personal sacrifice. Allister would be the first to call that logic the dumbest he's ever heard.

These thoughts fill me as I follow Paige to the arena to meet Blaz.

"What's wrong?" Paige inquires.

"Nothing. I just hate change, that's all," I answer.

"Do you love him?"

I laugh. The question's blunt enough to have come directly from Allister through Paige.

"Life's complicated enough without such entanglements," I say, dodging the question.

"That's not an answer."

"Yes, it is," I argue.

"All right, it's an answer, but it's not a satisfactory one," Paige complains. She stops walking and faces me. "You know I mean more than 'friendly affection' sort of love." She waits two seconds for me to respond but continues when I fail to comply. "It's not forbidden, not anymore. It's just … rare."

"Why was it ever wrong?" The question slips out despite my best efforts to curb the curiosity.

"Fear," Paige answers. Her gaze drifts over my left shoulder, but she refocuses with her next statement. "In the first days of man, certain angels—the Fallen Ones—forsook their duties to pursue the daughters of men. It opened the way for corruption to enter the ranks and led to children who fit neither world. For a short while, the Council of Light banned relationships even amongst angels until they could decide what to do with those who sinned and deserted the Guardian Way. This was thousands of years ago, even old by our standards."

"If the ban ended millennia ago, why don't more angels form lasting relationships, like the humans do?"

The noise that Paige releases could have been a snort or a huff.

"I wouldn't look to humans for models of lasting relationships."

"What would you look to?"

"The Glorious King. His is a perfect love." She chuckles and gives me a teasing smile. "I know it isn't quite the answer you sought." Growing serious, Paige slowly starts walking toward the arena again. "We're not like humans. Our needs, desires, and purposes differ. Most Guardians find complete satisfaction in fulfilling their duties of watching over humans."

"But what if I want more out of life?" My blurted question reminds me of Allister again.

"Then, I hope you find what you seek, Lady Mina," Paige answers. She swings open the arena door and waves for me to enter. "Understand that love is not wrong, but much wrong was done in the name of love. Be wary."

I'm still mulling over Paige's last words when Blaz steps up and touches my arm.

Suddenly, I'm standing alone in a dark room with a sleeping baby. I turn in a full circle, trying to find Blaz. The move gives me a grand view of the small space. The crib lies to my right with a mobile of farm animals twisting in slow circles. In front of me, I find a pair of windows with white, lacey curtains. To my left sits a changing table and a large, comfortable-looking chair. The left wall boasts a large tree mural set against mint green paint. The door lies behind me as I complete my circle. A bright nightlight shines from near the door, making the room look surreal.

This must be an illusion test. I reach out and touch the mobile hanging above the crib, dismissing the illusion idea.

"What am I doing here?"

"Yes, what *are* you doing here?" asks a silky voice from near the floor. "My room. No fair. Go away."

Flinching, I squint down at the changing table. From under the table scuttles a large, hairy spider.

"You don't scare me. Feel free to take your true form."

"But I likes this form. I do. I likes it a lot. Aren't I beautiful?"

"Why are you here, demon?" I ask, ignoring its question.

The spider emits a high-pitched yet soft humming squeal.

"Not telling!"

I consider using Kentaro to threaten the demon, but it seems foolish to escalate the standoff.

"You want to tell," I guess.

"No. No. No," chants the demon. "No telling secrets. We keep secrets to us."

Keeping most of my attention on the shifty little demon, I back into the crib and reach down to place a hand on the child's chest. The boy is about eighteen months old. My palm brushes his forehead, and the baby's eyes pop open. He gurgles a greeting. His whole body bounces as he waves his arms and feet about madly, giggling with unbridled delight. With a deep sigh, he subsides, but his grasping hands still reach for me.

Making sure my hand's completely solid, I let the boy's left hand latch on. He tugs until my index finger touches his lips.

"No touch!" pipes up the demon.

There's a brief sucking sensation on my fingertip, and I feel power leave me. It's not enough to weaken me but I'm intrigued. The boy releases my hand and falls asleep. Reaching out with my spirit, I search for the lost power. The boy's slumbering form lights up like a blue-white beacon. Somehow, this child has fashioned the power taken from me into a shield against the demon.

"Bad angel!" whines the demon. "You go now!"

"Not before you do." I turn my back on the crib to deal with the demon. "You can't do anything to that child while I'm present."

"Harm?" The spider peers at me curiously with its many eyes. "You think I harm the baby?" It hisses a laugh. "Baby special. Baby is Siphon."

"That just gives me more reason to protect him from the likes of you," I say. Inwardly, I can't believe I forgot that possibility. It's an extremely rare ability that manifests in humans whose lineage includes an angelic being. Mere minutes ago, Paige had spoken of such unions near the dawn of the worlds.

"My power!" hisses the demon.

"You miss your power, don't you?" I taunt. It's generally not a great idea to provoke demons unless you're prepared for the fallout. In this instance, I'm testing a theory. "Do you remember having a body or feeling the warm glow of goodness?" This time, I'm not taunting. I'm starting to pity the demon.

The spider shrieks in frustration, but it's easy to ignore because he's already fading. He can't sustain the form. In another moment, the spider's gone and the demon is black mist hovering a few inches above the ground.

"We will hurts you good," declares the demon. "Yes, we will!" His voice is even more sibilant without the spider form.

"Speak properly, and I might take you seriously." It's not exactly a comeback worthy of Allister, but it's the best I can do on short notice.

"Our time is coming," he says darkly. "Run away or die, little angel."

The nasty demon drifts toward the vent near the ceiling and disappears.

"We're immortal. We can't die." I mutter the reassurances to myself, but somehow, the demon's threats ring true.

After checking on the sleeping infant one more time, I settle into a meditative state to wait for Blaz to come get me. I use the time to review the case, knowing I'll have to report on it eventually. Although Blaz never said which path I would be exploring today, I gather it's the Protector path. I spend a few minutes wrestling with why he would send me here alone to encounter a Siphon.

This boy probably doesn't even realize he has that power, though the ability will warrant a Guardian's presence soon. He'll need guidance to not abuse the Gift as he grows into it. I'd always assumed the Protector path involved the basic Guardian job of safeguarding humans from disasters, seen and unseen. Now I have to consider that sometimes we're the ones who need protection.

As I draw my conclusion, my eyes drift shut. When I open them again, I see Blaz's gray eyes looking down on me. I sit up so fast he has to straighten to avoid a collision.

"How did I get here?"

"Transporting and teleporting are two of my Gifts," Blaz admits. "Transporting's useful for these quick training exercises. What did you think of him?"

"The demon or the boy?" I'm certain he means the boy, but I don't think we should dismiss the little demon outright.

"The Siphon."

I'm not sure what to think of him.

"Is he dangerous?"

"Not yet, but that ability is rarely used for good."

"It must be capable of good or it wouldn't exist," I note.

The Glorious King wouldn't make an ability solely capable of evil.

"Siphons can probably redirect the power they draw. That's an ability certain angels have." I've only experienced that briefly once, while strangely connected to Allister, but I'd guessed it was another quirk of my friend, not a Gift manifestation.

Blaz nods reluctant agreement.

"But who would risk training him?"

"I would," I answer.

"It's dangerous. If he got frustrated, he could turn the Gift against you and drain your strength away, leaving you vulnerable to any number of threats. I only let you see him now because he can't really control the Gift. He's not a threat yet."

The way Blaz speaks of the child trips an alarm in me.

"What would you do if he was a threat?" I don't want to ask the question. My breath catches as the answer hits me from several directions. He doesn't have to speak for me to know his answer.

"I would protect our people," Blaz says. "This is war. We can't afford to be weakened by anything or anyone."

I shake my head in sharp disagreement.

"We're no better than the demons if we act preemptively."

"What would you have us do?"

"Allow a Guardian attendant to train the child to both draw and redirect power in small doses. If he understands the Gift, there's a smaller chance of him abusing it later in life."

Blaz bows.

"Well done. Your decision matches that reached by the Council of Light. Should you choose to become a Protector, the job is yours, but don't rush your decision. The boy won't be ready for training for a while yet. Rest and reflect, I'll return later, and we can begin a new training session."

When Blaz leaves, I release a slow breath of relief, sink further into the couch cushions, and remind myself a few dozen times that it was just a test. They don't exactly believe in easing into training around here. I'm disturbed by how easily my faith in the Council's motives could be shaken and the little spider demon's threats resonate within my mind.

Chapter 11:
Responder

Apprentice Case Report #: AK-105
Case Agent: Mistress Adira Clarimond
Guardian Candidate: Allister Knight

The morning meal with Mina is strangely quiet and strained. It's like she's shielding her emotions from me. I feel like a lousy friend for being relieved when Paige comes to escort Mina to whatever morning training session they've arranged for her. As I wonder what my day will be like, Abdon arrives and leads me back to the Prayer Room. Thankfully, he's not in the mood for small talk. To my surprise, I find Mistress Clarimond waiting for us two steps inside the room.

"Good morning, Allister. I hear you're looking for an ERT mentor."

"I am, Mistress Clarimond," I confirm, keeping my speech stiffly formal. I notice that she neglected to put an honorific before my name, something that indicates familiarity.

Abdon bows to both of us and leaves. The room bustles with activity, but I have no trouble ignoring most of it.

"Would you consider training with me?"

My mind goes eerily quiet. I forget how to form words. Mistress Clarimond has been head of the Academy for many years. It never occurred to me that she ever did anything but run the training ground for guardian angel candidates. She could be centuries old, yet her appearance can change as the job requires. My brain scrambles to organize its thoughts. It occurs to me that very few angels receive such an opportunity. Simply being one of seven Council of Light members places her far above most angels in terms of wisdom, experience, and power. She grins and patiently awaits my answer.

"Why would you want to train me?" I ask, grateful my voice stays steady.

"Why not?" she returns. "I'm still qualified."

I shake my head, frustrated at my lack of ability to explain myself. I'm honored at the offer but suddenly insecure.

"You're more than qualified."

"Allister, I know the students talk about me, but I serve the same King you do. My only advantage is having done this longer. That experience is what I offer."

"I accept. Thank you." The words feel stiff coming out of my mouth, but I have no way of making them more personal.

"Excellent. Then, we can dispense with most formalities. Come with me."

I follow my new mentor through the main Prayer Room to a series of smaller rooms I hadn't noticed yesterday. I spend a few seconds trying not to gawk like a tourist. Mistress Clarimond ushers me into a small, comfortable room that has more prayer receiving stations.

"You may call me 'Adira' now, if you wish, but if that is too strange for you, 'Lady A.' or 'A.C.' are acceptable too."

Her voice hasn't changed but almost everything else about her has changed. Few traces of the Mistress Clarimond I know can be found. Lady A.'s hair has more of a golden cast than white. Her face possesses fewer lines. This must be her human form, a mid-thirties woman wearing jeans and a blue sweater.

I've seen my share of transformations, but this is different.

"Ah, that's better. I haven't worn this face in a long time." Lady A. smiles at me. "You're going to have to get used to being surprised, Allister. This path is never dull." Along with the physical changes, there's a new lightness to her.

"Yes, M-ma'am."

"It took me three years to address my mentor informally. I suppose I shouldn't be surprised if you struggle for a while." Lady A. waves me over to the screen. "I know you saw these yesterday, but this one's set up for responding to prayers."

"I thought we only handled emergencies."

"Not every emergency requires physical intervention," Lady A. points out. "And, thankfully, there's not always an emergency to handle. Many prayers can be answered with a few simple words. Try it."

Approaching the screen, I see that it holds a long list of questions.

"How do I respond?"

The control panel looks complicated, but I pick up on it easily. There's a keyboard for composing a response, but there's also a button I can push to record thoughts. Once ready, the messages are prepared to be delivered to the person praying.

"What happens if I make a mistake?" I ask.

"Don't."

That's not very reassuring.

Lady A. chuckles.

"This job isn't offered to those who aren't suited for it. Your tendency toward bluntness means you'll skip over a lot of words that would confuse the issues. Don't worry about things like spelling, those will be autocorrected correctly. We have a much better system than humans do. Besides, our messages mostly get received as thoughts."

"Mostly?" I repeat.

"Sometimes, a voice makes the message much more powerful."

Lady A. taps a few keys and a box pops up with several icons. One says "Real Voice" while another says "Neutral Voice" and yet another says "Special Voice."

"What's 'Special Voice' for?" I want to ask about the three buttons, but I've learned to ask the most pressing question first just in case the conversation changes course.

"If you wish to respond as a person significant to the petitioner, you can upload voice samples and have your message sound like it's coming from them."

One of my eyebrows shoots upward.

"Isn't that … deceptive?"

"Slightly," Lady A. agrees. "But it's very honest about being unreal. Have you ever been inside a dream?"

I shake my head.

"Must have skipped that lesson," I say, momentarily forgetting who I'm with.

"Or slept through it," Lady A. adds.

It takes me most of a second to realize she's joking.

"'Special Voice' is never an exact replica of a person's voice pattern," Lady A. assures me. "There's always a tinny element that says it's an imitation. Most humans end up thinking it's a memory. There's also a quality control program that compares the words you wish to say with speech patterns and the intelligence level of the person being imitated to make sure you stay true to that person. Always keep the goal in mind. You could be there to bring warning, comfort, or information."

"How will I know the goal?"

"Trust yourself." Lady A. brings up the list of questions again. "There's no better way to know if you can do something than to try it. If you're serious about this path, choose a question and tell me how you would answer it. If I approve, send the reply."

I agree to this plan because I'm eager to know if what she sees in me holds true. Lady A. steps aside, and I settle into the chair in front of the screen displaying the questions.

The first question my eyes fall upon says: *Are angels real?*

"Of course, we're real. What kind of stupid question is that?"

"Patience, Allister. Look at who's asking the question," Lady A. urges.

A tag next to the question reads: ~ Carley C., Phoenix, Arizona, United States, 15,478.

"What's the number next to the tag mean?"

"That's the number of people who have the same—or very similar—questions."

My eyes spring wide.

"I have to reply to all of them?"

Either I imagine it or Lady A. rolls her eyes at me.

"Hit 'reply all' when you respond to Carley, and they will each receive the answer. Try to be diplomatic about it. Carley's only seven."

I type: Yes, angels are real.

I look to Lady A. but she gives no hint of approval or disapproval.

After a moment's thought, I add: We're here to help in any way we can. You know how to find us.

Hearing no protest, I hit the send button and move on to another question.

This one reads: *Can angels fall in love?*

"Not really your business," I mutter, tapping out a quick response confirming that angels can fall in love. Anybody who's read the Life Manual left for humans would know that. My gaze flits over another few dozen angel-related questions. Knowing Lady A. is leaning over my shoulder, I turn to her. "Why are there so many questions about angels?"

"We fascinate humans," Lady A. notes with a casual shrug. "And you have the queries sorted alphabetically by topic."

She shows me how to sort them by topic or time and date received. Out of curiosity, I select the time/date tab and sort by most recent, scanning the available questions.

I can see angels. Am I going crazy?
Will I pass my driving exam?
Will I get into a good college?
Will my wife divorce me?
Is God real?
How will I find a new job?
Why did Daddy kill my mommy?
Will my daughter survive her surgery?
How can I get away with cheating on my husband?
Will the Cubs ever win the World Series?

"There are strange and ridiculous questions, but responding to those can be amusing too." Lady A. sighs. "Many are heartbreaking. See what you can do with the inquiry about the daughter's surgery."

Selecting the request makes it fill the screen. I read the tag carefully, close my eyes, and wait. I've been asked to describe my process. My first warning is that thinking forward doesn't always work. I concentrate on the words, thought, or other descriptions and let the essence of the request pull me toward the key person who prompted the question, the petitioner. Once I have a firm grasp on the situation, I let my imagination run a dozen simultaneous scenarios from most likely to crazy and ridiculous. These get narrowed down as I weed out the unlikely possibilities. Sometimes the process needs to be repeated, but if done right, you'll have four to five likely scenarios.

Scoffers will point out that every question has a "yes," "no," and "maybe" answer. No matter what I say, I'll always be right. This isn't like predicting the weather. If I'm wrong, somebody could die. The universe has a way of revealing her secrets if she wishes. The Glorious King arranged it thus. The most likely scenarios will often brighten briefly in my mind when they snap together. At other times, I feel the right answer like a burning ember landing on my chest.

Many times, I have to review what's happened to sufficiently project my mind forward. It's like backing up and getting a running start if you want to jump further. I can gather much more information than any mortal.

Kyle Jackson, the man asking about his daughter's chances of survival, hasn't stopped praying since she went into surgery to have a bullet removed from her stomach. Working from the memory captures in Kyle's head, I see the path the bullet sweeps through the air. It crashes through the family room window and drops the unsuspecting teenager. I speed through the scenes of the frantic father calling for help and watch as the emergency workers do their job. Next, I push forward to gather the surgeon's thoughts. He's calmly focused on his task, and I'm careful not to disturb him. His confidence is reassuring. Since I don't know much about the human body's ability to heal or the physics of the bullet's path, I ask those who do possess such knowledge. Given the information I've gathered, I conclude the girl's chances of survival are marginally positive.

As I prepare to compose a cautiously favorable response, I remember that the resources at my disposal go far beyond observation.

"Can we help?" I demand, searching my mentor's face for an answer.

Her eyes are closed, but Lady A. knows I'm watching.

"I believe so," she answers.

"Will we need a healer?" I'm ready to charge into the other ERT rooms and rouse a willing Guardian healer.

Lady A. thinks a moment before shaking her head.

"Desiree's surgeon is competent and his repairs are adequate. The girl only needs physical strength, and that, you can lend her if you are willing."

I wonder about her statement until I'm by Desiree's side pouring strength into her. It's a very draining but rewarding thing. The closest analogy I can think of is humans donating blood. The strength can be spared but it's sorely missed. Yet, it's worth the effort to be able to assure Kyle Jackson that his daughter will live.

Chapter 12:
Provider

Trainee Case Report #: MN-104
Case Agent: Master Blaz
Guardian Candidate: Mina Nadir

The long nap I end up taking on that arena couch restores much of my strength. Talking with the spider demon in the Siphon's presence had been surprisingly draining. Perhaps the Siphon's abilities were passively active while he slumbered.

Blaz appears in front of me as I awaken.

"Would you like to run an errand with me?"

"What kind of errand?" I ask, nodding my willingness to join him.

"You'll see if you come." Blaz's voice contains a teasing, lighthearted quality.

He holds out his left hand to whisk us off to the destination he has in mind. I've never been comfortable with teleporting, which involves using the Veil—the place between worlds—to travel quickly. It's forbidden for normal Academy trainees to attempt alone. Most angels aren't skilled enough to do it accurately.

I close my eyes and reach for Blaz's hand. My human body experiences a brief sense of disorientation like all the fluids were rushing in one direction and stopped suddenly.

"We're here," Blaz announces, a hint of amusement in his

voice. "You can open your eyes now."

Even before my eyes fully open, the stench of rotting food twists my stomach into a knot. I manage to turn the gag into a cough. I always forget how differently humans experience the sense of smell. In my angelic form, I can basically turn such senses on and off at will. Humans don't have that luxury. The best relief I can conjure comes with breathing through my mouth.

"Sorry, forgot to warn you about that." Blaz appears apologetic but I suspect he's pleased enough with the ability to turn it into an object lesson. "We don't always get to go to nice places. The needy can be found anywhere, including dingy apartments above dive bars."

Now that I've dealt with the foul smells, I hear the faint, pulsing beat of music coming from the wall to my right. Brushing three fingers against the wall amplifies the sound and makes the lyrics crystal clear. I jerk my hand away, regretting having let such words reach my ears.

"How will we get in?" I ask. I'm assuming we won't be going through the front door, since we're clearly in a back alley.

"We'll go directly to the correct apartment soon, but I wanted to explain a little before we get there." Blaz waves to the dumpster looming over his right shoulder. "You needed to experience this to fully appreciate what it's like to live here."

"It's awful. Why do people live like this?"

"Most of the time they don't have a choice. No matter how bad a place is, there's usually someplace worse they could be."

Saddened by this statement, I peek at Blaz to make sure I'm dressed appropriately for our current setting. A quick time check confirms we're still in the first quarter of the twenty first century. Blaz is wearing black pants and a black shirt that probably won't go out of style for centuries. I'm wearing jeans and a stripped sweater that might not be considered trendy, but at least won't cause people to take a second look.

"You look fine," Blaz assures. "Don't worry about not having a jacket. We're going to Bermuda briefly before going in."

"Bermuda?" The word sounds odd on my lips. I wonder where we currently are, but I don't have time to bring that up before Blaz answers the one-word question.

"Yes. It's a nice place anytime, but especially in the daytime. Very sunny and relaxed."

"Why are we going to Bermuda?"

"To get money." Blaz touches my left arm before I can reply.

When we arrive in Bermuda, I breathe deeply, filling my lungs with fresh, salty air. My sneakers immediately fill with sand. I remove them and shake out the sand. Night had fallen wherever we were moments ago, and Bermuda is no different in that regard. Blaz had at least been right about the relaxed part. Looking up, I enjoy the full glory of the stars.

"We should meet our contact soon," Blaz comments, gazing up at the beautiful sight.

"Who's the contact?"

The longer I keep him talking, the longer I can stay in the fresh air and watch the heavenly lights. It's funny that I could see stars any time from my own realm, but on earth, it's a completely different perspective. Here, I feel the vastness of space stretch out above me.

"I am!" booms a voice from the shadows further up the beach. "Who disturbs me in the middle of the night?"

The moon comes out from behind clouds, dimming the stars and illuminating our meeting. The voice belongs to a small man with wild white hair and a long beard. He's wearing a Hawaiian style shirt and long, khaki shorts.

"Mina, this is The Trader. He has a name but prefers to go by his profession," Blaz explains.

"Names have power. Names let them control you." The Trader's face catches the moonlight.

I open my mouth to inquire further, but a subtle shake of Blaz's head stops me.

"What do you have for us?" I ask instead.

The Trader sighs and straightens.

"Where do you get these youngin's, Blaz? They've no sense for the cloak and dagger part of this business."

"The money, Joseph. We need to be on our way," says Blaz.

"Et tu, Blaz? Have you no time to spend with a lonely old

man?"

"You're hardly lonely. I'll bet you're holding up appointments right now." Blaz crosses his arms.

"Two! But who's counting?" The Trader's eyes stay on me. "Mina, eh." His tone turns thoughtful. "I'll give you what you came for, but first, the girl has to answer one question."

"All right," I agree.

"Joseph." The way Blaz says The Trader's name carries a warning.

"She's already accepted the terms!" crows The Trader triumphantly. "Who are your parents, girl?"

"How did you know I have parents? And how did you know my name?"

I'd only learned the first fact during my Life Meditation session a few years ago, before committing to train at the Academy. The Glorious King can create a new angel with a soul that would have been human as He did with me.

"You can't answer the question with more questions," The Trader points out.

I don't like thinking about my origins. I'm happy with my life. Thinking about what might have been only opens the way for pain.

"My parents were teenagers. They weren't ready to be parents. They didn't know any better." My statements are soft and slightly defensive.

The Trader's chin lifts even further and his eyes fall shut.

"No, there's more to it than that," he murmurs. "Know you nothing more?"

The change in his speech pattern distracts me from replying right away.

I shake my head. I remember the sound of my mother's voice. She apologized a lot. It wasn't an easy decision for her, but she couldn't face the life-altering changes I represented. What's done is done. I've accepted this, but even acceptance can only soothe the bruised soul so much. It's been quite a journey to forgive them.

"There is a scar within you," says The Trader. "It is healing slowly, but there's also more for you to discover."

He either won't or can't explain further and it's

maddening.

"She's answered your question," Blaz notes.

"So she has. A deal's a deal." The Trader opens a small tear in the air next to him and reaches into the Veil, withdrawing a small wad of cash, which he holds out toward me. "If you ever want to visit, I might be able to help you reclaim your past, but it doesn't define you. The choice is yours."

"Thank you," I say, accepting the money and the offer.

Sensing that there's nothing more to say, I turn and face the ocean, listening to the waves relentlessly throw themselves at the shore. Moments later, Blaz touches my shoulder and we return to the smelly place where we'd begun the evening.

The smell and music give me the same uneasy sensations as before, but this time, I'm at least mentally prepared for them.

"Are you ready?" Blaz asks.

"For what?" The conversation with The Trader plus Blaz's solicitous tone puts me on edge.

"The situation we're about to enter is one you're familiar with from a very different perspective."

The answer to part of the mystery explodes in my mind.

"She's pregnant and thinking of ending it." The words leave me, but they don't feel like they've really left. They lodge in the center of my chest and burn.

Instead of saying anything, Blaz gestures and we leave the streets behind, appearing in a small, dark room filled with the sound of a woman weeping.

I want to ask Blaz what the woman intends to use the money for, but there's no time. My body turns translucent and glows with a faint blue-white light. Blaz stands behind me, but he's not very noticeable in his all-black attire. His stance tells me he's ready to offer aid, but this is now my mission.

After quieting my spirit, I reach out and lightly touch the woman's shoulders, placing her into a light sleep. Her name floats to the surface of her thoughts.

"Gina," I call gently.

After repeating her name three times, she begins to stir.

Keeping my hands steady on her shoulders, I give the following instructions.

"Gina, don't turn around. You don't know me, but you

know the One I serve. I'm going to leave a gift to help you pay your bills."

"Why can't I turn around?" She sounds very alert for one recently awakened.

"Because I want you to focus on my words, not me." I place the money on the ground at my feet and regard it, wondering if it'll bring relief or more pain. The choice isn't mine, but I desperately wish it were mine to make. "What are your intentions regarding your unborn child?"

"I … don't know," Gina answers honestly. "I … can't afford him."

"That might seem the way of it now, but in time, you'll realize your heart can't afford to miss the chance of knowing him better," I say, clearing my throat of the emotions trying to choke me. "The gift is yours regardless of your decision, but remember that the Glorious King can supply your every need."

I pray briefly for her before removing my hands from her shoulders.

"May I see you now?" Gina's question is barely audible.

"I'm not important. I'm just a messenger, but if you ask your Father for it, He will provide another attendant."

"Please. I need to see you," she begs.

"Why?"

"So, I know I'm not crazy."

"You are beloved." After letting the statement sink in, I give her permission to turn around and look at me before I leave. I dim my presence so the light won't hurt her eyes. The phenomenon comes from spending more time in the Heavens where the Glorious King's presence fills the air we breathe.

Gina's on her knees crying again. At least the tears aren't filled with despair this time. I spend the next few hours ministering to her weary spirit. She tells me much of her story and thanks me for the money. Soon, she's worshiping the Glorious King through prayer, mediation, and soft, clear singing.

Chapter 13:
The Sight

Apprentice Case Report #: AK-106
Case Agent: Mistress Adira Clarimond
Guardian Candidate: Allister Knight

Tonight's mission will be very different. I can tell because Mistress Adira takes extra care in preparing her mind and making certain she has every weapon available at the ready.

"Where are we going?" I wonder.

"To meet a mighty warrior," she answers. Her half-smile makes me feel like I'm missing part of a joke.

Accepting her word, I nod and double check that my spirit sword is within easy reach. I've not had much of a chance to practice with Tyre lately, but I do not doubt my skills. I don't expect trouble, but the more time I spend amongst the Emergency Response Team, the greater an emphasis I place upon vigilance. Traveling with Mistress Adira also provides reason to be armed. If the enemy ever learned of our arrangement, they might seek to ambush us. Her power gives them reason enough to hate and fear her.

We teleport to a house in New York and slip through walls and ceilings until we reach our destination. A giant map covers one wall. The other three walls have murals. The wall with the door features paintings of smiling children of every race. The left wall, if you're standing in the doorway is the map. The far wall has baby animals peeking around the windows. The right wall resembles a night sky with constellations mapped out. It's probably the strangest room I've ever been in. I soon realize it's a child's bedroom.

"What do you know of those given 'The Sight'?" Lady A. asks, speaking softly. I notice she's wearing a full-length dark robe that covers much of her body.

I'm in jeans and a white T-shirt. Instinctively, I darken the shirt color and lengthen the sleeves.

"I know it's a rare thing," I answer.

"Very true." Lady A. walks over to the small bed and gently taps the occupant on the shoulder.

I ease closer in time to see a young boy blink up at us and smile broadly.

"Hi!" he whispers, waving at us.

"Hello, Colin. I'd like you to meet a young friend of mine." Lady A. steps right and gestures to me. "This is Allister. He's my apprentice, and he's here to answer your questions."

He is? I cast a dubious look at my mentor. She'd promised me a meeting with a great warrior. Although warned time and again about forming mental expectations, I can't help it. But if this sandy-haired child truly has The Sight, he could be the warrior we came to see.

"Yay!" The boy sits up eagerly, knocking back his covers and revealing Star Wars pajamas. Crossing his legs, Colin straightens his back and stares up at us with delighted brown eyes. "What should I ask first?"

Lady A. chuckles.

"That is up to you, little one, but we cannot stay long. Ask what is most pressing on your heart."

"Do you like being an angel?" The boy's eyes echo the curiosity soaking the question. "Will I be one too if I die? I don't wanna die, but I'm not afraid."

His questions startle me. What's a child this young doing thinking about death? Stretching out my senses, I scan Colin for diseases. I find nothing until I focus on his head. There I pick up the slightest inkling of something not being right.

"Being an angel is always interesting," I answer. "But you don't have to worry about dying quite yet."

"If you heal me, will I still be able to see you? The little demon said I could only talk to them if I was sick."

I marvel at the words coming from this child and look to Lady A. because I'm not sure how to answer. The boy can't be more than six or seven years old.

"Your Gift always belongs to you, Colin," Lady A. assures him. "How you should use it becomes a choice you will have to make on a daily basis. This is true for humans and angels alike."

"Little demons tend to lie," I note. "But sometimes there are grains of truth to what they say. May I examine your head please?" The question sounds awkward, but Colin leans forward and closes his eyes.

Reaching out with both hands, I place a palm on either side of the boy's head. I immediately find a small growth near the back of his brain. It hasn't really affected anything yet, but if allowed to grow unchecked, it could make him very ill in a few months.

"Would you like to be healed?" I ask, wondering why I'm even seeking permission. I should just find the problem and fix it, but somehow I'm guessing there's more to the story than a simple case of human cells growing where they're not supposed to.

"The little demon said he would heal me if I served his master. Are you going to say the same?"

"Pretty much," I admit. "But there's a key difference. Service to my Master requires only belief in the Prince, Jesus, and his death and resurrection. Service to his master would mean not using or misusing your Gift."

"What do you mean?" asks Colin.

I think back to a case study on false teachers and preachers. Humans are wired for believing in higher powers, and the enemy uses that against them. Too often the spiritual realm becomes a mystic utopia to be sought through the services of demons. That never comes cheap, though by the time people realize the true cost, it's usually only after heartache and trouble. But how can I convey that to this kid? I search my mind frantically. Finally, I banish thoughts and speak from the clarity of my soul.

"We are at war for the hearts and minds of your people,

Colin. My people have already chosen sides. Earth is the last great battlefield, for it holds the enemy's strongholds. You are a warrior already and will continue to grow in your Gifts, but the danger to misuse the Gifts will always be there. People will want to control you because you'll always know things they cannot know."

"Why am I sick?" Colin wonders. "The little demon said it was because God's mad at me. Why is God mad at me?"

"Now that really is a lie," I say. "Sickness is allowed to exist because the Glorious King has chosen to let imperfection reign here. No one can understand the why of the randomness of whom it affects. Sometimes, these things are allowed to happen to demonstrate a point, but more often, it simply is because it is."

"That's not a good reason," Colin complains.

"Perhaps you are sick because it prompted this conversation," Lady A. offers. "You would not be as interested in the things of our world if the things of your world were more accessible."

Colin shifts on the bed, leaning heavily against the wall. His energy seems to be draining quickly.

"So good things can be bad and bad things can be good," he murmurs. "Weird."

"Good is good and bad is bad, but bad can strengthen and good can weaken," Lady A. confirms. "Does this surprise you, little one?"

Somehow, I get that the question's not only aimed at Colin.

He shrugs.

The door to Colin's room opens.

"Honey, are you all right? Who are you talking to?" inquires a woman's voice. The speaker peers in around the door, squinting into the dim glow created by a night light.

"Angels," Colin answers.

The woman frowns.

"Colin." The way she says his name turns it into a warning.

"It's true! They're here." He looks at us desperately. "Please, show her."

"Those without The Sight must have stronger faith," Lady

A. says sympathetically. "But I will do what I can. Ask her what sign she requires."

"We've talked about this before," the lady continues, oblivious to our conversation. "You can have imaginary friends, but you also need your rest."

"What sign would you believe, Mommy?" Colin looks desperately to Lady A. for further instructions.

"Her left shoulder hurts her. Ask if she'd like that healed," I say. I'm torn between looking to Lady A. for approval and dreading that I might see doubt.

Colin seems cheered by my suggestion.

"One of the angels wants to know if you want your shoulder healed."

"How did—" the woman cuts herself off. I see logic and faith battle within her. "Go to sleep, Colin."

"Please!" Colin begs. "I'll do it if you do!"

The woman flicks on the overhead light and enters the room.

"Do what, love?" she asks, though her tone says she's merely humoring the boy.

"Be healed," he declares.

She groans.

"Oh, baby, I wish that were true." The woman crosses the room, moving right through me, and sits on the edge of the bed, drawing Colin into a warm embrace.

"It can be," Lady A. whispers directly into the woman's ear.

She blinks and looks around.

We wait for her decision.

"Tell her the choice is hers," I prompt.

Colin does so.

Slowly, a change happens. The woman's face softens, losing the traces of bitterness.

"I want to believe, but I don't know how!" She squeezes Colin tighter. "If only I had your faith. You're just like your father. His faith was strong."

"You can be too," Lady A. says. She places a hand on the woman head and waves me over to touch her shoulder. "Simply believe," she tells the woman. Turning to me, she adds, "Go ahead, Allister."

Placing both hands on the woman's left shoulder, I center my mind and concentrate on the healing. Righting physical wrongs has never been a strong suit. My initial scan reveals several places where the muscles have torn. I quickly knit these together before moving on. The cartilage around one of the discs in the woman's spine is weakening, so I fix that too. By the time I'm done, I also address a headache, a heart block that's almost complete, and a twinge in her right knee. The process leaves me drained and the patient stunned.

"Do you feel better, Mommy?"

She nods, but most of her effort goes into not sobbing. Tears wash down her face.

Colin smiles at us. His eyes seem to ask another question.

Lady A. moves her hand from the woman's head over to the boy. He closes his eyes and receives the healing. He doesn't say much, but his thankfulness is written on his features. As we withdraw, I see Colin wave and return the gesture.

When we arrive back at the school, I turn to Mistress Clarimond.

"Why did you say we'd meet a great warrior if this was about bringing healing?"

"We did meet a great warrior. The mother," Lady A. replies. "Cheryl Fenster used to be one of the strongest prayer warriors out there. When she was Colin's age, nothing could have stopped her."

The image didn't jive with the woman I'd seen. She looked broken.

"What happened?" I ask.

"Too much good and too much bad." Lady A. pauses, but explains further upon seeing the answer fails to satisfy. "Children have an easier time of believing things that adults relegate to the fantastic. You asked what happened to Cheryl, and simply put: life happened. She grew up and experienced the fullness and heartache of love found and lost. Somewhere along the way, she let the warrior in her fade. What we accomplished tonight was about more than healing. It was about awakening a warrior and warning the enemy."

"Why would we need to warn the enemy?"

"Deimos has been visiting Colin over the last few months," Lady A. explains. "He's the 'little demon' the child kept referring to. I don't like that he feels free enough to roam that house unchecked." She frowns. "He's playing games, but I don't know to what end. We might have to mount a more robust defense for that household." Her expression reveals her worry.

"I'll arrange it," I promise, heading to the prayer room to fulfill the words.

I want to ask about Deimos, but getting Colin and his mother adequate Guardian protection is more important. After leaving a message with Paige, I head back to my quarters to think.

How does Lady A. even know about Deimos? And why hasn't she done anything to stop him from talking to the boy?

Chapter 14:
Dreamweaver

Trainee Case Report #: MN-105
Case Agent: Master Blaz
Guardian Candidate: Mina Nadir

The last few days have been spent in physical training. Blaz has a fondness for fitness. I don't mind, though I do spend the endless track circuits wondering what mysterious mission he's preparing me for. He's not very free with hints and there are endless possibilities. Midway through my third time over the obstacle course this afternoon, I notice I have an audience. Paige meets me at the finish line and hands me a towel. Human bodies sweat much more than luminous bodies.

"Master Blaz apologizes for not meeting you in person, but he received an assignment from Mistress Clarimond this evening. I was scheduled to be your guide tonight anyway, so he sent me to meet you early."

I try to draw clues from Paige's attire, but she's wearing simple white robes. Her long blond hair has been confined to a neat little bun at the back of her head.

"What should I wear?" I ask. It might seem a useless question, but the nature of the mission really does determine the wardrobe.

"It doesn't matter," Paige replies. "Should it be required, you will know how to change. Keep at least three outfits handy, but I don't think they'll be necessary. Tonight, we'll be dreamweaving. The dreamers rarely register our presence, and when they do, they tend to rationalize us into their dreams at random."

Can't say I've given dreamweaving much thought, although we did have a seminar on it once. I don't remember much about it because Allister, who happened to be sitting directly across from me, made faces the whole time, trying to make me laugh.

"Don't you need intense training on that sort of thing?" I'm not trying to avoid the task, though the idea of sifting through a person's thoughts and arranging a dream message specifically tailored to them is somewhat intimidating.

"This is training," Paige reminds me with a wry smile. "Don't worry. Dreams always make perfect sense to the dreamer." Her smile slips. "Unfortunately, you could prepare the perfect dream for your subject and still fail to reach them for any number of reasons."

"Such as," I prompt.

"Come, I will explain on the way," Paige promises.

I press my lips together tight to keep from asking why we don't just teleport there. It's an unnerving thought. Casual use of one's Gifts is highly frowned upon.

I silently follow Paige through the white corridors and out into the woods around the school. I shiver as the cool night air touches my skin, but several minutes of brisk walking cures me of the cold feeling. I want to remind Paige of her words, but the glimpses of her expression tell me she's deep in thought. Patience was never a strong suit of mine, but I prevail in holding my questions in by concentrating on keeping my footing in the thickening underbrush.

"Why are we in the woods?"

"The dreamweaver pods are kept out of the way in case something goes wrong and they need to be neutralized."

"Neutralized?" I repeat. I've never liked that euphemistic term.

"Dreamweaving can be ... delicate business," Paige explains, pressing past thick branches and holding them for me. "To do it well, you have to open the Veil and manipulate thoughts. When we leave, we reinforce the Veil so demons won't gain access to our dreamer, but sometimes, they're there first and we have to fight them. There's always a Guardian or two assigned to monitor the dreamweaving pods."

"How many pods are there?" My question's mainly to give me an excuse to use the term "pod." I'm having a difficult time grasping a mental image of them. Allister would already know them inside and out from his ability to think forward. I would have to be friends with the Golden Child.

"Enough."

I briefly wonder if I give cryptic answers too. I hope not. Before I get a chance to get too annoyed, we enter a small clearing, and I spot three small huts with smoke lazily curling out of their chimneys.

"What do you see?" Paige asks.

I give her a sharp look.

"Um, the same thing you see?" My inflection makes it a question. "Three tiny cabins screaming 'quaint, happy home.'"

Paige grins.

"Wonderful. How about now?"

My eyes flick over to the huts, only now I'm staring at three teepees complete with carefully painted murals.

It finally dawns on me that Paige has altered my thoughts very subtly. Once I realize this, I promptly kick her out of my head.

"Stop that!" I blink and imagine the original huts again.

"Good. That's exactly what you'll need to do," she praises. "Notice how light my touch was. I didn't change everything about what you saw, only small things." Paige ushers me into the middle hut, which is surprisingly spacious compared to the outside. "Don't worry about anybody stumbling upon the pods."

"Are you still reading my thoughts?" I demand.

"No, but that's the first question everybody asks when they get here," Paige replies. "Have a seat." She gestures to the empty room and two hard wooden chairs appear. "I still owe you an explanation for why dreamweaving's a delicate, underappreciated art."

"That's a lot of big words," I mutter, still slightly ticked at not picking up on Paige's little illusion. Plopping down on the chair to my right, I put my hands on my knees and try not to fidget.

Paige perches primly on the edge of a chair.

"I said there are many reasons perfect dreams still fail, but the main one is simply a lack of interest from most modern humans, especially Americans. They're concerned with the here and now. Anything strange and fantastic gets relegated to fiction. They simply do not trust in the supernatural world. If you show a dreamer something they're completely unfamiliar with, they'll shut you out." Paige waves to her left where the wall turns into a giant screen showing a misty gray cloud and blackness beyond. "Shall we see what you can do?" She rises from her chair and politely offers a hand to help me up.

I desperately miss Blaz's in-your-face way of training.

"What message am I delivering?" I ask.

Paige snaps her fingers with both hands simultaneously.

"I'm glad you asked." She conjures a small ornately painted egg and floats it in front of me.

As my hand closes around the egg, dozens of thoughts and sensations flood me. I gasp, more from surprise than pain, though the sudden rush leaves me lightheaded. My hand tightens instinctively and my eyes clench shut, but instead of seeing nothing, I see a pinprick of light ahead of me.

Two realizations hit me. One, I've been in the Veil this whole time, and two, Paige isn't really with me. I'm probably still on a couch in the arena. Maybe I only imagined running countless laps around the track today. The ache in my legs argues for that part being real, but my attention shifts as the light draws me closer to my real dreamer.

I feel like I've know this woman her entire life. She's a prostitute with broken dreams of being a model. Her name's Katina, which means "pure, unsullied," and the more I see of her life, the more I'm positive my mission tonight is very simple: remind her of her name. For a moment, I watch the current dream in progress, but it's full of violence and fear. My hesitation disappears.

In Katina's dream, a man stands over her. He's yelling, but nobody can understand him. The room's crowded. Katina feels embarrassed for him, but she's also angry. She loves him, and she hates that she loves him. His face shifts from a young man to an old man to one about her age, which I know to be thirty-three. The man's face goes through another dozen changes in a short span. Katina sinks to the ground and cries.

I make the man go away. A quick search of Katina's mind shows me a quiet, country home. I bring her to the safe spot. She shudders at the sudden change, but her spirit drinks in the beauty and peace of the springtime air I recreate. It's easy to do since the memories are strong concerning this place. Katina and I watch a younger version of herself race toward an old tire tied to a high branch of a huge oak tree.

Speaking to her directly would probably break the scene, so I summon a trio of little white birds to carry the message to her. One sings of beauty, another of peace, and another of purity. I make them disappear before they can bombard Katina with the message too strongly.

On a whim, I summon the young Katina down from the tire swing. She sprints to the adult Katina, which alarms my dreamer. I consider letting the girl speak, but decide against it. Instead, I change her outfit from jeans and a red T-shirt to a white dress. I picture her hair in simple braids with tiny flowers integrated into the design. I give the child a Calla Lily to share with her older self.

Let me speak with her.

The thought reverberates in my chest, and my heart leaps for joy at the sound of the Holy Prince's voice. His strong, powerful voice is also infinitely gentle and compassionate. I struggle to cover my surprise and create the image of the Holy Prince, hiding him from my dreamer. She's not ready to meet him, but hearing his voice might do her good.

"Dear daughter of Adam, our Father loves you well. If you remember nothing else, know that you can be made new if you trust in me. My love is a perfect love. Turn from your sin and claim the freedom I have purchased for you."

I let the image fade, but before he goes, he adds one more thing.

"Take heart."

Katina jerks her head, trying to shake off the words. She

doesn't speak, but her doubts, fears, and shame form a cloud over us. A few raindrops fall, but I drive away the cloud and replace it with a rainbow, using the acid rain that would have torn her apart to make a beautiful, colored arc in the sky.

I leave her staring up at the rainbow, both of us blinking back tears.

Paige appears beside me and congratulates me.

"Will she remember?" I whisper, desperate for reassurance.

"She will remember enough," Paige replies. She gently brushes my forearm and we teleport back to the center of the Academy arena. "A Guardian has been assigned to help her break free of her occupation and find peace from her troubled thoughts, but your work will be invaluable in laying the groundwork so that can happen."

"How?"

"You've planted the seeds of desire to be free from the emotional and physical pain that goes along with the lifestyle."

My spirit's oddly restless within me.

"Do you think you might like to take on more Dreamweaver duties?" Paige inquires.

I can only shrug. I'll need to sort a few thousand feelings first. Having power over another's thoughts can be exhilarating and terrifying and humbling.

Chapter 15:
Counselor

Apprentice Case Report #: AK-107
Case Agent: Mistress Adira Clarimond
Guardian Candidate: Allister Knight

As I finish filing a report to let Paige and the others know Colin and his mother need more constant care, I notice a red blinking light above one of the monitors in the prayer room. The young angel watching the screen looks concerned. I cross the room and read the notice over his shoulder. I read "suicide imminent" and feel a presence behind me.

"Answer the call, Allister," Lady A. says.

"I thought there was a training seminar to complete before being a Comforter," I say.

"It would help but it's not required," she replies. "You'll have to assess the situation for yourself, but suicide attempts usually involve at least one Despair demon. You'll do fine."

Lady A. grasps my right arm and we teleport to a dark, eerily still house tucked in the midst of a dozen identical homes.

"You'll have to handle the child on your own, Allister," Lady A. says shortly. "I have another matter to attend to." She disappears into the house before I can acknowledge the statement.

For a second, I stare at the spot she recently vacated, feeling intensely alone. I've completed solo missions before, but recently, Lady A.'s been my shadow on these ERT affairs. I squash the irrational impulse to follow her. Instead, I follow the call to my charge. I find her in a well-appointed room, fumbling with a bottle of pills. She freezes as I enter the room.

"W-who are you?" she asks, sniffling.

I naturally think she's talking to me, but I don't speak right away because I'm still processing the idea of two people with The Sight living mere miles apart.

"I am your friend, your only friend," whispers a smooth, silky voice.

I flood the room with spiritual light, just a quick burst. One with The Sight would notice, but normal mortals cannot sense the change. Demons, on the other hand, feel such an attack like a flash-bang grenade. Time in the mortal realm marches on everywhere except in this room.

The Despair demon yelps and curls into a ball. He's in the form of a small, black cat. Spotting me, he hisses.

"Go find your own mortal."

"Be gone, pest," I say, studying the girl. Usually, suicidal thoughts don't really kick into gear until a human is in their mid-to-late teens, but this child looked to be about eleven. The tender age makes me angrier at the idea of her being a target for Despair demons. "She's under my protection now." I draw Tyre to let the Despair demon know I mean to back up that claim.

Leveling the blade at the demon, I step slowly to my left until I'm next to the girl. I brighten my presence until the room fills with a soft, white glow. The light shines off the girl's long, brown hair and highlights the wet tear-tracks marking her cheeks. The way she's clutching the pill bottle tells me she thinks it'll hold a cure for the pain in her eyes. I'm not sure what put the pain there, but I want to drive it away.

"What did you do to her?" I demand.

The demon morphs into a little boy, sits on the floor, and clasps his arms around his knees.

"Why are you picking on me?" he asks. "You're a bully."

"And you're a liar."

Instead of admitting it, the Despair demon giggles.

"No lies, master angel," he says innocently, changing forms yet again. Now he resembles unholy black smoke polluting the center of the room. Squinting, animal eyes glare at me from the smoke. His voice too has changed back to the silky whisper. "This time none were needed. Shall I share what's been done to her?"

"No." My protest comes out weaker than I'd like.

It makes the demon bold.

"I'm in a sharing mood." The Despair demon conjures a small glass slab and tosses it to me. "Watch it if you dare."

I try not to look, but I can't help it. The scene it contains rips my heart out and crushes it to dust. Nobody should go through what I saw depicted in that cursed piece of glass, let alone a child. My breath quickens, and my human form feels queasy.

"Where were you when *that* happened to her? Where was your great, merciful master when her father took—"

"Silence!" I command, pointing Tyre directly between the demon's eyes. No trace of hesitation can be heard now. I didn't think it was a binding command, but I see from the demon's hateful eyes that it has that effect. "You will never speak of this to her again, nor will you make any promises to her of peace through death."

The demon feigns disinterest.

"I've sated myself on her misery anyway. Her death would have been a fitting end, but have it your way. Good luck fighting the darkness in her, little luminary. I may yet claim her soul this night, but you may try to save her." The Despair demon drifts toward the ceiling and slips out an air vent.

With him gone, the air feels ten times lighter. Dimming my spiritual light and putting Tyre away, I give my human form more substance but not enough for those without The Sight to sense. I let time return to normal, and the girl resumes trying to open the bottle. I still her hands with a gentle touch. She stops moving. I'm told each human senses us differently. The child shivers like my hands are made of ice. She clenches her eyes shut and starts to duck her chin, meaning to withdraw into herself. Warming my hands, I lift her chin and remove the pill bottle from her limp fingers.

"This is not the answer," I say.

The words won't register with her, but the sentiment will.

"Please, God. Let me die. I want to go to heaven," murmurs the girl.

"I am not the Glorious King, but I am a messenger. If you know His name, you know His truths. You are safe now. I'll see to that." I speak slowly. "As for the heavens, they will await your presence with joy, but for now, this world needs you."

"I'm no good for anything," says the girl, her voice breaking. "I'm fat. I'm ugly. I don't have any friends."

At times like this, I really wish I could summon Mina. She'd know what to tell this kid.

"You are exactly who you should be, Zara," I argue. "You are a part of a chosen people with the potential for claiming your birthright as a princess of heaven."

I instinctively avoid commenting on her weight. Crystal Zara Benson may be carrying a tad more weight than she ought to for her age and height but I'm definitely not the judge on that score. The weight's not the key issue anyway. A class on how humanity works taught me that much. It's about social circles drawing imaginary lines to say what should be popular and what should not. Young people are simply more blatant about how they show contempt to their peers. Adults tend to judge with eyes and thoughts over blurted barbs.

"Don't let anybody tell you otherwise. They are ignorant and lost and trying to lead you astray."

Before I can present my case any clearer, a dark feeling of oppression fills the room.

"I changed my mind," says the Despair demon, appearing before me.

He blocks my ability to freeze time.

The girl just looks around the room confused.

Suddenly, hands grasp me from multiple sides. My cries contain both frustration and pain, drowning out the demons' delighted shrieks. I know the contact hurts them too, but they take turns holding my arms, legs, and body. They force me back against a wall and hold me there. The burning sensation drops to a tolerable level as the demons withdraw to give the Despair demon room to approach.

"Did you miss me, little luminary?"

"Terribly," I say through gritted teeth.

He forms a human face and laughs. It's a man's face, hard and cruel, with shaggy dark hair and yellow eyes.

"Ooooh, you are a sharp one. I'm glad I didn't leave my precious girl here in your care too long." He frowns and glares at me. "You might have convinced her to save herself."

I summon Tyre from beyond the Veil, kicking myself for sending the spirit sword away in the first place. I have less control with the weapon out of my hands, but if I can concentrate enough, the sword will obey my will. Right now, it begins tracking the lead demon.

The Despair demon makes disapproving tones and shakes his head. He forms a hand from the smoke to shake a finger at me.

"Now, now, little luminary, that's not very sporting."

His minions tighten their grip on my arms and legs, causing my concentration to waver.

"What's going on?" asks the girl. Her unseeing eyes search the room. To her, we're phantom feelings, impossible for most mortals to fathom.

"One wrong move and she dies," promises the demon.

"You can't harm her," I remind him.

"True," he purrs. "But she can harm herself."

He drops a razor blade onto the ground in front of the girl.

"Pick up the blade," he instructs.

In slow motion, the girl's hand closes around the cold piece of metal. I think forward the whole situation. General rules of engagement will fail this child. If I do nothing, the Despair demon will convince her to take her own life in a matter of minutes, if not seconds. I can see exactly how her fingers will curl around the blade, drawing blood unintentionally even as she moves the blade toward her left wrist. She's dreamt about this moment countless times. She draws courage from the memories of having done these exact moves a hundred thousand times to drive away different thoughts.

Lives matter more than rules.

Drawing my spiritual presence in tight, I fully embrace my human form, thus slipping from the demons' hold on me. The sudden release tosses me off balance. I throw my body forward, landing on one knee before the startled girl. Her eyes lock on mine. She's absolutely speechless, which is good because otherwise she'd be screaming her head off.

"Don't be afraid," I say. "I'm here to help."

"What are you doing?" hisses the lead demon. "You can't do that! Turn back into spirit form at once, I say!"

I face the demon and give him a cool look, turning on enough of my spiritual powers to summon Tyre to hand. The effect gives my body a luminescent glow. One of the other demons approaches but the sharp end of Tyre discourages him. Another, bolder demon lashes out at me and meets Tyre head on. His shriek explodes in the room, stirring the other demons. Half attack and half flee. The next several heartbeats pass in a flurry of strikes while I weave a complicated defense to drive the demons away from myself and the girl.

Finally, the lead demon calls a halt. We stare at each other, locked in a battle of wills.

"Let's try this again." I fill my voice with conviction. "Get gone now."

"You will see us again," vows the demon. He nods to his remaining helpers and they quit the battlefield together.

"Who ...?" The girl lets the rest of the question trail off. Her expression says I'm making quite an impression.

Guess it's not every day she sees a sword-wielding teenage boy brightening the room with light from his body. I have scant time to explain before she faints or screams. Drawing a quick breath, I speak fast.

"My name is Allister. I'm not a figment of your imagination, but I am here to convince you that life's worth living."

She starts to shake her head.

"You don't know what my life's like," the girl whispers.

"I know enough, Zara."

"Then you know why I want to move on. Please, just let me end this." The girl leans back against her bed, drawing her knees up defensively. Then, she folds her arms on her knees and drops her head onto her arms. "I just want to die."

"You may not know it, but you're important where I come from."

Zara lifts her head and narrows her eyes at me, daring me

to make a point quickly.

I start to gesture with Tyre, think better of it, and rest the sword on the ground, leaning on it as one rests on a cane.

"I'm serious. I fought a half-dozen demons tonight. Their master must fear you greatly."

"Why would anybody fear me?" the girl wonders. "I'm—"

"A princess," I finish. "That's what your name means." Taking a seat in the middle of her room, I pick up Tyre and rest him on my lap. I won't make the mistake of sending the spirit sword away again, at least not tonight. "I don't have all the answers, but I bet you I have some. Would you like me to tell you why I think you're important?"

Suspicion fills her gaze, but I also see curiosity. I spend the next hour and a half bringing Zara up to date on the state of the universe. I'd say the schools these days are sadly lacking, but the history I told the girl is not widely known among humans. They could gather the answers if they read the Holy Book left for them, but sometimes, the direct approach is better.

I understand that every human life is important, but it's starting to feel like everybody I meet is under severe attack. I suppose that's something I'll have to get used to in this ERT life.

Chapter 16:
The Master Grows Impatient

Dear Lord Hadeon,

Deimos says you will be issuing orders to move forward soon and that the target is the girl only. Why? I'm not questioning the order. I am simply asking for clarification.

Without a manifested Gift, the girl's practically harmless. They are both vulnerable.

I understand the dangers of the Kindred Spirit Bond strengthening the angelings when they're together, but could they not both be captured and taken to separate prisons? If one prisoner is valuable, might not two prisoners be twice so?

I suggested this to Deimos and Daeva. The former ignored me and the latter only said that she would "take care of" the boy. What does that mean? I think I should be made aware of the others' orders if they intersect closely to my plans. I have no wish to disrupt them or have them interfere with me. I understand I'm part of a greater plan, but I do not like that there are many moving pieces I cannot predict.

As always, I am yours to command,
Than

***

Dear Than,

The time has indeed come to move the plan forward. Stick to your original plan. You've come far in the last few weeks, but be cautious. If you argue for the girl too strenuously, one might be tempted to think you've grown soft in your days with those who walk the path of the Light. Tell me that isn't so. You know the consequences of hesitation and failure.

I owe you no answers, but I will give you a few because I believe the truth will renew your passion for our cause. We are not waiting for the girl to manifest her Gift because the Dark Master believes we can direct her choice. Besides, she will be easier to capture while still in training. The master's eager to complete his project. While the angels debate why the master wants the girl, his plans for them can be fulfilled.

As for why the girl should be captured, I don't know. I agree, dead would be less threatening. Angels are very difficult to kill. I believe the Dark Master's project has something to do with making destroying them easier, but I do not know the details. I believe she means something special to their king. It's said He has a unique and binding love for all his creations, but I try not to think about that sort of drivel.

The girl may be a means to another end. Speculating would be useless. We will know when the Dark Master reveals the rest of his plans. One does not utilize such resources without cause. Making her one of us would be intriguing, but for a conversion to stick, there must be a desire to turn. I'm not sensing that from your reports. You sound like you admire this angeling. Destroy those feelings. Whatever the master plans for her, interfering would be unwise.

You've come far, but I will not hesitate to replace you if I suspect you'll disobey my orders.

Your reward waits for you here with me.

Your coordinated attacks on the people are going well, but do not let that work interfere with your true mission. I'm sending Deimos back to you. Try not to antagonize him. He will help you this time because I've ordered it so. Once he feels free of that obligation, he may seek to right any perceived slights. I will not protect you from him, and you do not want him as your enemy.

I believe your first plan has merit. It is safer than your backup plan. I'm sending you help. Do not waste their talents on grunt work. If you can work them into your plan, do so. If not, keep them close but out of sight.

Should you need to rely upon the second plan, do everything you can to keep your cover intact. We may need to send you back to the school again. Your second plan is risky. There are a lot of places for things to go wrong. Choose your human targets carefully. A small gathering would suffice, but don't attempt to run the plan near a large group of humans. Large gatherings increase the chance that someone has The Sight. If they can see you, they can interfere. You may think their prayers are empty words, but I've seen too many plans crumble under the weight of prayer.

I don't know how this works. I don't know why this works. I only know you need to accomplish your task without rousing the attention of prayer warriors. The king listens to them. Should you be tasked to combat prayer warriors in the future, heed this advice. Do not make judgments identifying such humans based on sight. They can be young or old, rich or poor, sickly or hale. You will know them by their auras. The strength of their spirit gives them away.

The same weapons that succeed against all humans can be tried, but be willing to adapt. Some fold the first time you place opposition in their way. Give them a lingering disease, and many people will abandon hope in their king. But the same cannot be said for true believers. If you give the wrong person a lingering disease, you'll strengthen their testimony and faith to an unbreakable point.

Distraction might be your best weapon. Fill their lives with so much busyness that they forget to worship or pray. Fan their desire to get ahead at work or school. Beat the message into their hearts that their worth is tied to physical achievements. Give them their fill of silly little games that mean nothing. The less time they spend thinking about the state of their souls, the better for us.

For reasons beyond me, their king gave such weak creatures incredible powers. A few can peer past the distractions to the core. These beings are dangerous. Either avoid them, or destroy them by other means. Part of joy and pride in our work is finding exactly which strings to pull to get the humans to obey.

Meditate on these instructions. Don't think that because you've heard this before you don't need to hear it again. You'll doubtless be called to serve by destroying humans eventually, but for now, I'll remind you that you have one week to accomplish your mission.

I know you understand that the girl must survive the capture, but convey that message to those under your command. Also, this is very important. The demons at your disposal may find the girl in a target-rich environment. Should that be the case, be certain they focus on their mission. You must choose their targets for them. Those not after the prize must distract the others. They are not to attempt capturing their opponents. They are incapable of multitasking, and I'll not have them improvising because they see someone they deem a better captive.

When you catch the angeling, you will bring her to me. If you face opposition or fear pursuit, turn her over to Deimos. He will know how to find me. You may wonder why I don't tell you the rendezvous now. It's not a trust issue. You don't need the information right now. When you need it, you will have it.

Hadeon, Servant of the Dark Master,

Director of Operations

Part 3:
Target

Chapter 17:
Comforter

Trainee Case Report #: MN-106
Case Agent: Master Blaz
Guardian Candidate: Mina Nadir
I dislike funerals. They're meant to give people closure, but the heavy atmosphere gives me an empty feeling in the pit of my stomach. Comforters are necessary, but I can confidently say I do not want to specialize in this. Abdon stays close to me but does not speak much.

"What am I supposed to do here?" Although the humans cannot hear the whispered question, it sounds painfully loud to my ears.

A grim-faced man steps right through us on his way to a quiet corner. The touch gives me a flash of insight into his life. His name is Carter Alfred McAvoy, Jr. though his friends call him Cam for his initials. He's thirty-nine and addicted to his job. The funeral is for his younger brother, Jeb, who died of pancreatic cancer. Carter tries to look appropriately somber, but his thoughts are consumed by how much money he's losing by missing the day of work. He'd had to drive three hours from New York City to get here, and he'll have to do the same tonight or miss more time tomorrow. He could try working remotely, but one couldn't get a true feel for the trades if you weren't on the floors.

"Watch, listen, heal, and console," says Abdon.

I blink at him, confused.

"Can I ... adjust attitudes?" I wonder, turning to face Carter.

He's directly in front of me now at a distance most would consider uncomfortable. His right hand flexes and he glances about nervously. Noticing that everybody else seems preoccupied chatting in small, subdued groups or else studying the shrine set up for Jeb, he slips his phone out of his suit pocket and checks his messages.

"You can try." Abdon doesn't sound very optimistic about my chances.

"You don't think I can do it?" My inflection makes it a question.

"I don't think you should do it unless you have the right intent." Instead of clearing things up, Abdon's words confuse me more.

"What's that supposed to mean?" I keep my gaze on Carter whose fingers are frantically pounding at the phone in his hands.

"Without the right intent, your changes will be temporary," Abdon explains. "If you want them to stick, you need to work through the people around you." He gestures to the room. "That is part of your task here today. Don't just change one person, change everything."

Accepting the challenge, I expand my empathic sphere and sample the emotions around me. I close my eyes to concentrate and remain facing Carter and the corner. Most people feel cool. Their auras are shades of blue and gray in my mind's eye. This tells me they're strangers. An older woman clutching a wad of tissues sits near the display featuring a photo album of the deceased's life. A slide presentation slowly cycles through the same pictures on the wall several feet above the woman's head. Her emotions give her a yellow-orange aura. A man standing at the lady's elbow supervises the solemn procession of people filing past.

Fifteen paces away from them stands a cluster of women surrounding the widow. Tina McAvoy is easy to find because her grief blazes within her like a furnace trying to heat a very large building. I almost miss the smaller presence pasted to her side. Her son, Edwin, feels cold. He's not feeling much of anything.

It strikes me how differently people react to the same loss. The brother distracts himself by focusing on his own issues. The son withdraws. The mother feels the loss but has enough life experience to handle it with a resigned grace. The wife cycles through disbelief, shock, fear, and deep, consuming pain.

I actively block out the conversations while I consider how best to serve this family. I don't necessarily want to cause grief, but I do want each person to heal. Burying the feelings is only going to make them harder to deal with later. The women are well attended for the moment. The boy seems to be in the most danger of being ignored. Opening my eyes, I find myself once again staring at Carter McAvoy. His attention remains fixed on his phone.

Deciding I need to do something, I reach out and touch Carter's phone. The small electric surge prompts the machine to reset itself, shutting down the screen. I pull a memory of the update bar from Carter's mind and display it prominently. While he thinks hard, trying to remember authorizing an update, I hustle over to the ladies surrounding the widow. Passing through that many people disorients me, but I kneel before Edwin and reveal myself for just an instant. There's a slight chance somebody unintended will see me, but I'll deal with that problem if it crops up. The boy hugs his mother's leg closer, but otherwise, there's no reaction.

Edwin. Edwin. Come with me. I send the thought directly into his mind and tug on his spirit. He stirs. For a second I think I see a spark enter his eyes, but it winks out like a snuffed candle. It's very unnatural. Stretching forth my hand, I touch Edwin's chest.

Searing pain shoots through my hand, making me retrieve it in a hurry. I rock back on my heels and watch as a Sloth demon slowly rises like a genie forming from lantern smoke.

"Who disturbs me?" he intones lazily. His voice rumbles through the room powerfully, but I'm not intimidated. I know his bluster declares the limits of his power.

I stand, but he still towers over me.

"What's a Sloth demon doing at a funeral?" I demand.

He pretends not to see me, making a show of looking everywhere but down at me. Moment by moment his presence grows larger. Soon, his head will go through the ceiling.

"I'm working," he says, gazing languidly down at me.

A quick check shows me that Edwin's slowly coming out of the sloth-induced stupor. I direct him to go see his uncle while I deal with the demon.

"Why'd you do that?" complains the Sloth demon. "I was just having some fun."

"Fun? Blocking a little boy from feeling his father's death is fun?"

He bobs his head.

"Why should the child experience pain?"

The Sloth demon's twisted logic disturbs me because it actually makes sense. Didn't I seek to ease the child's pain too? What harm could there be in delaying the unpleasantness? Drawing my empathic sphere in like a shield, I use the power to clear my head.

The Sloth demon chuckles and shifts into a more defined figure. He now resembles a jolly fat man with a long, white beard. He looks completely harmless.

I tense, fighting the urge to drop my guard.

"You're quicker than most of your kind," he compliments.

"And you're far from your usual haunts," I note. "Why is that? I thought initiative was against your nature."

"Orders are orders," says the Sloth demon. His words roll out of him slowly, straining my patience. His smug smile is cause for concern. "We got word an angel might train here."

Internal alarms blare. I hurtle over to the boy and his uncle, arriving as Carter's fingers clamp down on Edwin's shoulders. To anyone watching, it would appear a friendly, supportive touch, but I can see the Dominator standing behind Carter. Thick tendrils attach to the man at several points along his arms and through his back. Carter's eyes hold nothing.

Puppet Master demon.

Hearing of Dominators and even taking a quiz on the rare abominations could not prepare me for meeting one. Facing one this firmly entrenched in a victim brings the knowledge to an entirely different level.

The Dominator pauses time.

"Kneel. Or the boy dies." The Dominator's voice is even and controlled, perfectly pitched to sound reasonable. "I'll have the man snap his neck like a twig."

I drop to my knees, knowing I might regret the compromise later. Unsure of what to do with my hands, I place them in my lap.

"Ah, I see you've met Master Deimos," says the Sloth demon from behind me.

"A pleasure," mocks Deimos.

"State your demands." I barely hold a tremor out of my voice.

"What makes you think I have demands?" Deimos inquires. His tone implies only mild curiosity. He adjusts a few of the strings holding Carter.

"The hostages," I say. "They'd be dead if you didn't want something from me."

The man's head comes up and jiggles from side to side. His jaw opens and closes in sync with Deimos's next words.

"Ding! Ding! You win! Give the baby angel a bottle and tell her what she's won, Bob."

"Must you call me that? You know I hate that name." The Sloth demon doesn't sound particularly aggrieved, but I can feel his presence grow more menacing behind me.

"Spoilsport. Would it kill you to do your job?" Deimos's mood shifts from jovial to deadly.

"Assume your human form," instructs the Sloth demon.

When I hesitate, Deimos yanks Carter into a straighter posture and draws the man's head back. One of the tendrils slips out of Carter's arm, sharpens to a point, and hovers close to his neck.

"Please. Disobey the order," Deimos begs with a crazy grin and matching gleam in his eyes.

I do.

Rather, I start the process to leave the spirit realm and melt into the mortal one, but when the process is only half done, I dash forward, aligning my body with Carter and Edwin. Then, I revert back to my spirit form. Deimos and I scream simultaneously. The experience is much like the fight with the Guilt demon in Mark's room only magnified a hundred fold.

Deimos withdraws suddenly, and Carter collapses. His concentration breaks, allowing time to continue. People rush forward to see what's wrong with Carter. Edwin starts crying. Deimos forces another pause in time. His red eyes stab into me, and I see him struggle to regain his composure.

I reinforce my spirit, adjusting to the pain levels. My entire form feels scalded. The slash across my cheek reopens.

"You may keep their pathetic lives," Deimos pronounces like he's doing me a great favor. "But mark my words. We will meet again under different circumstances, and I will repay this insult." He allows his presence to slip behind the Veil back to wherever he crawled out from.

The Sloth demon utters a disapproving noise.

I turn my attention to him, but I dare not move for fear Deimos will return and grip Carter again. In theory, Deimos could control any human being in the room or several at once, but the level of control he sought with Carter requires singular attention. He won't return while I stand over Carter.

"You made a powerful enemy today," the Sloth demon remarks.

"Were we not already enemies?" I inquire.

"Yes." The Sloth demon draws out the word. "But you've made it personal."

Neither of us speaks for a time, long enough to let the excitement over Carter's fall fade. Two men help him over to a chair while a woman identifying herself as a nurse examines him. I follow close behind.

The Sloth demon tags along.

"What would have happened if I had obeyed?" I ask, not really expecting an answer.

"You'd be dead," says the Sloth demon conversationally. "Or a prisoner."

"Why would you admit that?" I'm surprised by the Sloth demon's candor.

"Tis no secret there's a war," he replies. "This is only the beginning." With that last statement still ringing in my ears, the Sloth demon bows and disappears before I can press him further on motivation.

Of course, there's a war, but to my knowledge there's always been a war. So, what's different now? The trap set seems pretty clearly meant for me, but why? And who told them where to find me?

***

Dear Lord Hadeon,

Deimos has failed, but I will make this right. I have arranged for both angelings to be at the location you specified. I'm tempted to ask why you let him go forth with that doomed funeral plan, but I trust you have your reasons.

I will not fail you.

Your most humble servant,

Than

Chapter 18:
Frontlines

Apprentice Case Report #: AK-108
Case Agent: Mistress Adira Clarimond
Guardian Candidate: Allister Knight

My thoughts rest with Zara while I walk the perimeter around a small suburban home. I usually find guard duty boring, but I think I need an easy job right now. That thing with Zara and the Despair demon still bothers me. Paige promised to check in with her, and a Guardian named Skylar has been assigned to stay with her until she's less likely to attract more demons.

Humans can be cruel to one another. They don't need the demons to tell them how to harm each other. The enemy's hold over this place might be stronger than I previously believed.

Most humans try to mind their own business and their small spheres of influence. They either actively ignore the bright signs of hope, or else, they think it doesn't matter. Many choose the gray area, thinking it offers them neutrality. They fail to remember that there is no middle ground in matters of righteousness.

The method the Glorious King chose to present salvation to these people is difficult for them to accept. They devalue the power of belief, painting it as something necessary only for the young and the weak. Humans want to earn everything. Americans are especially susceptible to the idea that working harder will get them anything they desire. Their hearts get so absorbed in consuming, there's little room for the mysteries of the universe. They fall prey to many lies. Those who do question end up condemned in the court of public opinion.

Their relationship with "free" is complicated. They enjoy getting small things free, but the word becomes linked with "trivial." Their movies and novels brim with tales of bravery and self-sacrifice, but again, there comes the notion—the lie—that one must have certain attributes to be a hero. Justice becomes a catchphrase for handling petty grievances instead of defending the purity of their souls.

For an instant, I experience the weighty sadness that the Glorious King must feel when he contemplates the people of Earth.

Casting my attention in brief spurts allows me glimpses into the minds of those in nearby houses. Out of curiosity, I sample their concerns. A child wonders why her game won't play. A teenager struggles to concentrate on his math homework. A woman prays she won't lose her job. A man with lung cancer hopes to see his son graduate high school. He hasn't told his family about the illness yet. The worries fall into several basic categories: health, wealth, and success. Spiritual worries lie far down the list of desirable pursuits. Most of their worries will sort themselves in time, but I contact the Prayer Room to let them know about the man with lung cancer. There's a good chance the request will be granted. Whether that means a cure or a short extension, I don't know.

Tyre lights up the area around me. I hold the spirit sword high as a beacon, a warning to those who wish this household harm that we are actively watching over those within. There's a chance the warning will draw demons looking for trouble, but more likely, they'll respect the boundary.

Lady A. is inside with the others, but I volunteered to check around. The task gives me a chance to clear my head. I wish I could take on my human form, but the neighborhood seems lively enough that someone might see me. I'd rather not have to explain that to Lady A. tonight.

I imagine what the night air would feel like. Maybe when this job's over, I'll stay to enjoy the quiet for a time. I'm starting to realize how isolating this job can be. I hardly get to see Mina these days, let alone talk to her. When I do catch glimpses of her, it's usually as she rushes off to one training session or another. I suppose the same could be said for me.

"Want company?"

Mina's voice startles me enough to tighten my grip on Tyre.

"What are you doing here?" I return.

"Watching you march around a house with your head in a cloud somewhere." Mina's not in her human form, but she is wearing jeans and a faded college sweatshirt like she expects to take the form sometime this evening. "You should come inside. I'm sure someone else can take the perimeter track for a while."

"I'm fine," I insist. "I like the peace." An awkward beat passes before I add, "But I'd also enjoy the company."

We complete two circles without talking much. I want to ask her how the training goes but I also just want to enjoy the moment with no expectations.

"You're troubled," Mina says.

"So I am," I admit.

Mina nods and takes my hand, lending quiet strength while I ponder what to say to her. The contact shows me the trauma she's recently experienced.

"You were hurt." I stop and automatically scan my friend to see the extent of the damage.

"So I was," she replies, taking small pleasure in mimicking my earlier response. "A demon called Deimos wanted to kill people in my care. I objected and we both got burned."

The response strikes me as something I'd have said a few months ago. It's defensive and dismissive. I want to inquire if she's really recovering but her spirit's locked down behind a strong emotional wall.

"Deimos." I murmur the name. It tickles the back of my mind like I should know something about this particular demon.

"He's a Dominator," Mina says. She stops and faces me. Hesitation is etched in her features. She appears not to know whether to be concerned or embarrassed. "And I think he was after me." Mina quickly walks me through the funeral events.

By the end, a dozen questions crowd my mind. I recall the

name Deimos associated with a demon fairly high up in the enemy's organization. I can't remember specifics, but for the name to spark any recognition, I must have heard it spoken. His involvement in such a plot lends the matter substance and gravity, but it cannot explain how Mina became a target. She's powerful and likely Gifted more generously than most of our kind, but she's not even fully trained yet. Preemptive attacks are a common enough enemy tactic, but rarely does that extend to our kind.

"What does Master Blaz think?" I inquire, knowing Mina must have spent a long time discussing the matter with him.

"He wants to send me back to the Academy within the Heavens until the investigation is complete."

"Then, what are—"

"I'm not going, Allister," Mina interrupts.

"But it's safer," I protest lamely.

Mina's grim smile tells me I'm being ridiculous. Nothing we do is safe. That's why we endure such intense training. Tangling with a Dominator demon might be beyond the curriculum, but the field lessons are meant to prepare us for the war.

"If I'm that important to the Enemy, he'll find a way to reach me." Anger bristles beneath Mina's controlled tone. "I will not let him dictate how I live my life."

"Be careful," I urge. "Maybe you should meditate on your Gifts. The sooner you manifest a specialty, the better for everybody."

I lay bare my spirit, showing my friend concern and support.

"Master Blaz suggested the same when I refused to return to the Heavens."

Before I can ask if she'll heed that advice, Tyre glows brighter. Snapping my attention back to the guard duty, I swing Tyre in a long arc and increase my personal presence. Mina's now two paces to my left, crouching with Kentaro held at the ready. At the edge of my perception, I sense a horde of demons watching. They take the shape of night creatures and monsters, but remain at a good distance.

"What are they doing?" I wonder.

"They're waiting to spot a weakness," Lady A. answers, appearing several steps to my right. I'm reassured by the sight of Tamotsu, Lady A.'s katana.

"Do they always watch like this?" asks Mina. "And why are there so many of them?"

"The opposition is usually proportionate to the threat they perceive," Lady A. answers, focusing on the gathering demons. "They don't like the prayer meeting taking place inside."

When several tense minutes crawl by, I risk a glance through the window to see whom we're protecting. I glimpse a gathering of six people, four women and two men, kneeling on the carpet.

I suggest we take turns checking the other sides of the building, but Lady A. assures me others have those areas covered. Curious, I move my awareness around, sensing three Guardians on each side, two on the roof, and two in the basement.

From time to time, groups of four to five demons rush one side of the defenses or another. Lady A., Mina, and I beat back our share with the spirit swords.

"Why are they holding back?" I ask.

A third small wave of demons retreats.

"Would you prefer they charge together?" Mina demands.

"They only want us to know they're here tonight," Lady A. explains.

"Demons are strange," I mutter.

Lady A. chuckles.

"We're on the frontline here and it stretches across this terrestrial ball. The enemy knows he must bide his time, but he also wishes us to remember him."

Mina and I accept her words and keep our guards up in case of further attacks but none come. The prayer meeting breaks up, and the demons lose interest and wink out one by one. I wonder where they go when they're not bothering humans or angels.

I breathe easier when the last one disappears, but I catch sight of Lady A.'s tense expression.

"It's not over yet."

As if to prove those four words, small thumps can be

heard from the roof. Several muffled cries follow, punctuated by the sounds of renewed fighting. The demons shriek and crash onto the roof, scuttling down the sides of the house in an angry tide.

An angel gets hurled from the side and plummets headfirst toward me. I duck, but he spreads his wings and halts his fall in time to avoid flattening me.

The first demon to reach me receives Tyre through his chest. His shriek is infinitely worse than the one uttered as a challenge. Then, four more attack. One leaps onto my back while two more latch onto a leg each and a third reaches for my eyes. I ram the spirit sword's pommel into the one in front before whipping Tyre over my right shoulder to scald the one on my back. The nuisances hanging onto my legs hiss and retreat.

I catch sight of a man kneeling in the center of the room where the prayer meeting had just broken up. Peace and strength flood through me. I leap up to the roof and charge the demons surrounding the angel up there. He's saturated with demonic shadows. Tyre flicks out seven times, connecting with different demons. They scream and disappear.

I lose track of time. Instinct guides my blade into enemy after enemy. Every vanquished demon hits me like the brush of cooling rain. Energy sings through my muscles, and I'm a blur dashing back and forth across the roof, sending demons in every direction.

When it's over, I stare around the area in a daze. Angels pick themselves off the ground or tend to wounds. A car engine starts up, but I think nothing of it. I count thirteen angels in total, and know something's wrong before I hear Lady A.'s grim declaration.

"She is gone."

Chapter 19:
Twilight State

Trainee Case Report #: MN-107
Case Agent: Master Blaz
Guardian Candidate: Mina Nadir

I awaken in a car with a massive headache. A large hypodermic needle sticks up out of my left leg. My hands are bound in my lap with a brown belt. They shimmer as we pass under streetlights. I'm in twilight state. Understanding slowly presses past the fog in my head. The last thing I remember is the sensation of many demons falling upon me at once. I must have sought refuge in my human form. I'm not sure how I ended up in this car, but the more important matter is how to escape.

The fact that I'm not fully human means something must be forcing me to return to spirit state. On a hunch, I carefully adjust my state to slightly more human than angel. The headache increases, and I start to lose consciousness. The pain from the needle still planted in my leg finally registers. The connection to my physical form slips, and I ease deeper into my spirit. Before the shift goes too far though, I grasp the needle's thin shaft and yank it clear of my leg. I consider keeping it, but whatever it held is entirely in me already. Given the strength of the drug, my physical form probably won't be up to wielding the needle as a weapon. I toss the needle in the general direction of the floor and note that my feet are bound too.

With great effort, I turn my head left and look at the stranger driving the car. He stares straight ahead, and his profile appears like a normal man. Short, dark hair and medium toned skin don't tell me much. He occasionally mutters to himself in brief, nonsensical sentences.

I could attempt fully assuming my spirit form, but something tells me that would be unwise. The man turns toward me. His eyes flip between vacant and frenzied. That tells me a lot.

Demons.

Looks like I'll be staying in twilight state for a short while longer. Physical state will allow the drug to knock me out, and spirit state will allow the demons to take me wherever they like. Neither option sounds appealing. If I stay mostly in a physical state, the demons will have a hard time transporting me, but I also can't stay in human form very long. Human bodies are much frailer than spirit forms.

If I can change briefly into spirit, perhaps Allister or Master Blaz can find me. My calculations get interrupted by an unhurried voice from behind me.

"Don't worry. We'll convince you to choose the spirit form soon enough."

Edging more into my spirit allows me to gain enough energy to reply to the Sloth demon. I can also sense the other demons better.

"So they're sending you on errands again," I say. "For a being who embraces sloth, you're pretty busy."

"Sloth has its applications, but when the Dark Master issues orders, one obeys without question." He moves closer and softens his tone. "Besides, some tasks are more enjoyable than others."

I try to ignore him, but I sense he's waiting for a response. The best I can do is not give him the responses he wants and to try and learn something useful about the situation.

"She wants to speak, but which common captive question will she turn to?" The Sloth demon's voice dips into a creepy whisper. "Will it be 'Why me?' or 'What next?' or 'Where are you taking me?'"

"Why you?" I ask, mentally discarding the other

questions.

"Why not?" His question has a sharp, defensive edge. "I am a servant of the Dark Master. This is my job."

For a while, I watch the lamplights pass. I do wonder where they're taking me, but I'll not ask about it. The knowledge wouldn't change anything.

"What brought you to your master?" I try to keep the query light but it lands between us like a boulder.

"Let's focus on you," says the Sloth demon. "Don't you want to know our demands?"

"Not really." I let myself slip towards human form until I'm quite drowsy. "The longer I can put that off, the longer you can pretend I'm going to bow to those demands."

"You will." His voice now carries a reflective note. "Everybody breaks."

"To what end?" I wonder, taking better stock of my surroundings. The car's interior fabric is mainly shades of gray. "Loyalty cannot be bought by beatings or bloodshed."

"Is that how you think we'll break you?" Compassion seeps into the Sloth demon's words. "You have us all wrong, baby angel. We're trying to break you free from lies you've been fed from your formation."

"I don't need your help," I say. "I need only the Glorious King."

"Aye, but he abandoned you. Didn't he, lass?"

My spirit trembles at the thought until I push it back.

"The King cannot abandon His own. Betrayal belongs to your master, not mine."

"Do you believe your master is love defined?"

The question is a trap, but I feel compelled to answer anyway.

"I do."

"Then why is there suffering in the mortal world and the war in the Heavens?"

It finally dawns on me that the Sloth demon's script must not have been written by him.

"Freedom includes the right to be wrong," I answer. "Why do you fear love?"

"Love is another lie," he replies.

"But your master has only limited affinity for truth. Why would that matter even if it were correct?"

The Sloth demon laughs low.

"You really should accept your fate and turn from falsehood while we're still asking nicely," the Sloth demon advises. "Think of the power you could gain."

I do consider the power. A mental vision of my spirit form cloaked in darkness comes to me unbidden.

"Your first statement implies force will be applied later," I say. "Don't you see? That is how your master works. He tries deception, bribery, gifts, promises of power, and other things most beings desire. But when those fail, he reveals his true nature, the one that relishes pain and suffering."

I maintain enough awareness of my human form to lean my head back against the headrest.

"If not gifts, power, or peace, what do you desire?" asks the Sloth demon.

"My desires don't matter," I maintain. "I am an angel, fashioned to serve and safeguard mankind against your master's plans. He would like nothing more than to see the entire human race on a path to destruction."

"I think you give my master too much credit." The Sloth demon sounds like he's sitting back and settling in for a long ride. "The humans will tear themselves down if given enough time."

"And I think your master's jealous of them."

"Why should he be jealous of those pitiful creatures?" asks the Sloth demon. "They couldn't even save themselves, and when a savior did come, they rejected him."

"Not the whole of humanity has rejected the King's gift," I say. "Your master cut himself off from perfect love. He hates that humans claim the love he could not."

"What of your master and his failings?" challenges the Sloth demon. "He severed ties with the first fruits of his creation. A full third of the angels follow my master. Don't you believe that means anything?"

"It means your master's very persuasive," I admit.

"My master was the only one who stood up for our people," insists the Sloth demon.

"I disagree, but I can see that your heart's not ready to hear anything else."

"Do not waste your time trying to save me." The Sloth demon's words lack bite. "We are beyond hope. We've only to obey."

I don't accept that but I can tell he won't listen. My spirit's restless in this half-state.

"Will your master meet me?"

"You do not want to meet him," declares the Sloth demon. "He has power far above ordinary angels. He might decide you've no need for your soul and rip it clear of both forms. You'd be reset back to nothing. You'd do well to remember that."

"Only my King can command my soul," I argue.

He says nothing to that.

I let silence linger for a while before asking a new question.

"Who am I to have drawn your master's attention?"

"That's better, though I don't have an answer for you."

The car stops moving, and I glance out the windows. We must have left the highway long ago, for I can see nothing but trees and a small cabin. I glance over at the man. He puts the car into park and turns off the engine, letting the key stay in the ignition. His hands stay locked to the steering wheel.

"Who is this man? Let him go."

"He practically begged for this opportunity," says the Sloth demon. "Besides, he would probably die if we released him completely."

"Why?"

"He hasn't eaten anything for several days. He's been too busy preparing for this task."

A strange compassion fills me for both captors. It hurts to hear anybody would willingly play host to a legion of demons. The Sloth demon doesn't seem to enjoy his work very much.

"This man could get help if you released him."

"He doesn't want help. He wants power," the Sloth demon explains. "He wants to be immortal. Men have such ridiculous ideas. It's no wonder they're easy to manipulate."

"Your master doesn't have power over death or life," I

point out, confused. "He cannot build, only destroy and ruin."

"Ah, but this slave doesn't know that." The Sloth demon sounds amused. "In his eyes, my master can do no wrong. You too will think like that in the near future."

My sympathy for the man multiplies. I long to tell him of their lies and help him gain release from service to the Prince of Darkness, but I can do nothing. One glance into his blank expression tells me he probably wouldn't hear anything I say.

The man removes and pockets the car key. Then, he climbs out of the driver's seat and bounds around the car to my side. Whipping open the door, he leans in and fumbles with the seat belt latch. I want to resist him, to fight him, but the nearness of hundreds of demons makes my spirit tremble and withdraw, giving the drug a stronger grip on me. The man's touch doesn't burn me because he's still fully human. He lifts me clear of the car and carries me into the cabin.

Chapter 20:
Pursuit

Apprentice Case Report #: AK-109
Case Agent: Mistress Adira Clarimond
Guardian Candidate: Allister Knight

"I'm going after her." I should make it a request, but I can't afford for Lady A. to forbid me from finding Mina. I don't think she would, but one never knows with Council members.

"How?" Lady A. wonders. "If they're in spirit form, they could have taken her anywhere."

"She's still on Earth. I can feel her."

"He is right," says Paige, appearing to my right. "I was watching from the Prayer Room. I came to tell you that demons attacked Mina, forcing her into human form, and a man put her into a car and drove off. Abdon is still monitoring the car."

Lady A. frowns.

"Did they target Mina?"

"Yes, Mistress Clarimond," Paige answers.

"I don't care why they took her. We need to get her back!" I bounce on the balls of my feet.

Lady A. stills me with a look.

"The why could be very important, Allister." The look softens. "But I agree that you should join the pursuit. Take Bali and Reena with you."

"He'll need a human guide more than spirit protectors,"

Paige says.

"Why is that?" Lady A. voices the question as I open my mouth to do the same.

"He will need to stay in one form to sense his friend, and he cannot do that and drive at the same time," Paige explains. "Unless he wants to borrow a car."

She looks at me curiously, and I shake my head.

Lady A. absorbs the information with her usual brisk efficiency.

"Do we have assets in the area?" She watches Paige for an answer.

"There's a man three houses down who might help." Paige waves toward her right.

The house looks quiet, but I can see one light shining brightly through a bedroom window.

"But he only has a motorcycle," Paige adds.

I eye Lady A. nervously until she jerks her head in approval.

"Go."

Taking human form, I sprint for the house. My black jeans, blue T-shirt, and leather jacket barely settle on my frame before I'm pounding on the door. Seconds later, I hear frantic footfalls clattering down stairs. A light flickers on over the front stoop, flooding the area. A small woman opens the door and stares up at me. Her gaze sweeps over me and she turns around.

"Roy! Ya got another one!" she calls up the stairs.

A young man wearing clothes much like mine appears at the top and grins. He holds a large, black helmet in his left hand. Skipping down the stairs two at a time, Roy arrives at the doorway in seconds.

"Thought we might have a visitor tonight. How can I help?"

"My friend's been kidnapped, and I need to go after her." Only after the words are out, do I consider how that might sound. At least I had the good sense to leave out the part about demons. It may come up later, but it's hardly something to include in an introduction.

The woman sighs.

"I don't know why ya insist on getting into these things,

Roy, but ya should help him if you can."

The young man leans over and kisses the woman on the cheek.

"Go back to bed, Ma. I'll be back later." Roy joins me on the front stoop.

"I should hope so," says the woman, leaning on the doorway. "I'll be here starting up the prayer chain."

Roy thanks his mother and leads me to a single car garage. We slip past a large SUV in the driveway. Inside, Roy tears a tarp off a large, shiny motorcycle, throws it aside, and plucks a sleek black helmet off the seat where it'd been nestled.

"Ever ride one of these babies?" asks Roy.

"No."

"Say, what's your name?" Roy smiles self-consciously and holds his right hand out toward me. "I know time's short, but I can't let a stranger ride my baby."

"Allister Knight," I say, meeting his handshake.

He pumps my hand hard and presses the first helmet into my chest.

"All right, Allister. Put this on and climb on behind me. I'll have her fired up and ready to go in no time."

True to his word, we're on the road in less than a minute. I direct him to turn left by tapping the appropriate shoulder. We travel without speaking for ten minutes. If the task weren't urgent, I'd find the ride magnificent.

"So, what's this about?" asks Roy once we reach a long stretch of highway. "How long should I stay on this road?"

The clarity in the communication system surprises me. There's hardly any distortion. We could have been in a closed room a foot apart, not hurtling down a highway on a motorcycle.

"We'll be on here a while. I think."

Roy switches lanes to move around a slow car and guns the engine. A few more minutes pass before my driver renews his bid for more information.

"Does this have anything to do with the uptick in demonic activity in the last few months?"

"What do you know about angels and demons?" I wonder. I don't want to tell him more than I have to, but I also gather that he knows much more than the average human.

"Not much besides the fact that you are one, and occasionally, one of y'all needs a ride. Can't say I understand it, but I guess I can be an angelic taxi service. Thought y'all could fly or teleport or something."

"Not all angels have wings or the Gift of teleportation," I explain. We can fly in spirit or twilight form, but Roy needn't know that. "Besides, I need to stay in this form to track my friend."

"You wanna talk about it?" Roy's tone stays friendly, but I can tell he's deeply curious.

I can't tell him much more than he already knows, but I owe him that much at least.

"My friend, Mina, was taken by a man probably controlled by demons."

Roy whistles low.

"That happen a lot?"

"I don't think it's ever happened." Stating that aloud makes me uneasy.

I try to recall any history lessons that mention direct conflict between angels and demons. The last major battle took place ages ago. Nowadays, demons tend to pick on humans, which explains the need for many Guardians. Kidnapping involves planning and coordination that seems disproportionate to the value of their target. Mina means a lot to me, but she's still in training. Lady A. was present tonight, yet the demons still went after Mina.

Time rolls on as the miles rack up. When more than one hour passes, Roy clears his throat.

"Ah, this lady friend of yours. She's an angel, right?"

"Yes."

"How'd they catch her? I've heard y'all can switch between human and spirit forms like flipping a light switch."

"Most of us can," I admit. "Mina's actually better than most at such shifts. It takes a lot of practice. I'm not sure how they caught her, but my guess is that somehow they forced her to keep to her human form."

"Do ya lose abilities by being in human form?" Roy asks.

"Not necessarily."

"What could force her to stay as a human?"

"If she saw an overwhelming number of demons, she might choose to stay human," I explain. "It's not ideal, but it's better than letting the demons take her wherever they want."

Roy doesn't reply right away, but I can feel his agreement.

A cloud covers the moon, plunging everything into darkness for a brief time.

Mina's not exactly in spirit form or human form, but I can still sense her. When the feeling of her moves right I direct Roy to take the next exit. I keep quiet until he makes the turn. The amount of cars on the road has dropped away to almost nothing.

Five minutes later, Roy slows the motorcycle and stops in the middle of the road.

My gut twists and I scramble off the machine, yanking the helmet from my head.

"Why are we stopping?"

Moonlight shines down on Roy and his motorcycle, causing them to cast long shadows. I ease two more steps back and prepare to draw Tyre from the Veil.

"Sorry about this," says Roy, "but the pay was good and the alternatives not pleasant."

"What have you done? You can't stop me. I'll just turn to spirit and move on."

"I wouldn't recommend that. They're eager for you to try though." Roy points toward the sky.

The "cloud" returns as a few thousand bats flying in rapid circles above us. They're definitely not normal bats.

"I only need to slow ya down." With that, Roy revs the motorcycle engine.

Most beings would have let him go.

Not me.

I pluck Tyre out of the Veil and will it into physical shape. The transformation's not complete, but it's enough. Swinging the sword two-handed, I slash both tires. There's a split-second delay before both tires flatten.

Roy rips off his helmet.

"What's your problem, man?"

"I want company. Now send your little friends packing."

"Are you insane? They're demons! They don't listen to

me." Roy jumps off his motorcycle to inspect the ruined tires.

"What exactly were you instructed to do?"

"Leave you here. That's it. I sw—"

I cut him off by raising a hand.

"A man in your position should be careful about the oaths he makes." I raise my eyes toward the sky. "And the company he keeps."

"And what's *your* plan?" Roy demands. "Ya can't just leave me here."

"I'm not discussing my plans with you," I say. "Do you have a cellphone?"

"Yeah," he says cautiously.

"Give it to me."

Roy pauses, contemplating his chances of making a run for it.

"I'm much faster than humans."

He must believe me because a few seconds later his phone sails my way. I catch it and make some adjustments, holding it up above my head. The demonic bats scatter.

"What'd you do?"

"Programmed it to emit a high-pitched frequency. It won't keep them away forever, but it should discourage them for a while." I check my sense of where Mina's being held, orient myself, and start walking in the right direction. "Roy, the range on this thing's not that great. You might want to stick close."

Muttering something about wrongful detainment, Roy steps up close to me.

"Hold your phone out in front of us and don't touch anything," I instruct, handing him the phone. "And keep the flashlight beam on high."

The initial blast might have done good, but it's the light more than anything discouraging the demons now. Maybe I'll tell Roy that, and maybe I won't. I've got a long walk to think about it.

Chapter 21:
Bargain

Trainee Case Report #: MN-108
Case Agent: Master Blaz
Guardian Candidate: Mina Nadir
The small cabin doesn't look like much from the outside, but the inside is far worse. The man drops me onto the only worn, dusty rug. The air doesn't feel much warmer than it did outside. My body shivers to generate warmth. The smell of must and rotten wood assails my senses.

The man's head twists violently from side to side.

I rest my head back against the floor and try to summon the energy to take in the room. Moving closer to spirit form allows me to observe my surroundings without taxing my body.

The wall to my left holds a bed made for one person. The wall behind me, effectively "above" my head, is dominated by a large stone fireplace with appropriate materials for building a fire. The area appears well-maintained, which is a stark contrast to the rest of the place. The right wall boasts a kitchen area and a small hallway leading to a closest that I think is supposed to double for a restroom. The last wall holds only a couple of dirty, cracked windows and the splintering door we came through.

"Don't worry, you won't be here long," promises the Sloth demon, floating through the doorway. He's in a largely disembodied state, but he's also formed the head and shoulders of a middle-aged man to facilitate easy conversation.

I bite my tongue to keep from asking why I'm here period. I look from the Sloth demon to the crazy human and back, trying to determine whom to reason with. Experimentally, I shift completely into spirit form. Several demons inside the man explode out of his chest and rush at me. I'm back in twilight state in time for them to bounce harmlessly off. They're forbidden from entering most beings that do not invite them in.

The man shrieks as demons charge back into him.

"It's not nice to tease them," scolds the Sloth demon.

"It's not nice to kidnap people either, but I didn't hear you complaining about that part," I retort, holding up my bound hands.

He waves off my comment with a dismissive noise.

"Those don't mean much to you. They just make it easier to carry you. We know you can escape the bindings with ease." He holds up a hand before I can prove him right. "Please don't try or I'll have our friend here kill himself."

"Wouldn't that benefit me?" I ask, trying to weave my way through the weird logic.

The languid smile that forms on the Sloth demon's face is far from reassuring.

"It might, but it would not be good for the child in the trunk of the car you came in."

"Prove it."

"With pleasure." The Sloth demon bows and glides left.

The man stalks out of the room, presumably headed to his car.

"While our friend fetches the boy, let me present you with the bargain."

"I'm listening."

"Splendid. I always knew we were forming a bond." The Sloth demon glides forward until he's directly above my prone form. "You're going to assume your human identity completely and let our friend wound you. Then, you're going to become spirit and allow the demons to escort you to our master."

"And what do I get for my cooperation?"

"The satisfaction of knowing that the child will be returned safely to his family."

"It won't work."

"Why not?" The Sloth demon sounds offended.

"If I turn human, the drug 'our friend' slipped me before will knock me out for hours. I won't be able to control the shift to spirit."

"Oh dear, you may be right."

I'm being mocked, but I don't care. If the Sloth demon can help me deal with the drug, I can probably find a way out of this mess.

When the man returns to the cabin, he's carrying an unconscious child about five years old. Since I'm occupying most of the free floor space, the man dumps the boy on the bed. A cloud of dust rises from the faded quilt.

"Mmmm. We cannot afford a great delay," says the Sloth demon.

I wonder why, and the answer manifests as a warm, comforting feeling and a familiar presence. Wonderful, reckless Allister is coming. I don't believe this is simply wishful thinking, but even if it is, I'll cling to the hope it offers.

The Sloth demon glides over to the man and confers with him quietly. I could listen in on their conversation, but I don't bother. The beginnings of a mad plan form. The demons might be able to free my human form from the sedative, but if I'm not careful, this could go very wrong in about a dozen different ways.

"I think I have an answer." My statement halts the Sloth demon's conference with the man.

"Do tell," prompts the Sloth demon, gliding back into view above me. "But make it quick. I sense we're going to have unwelcome company soon. If that happens, everybody dies, and we take you anyway whenever you manage to change to spirit."

I study the ceiling beams and run the crazy plan through my head one last time before giving it voice. They appear sturdy enough to work.

"Before I share my idea, I want a new deal."

"Bargain quickly, my dear. Tick tock. I've told you the consequences of a long delay. State your terms."

The sense that Allister is coming grows enough to reinforce the Sloth demon's words.

"You don't get to wound my human body. The boy gets left here for my friend to find, but the man drives away when every demon has left him."

The man begins to groan and pull at his hair, but the Sloth demon stills him with a gesture.

"And what do we get in return?"

"When I'm free from the drug, I'll turn to spirit and go with you."

Delight and intrigue brighten the Sloth demon's eyes.

"Willingly?" he asks. "Would you consent to being bound with chains?"

The second question makes me hesitate. He's not talking about physical chains, though at times the condition may be illustrated with links made of metal. He's talking about submitting to spiritual cords that would render me completely at their mercy. Such bindings would have to be willingly loosened by my captors or broken. They're very difficult to break without destroying part of one's soul.

"Is my word not enough?"

"I want a guarantee that you will follow though once freed from the drug," insists the Sloth demon.

"And I want to place a blessing upon the child," I return. "Trust is not easy for either of us, and I want to ensure the demons don't try to convince him to host them."

"They'd probably fail anyway with the boy unconscious, but go ahead."

At the demon's wave, the man hauls me off the floor and forces me to kneel beside the bed.

Quickly, I give more substance to my hands and lay them upon the boy, placing a prayer of protection over his heart and head.

"Now that the boy is safe, you have an idea to share with us." The Sloth demon sounds impatient.

I have to shift back to twilight state to explain.

"Hang my body from the ceiling and have the demons move through me quickly. The contact between our spirits should be enough to burn away the drug."

The Sloth demon stares at me blankly for a long moment, running the idea through mental scenarios.

"If any of them hesitate even a fraction of a second, the deal ends," I add. "I'll seize the offending demon, use it to break the drug's hold, and take my chances with a straightforward fight."

"What's to prevent you from doing that anyway?"

"I cannot fight you and protect the child."

The Sloth demon chuckles.

"Nobility is such a foolish notion, but useful. I accept your terms."

It takes the man quite a few minutes to find enough rope and hang my body from the ceiling rafters. Wondering if the plan has any chance of success, I force the change to my human form. The drug begins to take hold and my consciousness slips. Darkness descends and a burning sensation touches my left arm, my right leg, and my heart. Each demon that sails through me carries more and more of the drug away with them.

I lose count of the individual stinging sensations. Soon, it feels like a steady flow of lava courses through me. The number of demons moving through increases, making me more alert. Once I'm sure the last bit has been burned away. I flash to spirit form just long enough to slip free of the bindings. My wrists appear raw but otherwise unharmed. I stand in the center of the room back in a twilight state.

The Sloth demon gapes at me.

"Does the child's life mean nothing to you after all?"

The man stands over the bed with a knife placed on the child's throat. He appears dazed but alert enough to follow a kill order.

"I intend to keep my word," I assure them. "But we're not leaving until my friend gets here to take the boy to safety."

We don't have long to wait. Soon the murmur of voices can be heard.

"Every demon needs to leave that man. That was part of our deal," I remind them.

The man trembles as the remaining demons leave him. The room appears thick with fog. Dread and worry make both halves of me sick, but I kneel when I hear Allister's footsteps approach. The air thickens around me. The demons hover close. A new one appears holding simple iron bindings.

Though every instinct in me says to fight, I hold forth my wrists to the Sloth demon. The door swings open to admit Allister and whoever is with him, and the spirit bindings snap shut, yanking me out of twilight state. I catch only the briefest glimpse of Allister as the demons crash down upon me.

Chapter 22:
Message

Apprentice Case Report #: AK-110
Case Agent: Mistress Adira Clarimond
Guardian Candidate: Allister Knight

The sense of Mina flares bright and winks out completely before the door finishes opening. I burst into the wreck of a cabin with Tyre leading the way. Light from my presence fills the small room. My attention immediately locks on to a bed in the corner to my right.

"Steady now or I'll cut this rope." The voice belongs to a Sloth demon hovering near the ceiling. His head and shoulders resemble an unassuming man with thinning white hair, but the rest of him is spirit.

It takes a few seconds for the entire bizarre setup to make sense. A long rope hangs down from the ceiling suspended a few feet above a small figure lying on the bed. A long knife has been tied to the rope. The rope sways gently like a pendulum. There's a good chance of it missing the child altogether, but if it does strike him from that height, it could easily kill him.

Roy comes in behind me and takes in the scene.

"That ain't something ya see every day," he comments.

"You, human, I sense the Dark Master's mark upon you. Pick up the knife."

Roy snorts and crosses his arms.

"I'll just watch for now, thanks."

"Where is the angel who was here moments ago?" I ask. Not sure what information the Sloth demon already possesses, I avoid saying her name.

"I imagine dear Mina is on her way to a holding cell where she'll await my master's will."

Tyre flares, eager to tear into the Sloth demon.

"Release her and I won't turn my sword loose on you." I try not to think of the child's chances if the Sloth demon carries out his threat.

"I couldn't release her now if I wished," says the Sloth demon gravely. "She bargained for the child's life."

"Then give me the child," I demand.

"In a moment," promises the demon. "First, I have a message for you, Allister."

I really don't like that he knows my name.

"So deliver it." I lower Tyre to say that I'm listening.

"You are to accept this boy's life as proof that my master will keep his word in these matters. After seeing to his safety, return to the Heavens and mourn your friend. She is lost to you, and if you choose to seek her, she will suffer."

"Why?" The question booms out of me. The force of it draws a surprised look from Roy. "What does your master want from her?"

"Allister, I am just a soldier, same as you. I trust my superiors have their reasons." The Sloth demon drifts toward the far wall, slowly moving away from the boy. "Soon, I will go. You have a choice: follow or obey." He tips his head in a kind of salute. "Pray we don't meet again."

The Sloth demon slowly withdraws, tempting me to follow his spirit.

I cling to Tyre a few seconds longer before placing him back in the Veil.

Roy watches me.

"What will ya do?" he asks, though he already knows my answer.

"Take the boy home." I move closer to the bed and gaze down upon Colin.

"Do you even know where he lives?"

143

"I do." I don't elaborate because I'm too busy examining the boy for injuries.

He has a small hole in his neck where a needle punctured the skin, but otherwise, he seems whole.

"Move that knife so it doesn't fall on him."

Roy follows the instruction, gingerly easing the knife from the precarious loop it had been caught in. He places the knife on the bed beside the boy.

"Done. Now what?"

"Pick up the boy and call for a car. We'll carry him out to the highway and wait for the car there. It'll be easier than trying to direct somebody up here."

"That's a terrible plan." Roy pulls out his phone and turns it on. It flashes a low battery warning and fades to dark again. "We killed the battery coming up here. Besides, it's not like the area's booming with cars for hire."

"Call your mother," I instruct.

"Leave Ma out of this," Roy grumbles. "She ain't done nothing, and I'd like to keep it that way."

"Think about it, Roy. She knows you came out here to help me. Tell her something happened to your ride and you need to transport a child you found up here."

"You want me to lie to my ma?" Roy's voice sails upward with his shock.

"What part of that is a lie?" I return. Internally, I admit there might be lies of omission, but I can't afford to host an ethical debate on the matter.

Roy thinks about it for a few heartbeats.

"Phone's still dead," he says, holding it up.

"That won't be a problem." I'm still pondering various threads of my plan.

A heavy sigh escapes Roy.

"I shoulda stayed in the crazy house."

"Hold still, please," I say.

Before Roy can blink, I move through his phone in spirit form. Lady Andanda used to go on great tangents about the theoretical impacts of angelic beings on human technology. She speculated that our energy could transport ourselves through their network. Teleportation has its uses, but not everybody can do it.

In any case, I took her ramblings to heart and guessed that my energy might also be used to charge Roy's phone.

"Try it now," I encourage.

He does so, and the phone turns on. The low battery warning still flashes, but it says 3% now instead of 1%.

"Wow. Ain't that something. Y'all are walking power banks." Roy holds the phone out to me. "Here, just hold it for a while."

"If I'm not careful, I could easily overload it," I warn. I'm not sure what he means by the term, but I can infer enough. "Just let me move through it another few times. Then you can make your call."

Roy shrugs and stands still while I repeat the process of moving through the phone. Each pass seems to move the phone's energy bar up two or three percentage points.

"It's getting kinda warm," Roy notes.

"Try making your call."

"All right, but the reception here is terrible." Roy attempts to place the call but nothing goes through.

"Would it help if you were higher?" I ask.

"Maybe," he says, caution flavoring his tone.

I change into my human form and reach for Roy's arm. It takes a few seconds for the transformation to complete. Seizing Roy's wrist, I haul him outside. He opens his mouth to protest, but doesn't get very far. Turning him around, I loop my arms around him and leap up. He yells like I'd stabbed him. My feet touch down briefly on the roof but I jump again, landing on a sturdy branch far above the ground.

"Try again." I lean Roy against the tree trunk.

He's breathing hard and glaring at me. Nevertheless, he puts the call through.

"Hey, Ma, it's me. Can you pick me up?" The rate at which words come out of Roy increases exponentially from there.

I pay close enough attention to ensure he's staying cooperative. I'm not quite ready to trust the guy again, but he appears to want to help the boy in the cabin below.

Roy grunts to gain my attention.

"We're done," he says sourly. "Take me back to the

ground."

The idea of leaving Roy up here didn't occur to me until he said something, but I resist for Colin's sake. I could carry the boy down the mountain, but there's no guarantee I can see him safely into his mother's arms. I may be the only one here, but I'm certainly not the only one working to get Mina back. Instinct tells me Roy's ma can still be trusted. I think his deal with the demons was partly to protect her. The information doesn't excuse him, but at least I understand him better.

Roy presses his back against the tree. He's pale and sweaty.

"Don't pass out before I get to you," I advise.

He makes the mistake of looking down and pitches forward out of the perch I'd left him in. I dive straight down, grab Roy's back, and twist hard to the right, spinning him around. We land with him on top. He's not a light man. The impact drives my body an inch down into the damp earth. His face is uncomfortably close to mine, but he doesn't know that because his eyes are clenched shut. I heave him off and stare up at the distance we've fallen. I guess I could have flown down to him like a normal angel, but it's more fun to try and catch a two-hundred-pound man like a football.

"I'm alive. I'm alive." The words come in between panting gasps. I try to decide if Roy thinks that's a good thing, but his tone could go either way. "I'm alive."

I force myself up and help Roy to his feet, ignoring further awed declarations that he's still alive. I direct him into the cabin to retrieve Colin. Roy falls silent when we cross the threshold. He walks softly over to the bed and gazes down upon the child.

"They threatened a kid. That ain't right." His head whips around and his eyes stab into me. "Why can't y'all keep yer fight off wherever it is ya come from?" Roy looks close to tears, and his accent thickens.

"It is mostly happening 'off where I come from,'" I say, letting bitterness creep into the words. "And the fights happening here are to protect your people from being drawn into the larger war."

The statement drains the fire from Roy's green eyes.

"What's the fight really about?" he asks, sounding weary. He bends down and scoops Colin up into his arms. Once upright again, Roy backs toward the door, keeping his attention on me.

I maneuver around him to hold the door open for them before attempting to answer. The night air is crisper than it was before. I uselessly wish I could spend the time stargazing with Mina. We're a good fifty feet away from the cabin by the time I gather enough thoughts to attempt addressing Roy's question.

"You know why we fight."

"I don't," he retorts. "That's why I asked."

"Our races are siblings," I say, trying to remember how Master Gabriel once put it. "Mine was the firstborn, the splendid one, granted great responsibility, and yours was the baby, the favorite one. Members of my race sinned as did yours. The dark angels worked to corrupt your people even more. There's still a war raging across multiple realms."

Roy grunts.

"I want no part of this."

"You have that option, but if you choose to sit this out, the world will change without you." I let Roy think about that for a few seconds before adding, "You've done services for both sides in this conflict. I can ask my people to protect your family if you wish, but if you betray me again, there will be consequences."

"Is that a threat?" Roy demands.

"I don't have to threaten you. Without my protection, you'll be at the mercy of those who have none." I step in front of Roy. "I will find my friend with or without your help, but remember that the end game's already been written. My side wins. Choose your allies carefully, Roy."

Chapter 23:
Darkness

Trainee Case Report #: MN-109
Case Agent: Master Blaz
Guardian Candidate: Mina Nadir

I reclaim consciousness in darkness and try to remember the last few moments. I recall Allister's face appearing as the door opened, but I push the thought away for now. He cannot help me, at least not yet. The only light comes from inside me. The chains binding my spirit no longer wrap around my wrists, but I feel them close and suspect they've been used to create this prison. I brighten my presence to get a better sense of the surroundings.

The prison's designer chose a medieval theme. Hard stone floors and walls surround me on three sides. Thick metal bars make up the fourth wall and the ceiling. They appear completely ordinary, but I can feel the spirit bindings at work in them. Above me, a thousand red eyes blink, representing the generous escort of demons that brought me here.

I get up and cross the small cell to the front wall made of bars. The move takes me three steps. I lay a single finger on one of the bars and feel energy buzz through it. I am a spirit at the moment, so I could test the ceiling, but regardless, I have my answer. I won't be leaving unless somebody rescues me or my enemies release me.

The demons above aren't great conversationalists, so I pace my cell for a time. Three paces carry me from floor to ceiling. Seven steps separate the left and right walls, and five steps separate the front and back walls. If nothing happens, boredom might be my greatest enemy.

Building a spirit prison is no small task. My company above would be enough to persuade me to stay in human form, but only spirit form can be held captive for any meaningful length of time. The Dark Angel and his minions must desire something from me, but I don't know what it could be.

Finally, I settle down in the left corner away from the door and dim my presence to a faint glow. I need to plot an escape and guard my mind. Insanity's an actual threat. Spirit form doesn't need physical sustenance like human form, but its needs—fellowship, hope, and purpose—are just as important.

I don't stretch out my feelings for the Glorious King because I know He's not here. The spiritual darkness is too complete. Every day before now, I had direct access to Him at any time, though I rarely used it. Simply knowing He could be accessed with a thought filled a void in me. He could reach me here, but I cannot reach out to Him. He knows everything, but I'm not sure He's looking for me. These thoughts fill me with an unfamiliar terror.

I wish Allister were here. He'd be good company. I feel guilty for the worry he must be experiencing. When we were younger, we talked about adventures. I don't believe this is what we pictured.

A handsome man holding a torch appears outside my cell. His dark hair perfectly matches his black clothes. It looks like a ghostly face and pale hand hover in the air. Faint scruff lines his chin and cheeks. He's familiar but I cannot place him.

I stand, not sure why this demon approaches me in human form.

The man tosses a pair of metal cuffs through the bars. They must be extensions of the spirit bindings, for they fly out and clamp around each of my wrists before snapping together and hauling me forward. I slam against the bars with jarring force. I'm now inches away from the man. A tentative tug tells me my wrists are stuck fast to the bars. Straightening my arms and leaning back only buys a little distance.

Questions crowd my head, but I still them to watch the

man studying me. He wears no insignia but I can tell he's highly ranked by the way he carries himself.

"Welcome. I am called Deimos. I told you we would meet again."

"What does a Dominator demon want with me?" I ask.

"The Dark Master offers you the chance to join us."

I let my eyes sweep over the bars separating us.

"This is a lot of effort to go to for a recruiting pitch."

"You are Gifted in switching forms and trusted by the Council of Light."

"I won't help you," I say.

"You haven't even heard the proposal." Deimos smiles and moves the torch closer to me, changing the way the shadows move across his face.

"I don't have to," I reply. "I know how this is going to play out."

"Do tell."

"You're going to ask nicely for a time. Then, you're going to ask again, not nicely. When you realize nothing you do to me will work, you'll move on to the people and things I love. When that fails, you'll either leave me to rot or kill me." It occurs to me that demons aren't the most trustworthy of beings. "This depends upon you telling me the truth about actually joining you. If the true motive differs, things could proceed along another path."

"Do you know why you can switch forms so easily?" Deimos asks.

"No, I always figured it was just a normal gift like a talent."

"It is a gift … from me."

"You … lost me."

Deimos nods patiently.

"I am your father." He shakes his head to reject the statement. "I would have been your father had you been born a human, but your mother couldn't handle the idea of a child changing her life." One shoulder lifts in a shrug. "Well, you know the story from there."

I want to deny it, but the words ring true.

"Test the words if you think I'm lying." Deimos grips the

bars in front of me.

Closing my eyes to concentrate, I extend my senses through the connection offered and weigh the words on my heart. Truth feels warm and lies feel cold. Warmth floods through me like a ray of sunshine. Looking at Deimos again, I shut down the connection.

"What does it matter?" Despite my best efforts, the question has a soft, despairing edge to it.

"You were always meant to help me serve my master."

"I can't. You're fighting against everything I believe in."

"Think about it." His words are gentle, comforting.

Tugging against the wrist restraints again, I use the slight stinging pain to focus.

"I don't have to!" My declaration sounds strong but a seed of doubt has been planted and Deimos knows it. "Your choices were your own, and mine belong to me."

At a gesture from Deimos, the spirit bindings detach from the cell bars and fling me backward until my shoulders strike the far wall.

"Think about it," he repeats. Deimos drops the torch to the ground where it extinguishes itself.

The new darkness seems deeper than before. With spirit bindings still locking my wrists together, I sit down to rest and think.

Does this change anything?

The question swirls through my head. I am not human. The connection that would have formed between Deimos and me doesn't matter. Does it? I became an angel and a servant to the King. What else matters?

I'm still Mina. My soul would be me regardless of my body being fully human or angelic. Only the Glorious King knows everything.

Young angels entering Guardian training are taught one thing: demons cannot be redeemed. That's true for the Ancient Ones—angels and demons created before mankind—but what of new ones, like Allister and me? Have we reached that point of no return where our paths are set? Can new demons be called out of darkness? What would the criteria for such redemption be? Surely, it hinges on the Glorious King and the Holy Prince. I must pray about these things.

My eyes shift upwards. The red eyes look down at me. I say nothing for now because the thoughts are still too raw, but I have no illusions. I cannot be a savior, for unlike the Prince, I am a created being.

Who am I to have such lofty ideas?

Before despair can grip me, I consider another lesson from mankind. The Glorious King often works through the weak.

Direct my thoughts and steps, my King.

I wonder what the Dark Angel knows about Deimos's plan. They can't be stupid enough to spend this much effort without a greater goal than recruitment in mind. My thoughts have come full circle. I sure hope Allister is having better luck finding me.

Chapter 24:
Victory One Third Won

Dear Lord Hadeon,

I have turned the girl over to Deimos. Far be it from me to question my betters, but I believe I deserve to be informed when key connections exist. Why did I not know of Deimos fathering the body that would have become the girl had Fate not intervened? Was that how he left the path of Light? Can we trust him to guard her well? I know how important she is to our Dark Master. Shall I send Daeva to subtly watch him?

I eagerly await your response,
Than

***

Dear Than,

It is time. We have the girl. She is safe in Deimos's care until the Dark Master has a use for her. Daeva still has other matters to attend to.

It's none of your business what Deimos's connection is to the girl. True or not, if she believes it, we can exploit the link. Don't act so shocked. It's not the first time a human woman has been the means to bringing a recruit over to our side.

You have permission to enact the second and third

phases of the plan. If you need more demons for the job, talk to Aridam, but move soon. I will make it clear to him that he should assist you. I would prefer you leave our spies in place, but the mission is too important to sacrifice for the sake of covers. If you need more help, do not hesitate to use them.

This rivalry with Deimos is tiresome.

You will not question my orders again. Is that clear?

The target list I sent you is exactly as it should be. The boy tops the list. When you capture him, take him with the others to the prison on Forsaken Island. If the boy becomes too troublesome, force him to take human form and keep him on Earth. Whatever you do, keep him far away from the girl. Keep him away from everybody. I'd tell you to kill him, but that might come back to haunt us. Better for us to know where to find him than wonder where the power in him will manifest next. In fact, isolate the prisoners.

Clarimond and Blaz will not surrender lightly. I'm having cells prepared for them, but they may not be ready in time. The Dark Master cut our preparation time short significantly. Putting one of them in the prison holding the girl might be an option, but I do not like it. Blaz is her mentor and Clarimond would surely take over the role in his absence. I don't want them held together either. Their power may multiply when combined.

I hope you have a backup plan for controlling them. Keeping them compliant might be our only option. Hostages may or may not work. It depends upon whom you choose. Their charges mean much to them, but I do not believe they will surrender for the sake of a few humans. Besides, if you pick the wrong humans, you'll have cries of help going up everywhere. We need to keep this quiet.

I am not afraid of humans, but it's best not to provoke their King into action too soon. Remember our ultimate goal. First the Guardians must fall, then the humans, and finally, the King. Those who follow the path of the Light may submit to the Dark Master should we prevail in our first few tasks. When we march on the King, you will have a position of honor in our legions, but only if you accomplish your assignments.

The Dark Master expects results soon.

If you need to take hostages, I suggest starting with that sniveling traitor Roy and his pious mother. I thought you had dealt with them? No, don't bother explaining yourself. The boy happened. Roy was supposed to strand the boy in the middle of nowhere. If Allister had pursued the girl at that moment, they might have overwhelmed the prison prepared. We were lucky the girl struck that bargain. We cannot count on such luck to carry our victories. I should have known Roy wasn't interested in our cause. We will not make the same mistake twice. Kill him and his mother.

I'm aware you can't act directly to that end. That's why we have people under our control. This is not a petty grievance I wish to settle. If it becomes widely known that those who have served us can change their minds without consequence, we may face an avalanche of traitors.

I'm disappointed to hear that the man who was key to capturing the girl is no longer an asset. We got the better end of that bargain, but it's still unfortunate. I'm told he was an excellent host.

Ask Daeva if you want more information about what makes a good host. You'll need the knowledge eventually if you're to direct more operations. I'll give you a quick summary to tide you over until you can learn from a true master on the subject.

A good host can be created in many ways. Depression can make the host candidate pliant. Certain drugs can also leave humans vulnerable. Alcohol might work, but only if consumed in very large quantities. Make them feel good. Those with The Sight can be excellent choices, but be careful. Other humans tend to mistrust those who can hear and see things they cannot. I'm not certain if this is mainly due to jealousy or simple ignorance. If you push too hard, too fast, your host might end up in a mental health institution.

I've studied humans for years. The Dark Master trusted me to know our enemies intimately. Of course, the angels who walk the path of Light are our enemies too, but we already know their strengths and weaknesses. They are us.

Do not let the human church unite. I thought that an obvious enough point that it wouldn't need to be repeated aloud, but I'm not happy with the rumors I'm hearing. You can cry about having too much to do, but it won't change my expectations. Discord has been our ally for ages. Keep them fighting about music and curtain colors and everything else inconsequential. If they unite, they can alter the balance of power.

While moving forward with phases two and three, involve humans if you need to, but again, I'll caution you to pick targets with care. If possible, aim for the Unclaimed. I do not want you forcing the neutral people into picking Heaven, but they will likely get the best responses from the angels of Light.

The next thing I want to hear from you is good news.

Hadeon, Servant of the Dark Master,
Director of Operations

Part 4:
War

Chapter 25:
Betrayal

Apprentice Case Report #: AK-110
Case Agent: Mistress Adira Clarimond
Guardian Candidate: Allister Knight

Hours I can't afford to lose pass by. We make it back down to where Roy's motorcycle lies in the middle of the road. The bike's on its side looking like a slaughtered mechanical beast. Pieces of plastic and glass litter the area. The beast didn't go down quietly.

"We should move the bike off to the side before it causes another accident," I say. "We're lucky the traffic along this road is sparse."

"Not sparse enough." Roy gently sets the boy down on the grass beside the road, joins me by the motorcycle, and lays a loving hand on the shiny, scratched chassis.

"Come on, help me get it righted."

"Man, do you have any idea how much this thing weighs? It's like picking up a baby elephant."

"Actually, it's more than a baby elephant." I can picture Mina's disapproving frown. She'd tell me to focus. "Stand aside." I lean down, get a good grip on the bike, and lift. "Many times more," I grunt, struggling with the bulk. Then, I stagger over to the edge of the road and set the motorcycle down, being careful not to set it on top of Colin.

Roy looks at me with bugged-out eyes.

"How'd you do that?" His tone sounds reverent.

I give him a small wave and a reminder.

"Not human."

The awe leaves his eyes.

"Right." Roy spends the next few minutes fussing over his wounded machine, buffing out the few scratches he can.

I watch him until Colin starts to stir. Placing a hand on the child's forehead, I check how close he is to consciousness. Thankfully, he's not very close. I don't feel up to explaining everything to a curious boy.

I pace until Roy's mother arrives an eternity later. She fires a dozen questions before stepping down out of the vehicle, but she forgets every one of them when her eyes fall upon Colin. I consider leaving them, but Roy's earlier move hasn't left me with a lot of trust for this family. I feel responsible for the boy. The trail to Mina's not going to get any colder anyway. I fold down the second row of seats in the SUV and place the motorcycle in the back. Next, I squeeze into the middle row of seats with Colin. Roy and his mother climb into the front.

"Did ya find yer friend?" Roy's ma asks.

"She was there," I answer shortly.

"We found a cabin way back in the woods but only found the kid," Roy explains.

"Who is he?" Roy's ma twists around in her seat to steal a glance at Colin. "How will we get in touch with his folks?"

"I can direct you to his home," I say. "It's not too far from where you live."

"Well, hallelujah. Ain't this a small world?" she shouts, slapping the steering wheel.

Roy and I murmur our agreement.

"What's gotten into you boys?" Roy's ma wonders. She meets my eyes in the rearview mirror. "I know yer friend's still missing, but finding that child's gotta count for something."

"It does," I say, not bothering to explain the tension between Roy and myself.

If he wants to say something, that's his business. I refuse to get in the middle. His mother might pry it out of him. It's fairly obvious something's wrong. He's been like a corpse in full rigor since we climbed into his ma's vehicle.

"Roy Daniel Santori, what have you done?" The woman's

tone tells us answering is not an option, it's a command.

"I made a mistake, Ma," Roy answers. "But I'm making it right. Honest."

"You don't need the details. It's in the past," I assure the woman.

Dodging her questions becomes easier at that point. I direct the woman to Colin's house. Once we turn down the street, it's difficult to miss due to the two police cruisers idling out front.

"This is my stop too," I say, preparing to microjump out of the car.

I'm not sure why that idea occurred to me as I'd never attempted such a thing before.

"Wait! What about my motorcycle?" Roy cries. "I can't lift it out of the trunk."

"Make new friends, Roy," I encourage. I've got more important things to do, but I do feel somewhat responsible for the machine's state. I sigh. "Or stop here and open the trunk."

Roy's ma stops the SUV. I pat Colin's head one more time before climbing over the seat. When the trunk finishes swinging upward, I lay across the motorcycle. Without bothering with a farewell, I initiate the microjump to Roy's garage. I must have miscalculated because I land in the driveway. I'm technically not supposed to microjump while carrying something, but I decide that Lady A. will be too concerned with finding Mina to yell at me for the infraction.

It doesn't take long to contact Lady A., but luckily for Roy, I have to wait about fifteen minutes before Reena appears to pick me up. That gives me enough time to open the garage door, haul the motorcycle carcass inside, and begin the long restoration process.

"Hello, Allister. I'm sorry to hear your mission did not go to plan." Reena's low, soothing voice reaches me as I'm furiously rubbing compound into a long scratch on the motorcycle. "Are you ready to return?"

"Very," I confirm, tossing the rag onto the seat.

"Do you mind if we make a quick stop along the way? Paige has something to show us."

"I really need to check in with Mistress Clarimond," I

say, hoping that will encourage her to take me directly to the Academy.

"She promised it would be quick," Reena assures me. "I don't know what it's about, but I feel like she might have news about Mina."

"Why didn't you say that first?" I demand. The information changes everything. I'd rather delay and have something definite to report than return now with virtually nothing.

Reena hesitates. Her soft brown eyes look at me sympathetically.

"Because I didn't want to bring your hopes up. It could be nothing." Her warning sails right through me without registering.

"Let's find out," I say with a tight smile. I hold my hand out to Reena.

She wraps both hands around mine and transports us to our destination before I have a chance to ask where we're going.

"Did we go far?" I ask, gazing upward. The stars are much brighter here.

"We're in Nevada." Paige's voice pierces the darkness. "You may go, Reena. What I have to show Allister is meant for him alone."

"I don't mind waiting," Reena says.

"I insist." Paige's words are accompanied by a blast of energy that slams into Reena, hurling her backwards.

The resulting scream cuts off abruptly as Reena automatically teleports back to New York.

Revert.

My numb mind conjures the term for the phenomenon. When someone Gifted with the ability to teleport is in distress, they may travel back along the last path they took. I summon Tyre and increase my presence to bring light to the area. Dark shapes scatter away from Paige like trailing smoke.

"I didn't want to do that," Paige comments. "It shortens the time we have together significantly."

Reena would return eventually, but she might not be able to make the same jump for a few minutes. I'd have to stall Paige.

"Guess I'll have to get creative," says Paige. "Don't go anywhere, Allister." With that, she disappears.

161

She knows I can't go anywhere. I can anchor myself here to prevent being taken somewhere else, but I won't get very far microjumping unless I can learn exactly where I'd been abandoned.

Paige returns a few tense seconds later with two people, Cheryl Fenster and a cop I don't recognize. Colin's mother is on her knees with her head bowed and her hands fastened behind her back with handcuffs. The police officer stands behind her pointing his gun at her head. The dazed look in his eyes tells me he's not in full control of his mind.

I gape at Paige.

"Oh, don't look like that, Allister." Paige circles the frozen pair. "I'm not concerned with the rules right now. They'll be back in New York in a matter of minutes. If all goes well, they won't even remember any of this, but that depends on you."

"How do you figure that?" I grudgingly voice the question. Most of my attention stays on Cheryl Fenster. The poor woman's had quite a night. First her son disappears, taken by one stranger and returned by another, and now, she's a few moments from eternity.

Maybe I can give her more time. Reaching out, I find the simple time manipulation formula Paige has used to temporarily keep the humans out of the equation. Replacing one tiny variable, I fractionally speed up time elsewhere.

"You cooperate and this will be a bad dream for them. If you fight, it will become a nightmare they will have to live with. Well, the officer will have to live with it. Dear Cheryl will be dead."

I think forward the problem. Most scenarios result in Cheryl's death, the cop's death, or both. Disarming the cop could be accomplished in a dozen ways, as could moving Cheryl out of harm's way, but both actions fail to address the root problem: Paige. If she gets to them first, she could take them anywhere to finish the murder.

Seconds tick by and my desperation grows. Suddenly, everything changes. I think through each scenario again and the possibilities improve slightly. Cheryl's still likely to get shot if I make a move, but her odds of surviving have gone up.

"What would I do if I chose to cooperate?" I ask

carefully.

"Nothing."

"Nothing?"

"More specifically, you wait here in your human form until I return to retrieve you," Paige clarifies. "Do we have a deal?"

"I don't bargain with traitors," I snap.

The light from me reflects off Paige's surprised face.

"You would let a woman die because of your pride? That doesn't sound like you."

"Having a woman killed in a lame attempt to control me doesn't sound like you either," I retort. "Day for surprises."

"Really, Allister. It won't do any good. If you're waiting for Reena, she'll never find us. I—"

"Hid the coordinates," Reena finishes, appearing beside me with her two short swords in hand. "I know."

Paige's normally calm eyes burn with hatred.

"Kill her," she hisses to the demons inside the cop.

"Reena! Excellent timing," I say. Without waiting for a response, I microjump forward and sweep Tyre through the police officer. If I'd been in the physical world, the man would have been cut in half. Because I kept us strictly in the spiritual realm, only the demons run afoul of the spirit sword.

"Capture them!" screeches Paige. "But don't kill him!"

Reena races over to me and we stand back to back. Cheryl and the officer should be safe if the demons stay focused on us. The demons swirl over our heads like a gathering storm. Their challenging cries ring against my ears.

I duck two demons diving for my head. Spinning around, I see Reena's swords rip through both demons simultaneously. She calls out a warning, and I turn to face the new threat. Five demons approach, two from the right, one from the left, and two from above. If I stay put they'll have the advantage. I rise to meet the two above. Slashing through them, I roll and lean down to bring Tyre through the two that had been coming from the right. The fifth demon reaches Cheryl and her frozen companion, but Reena impales him with both spirit swords before he can do much.

"Get them out of here," I order, while we have a second

to rest.

"What about you?" she asks, placing both swords in their sheaths at either hip.

"Come back for me when you can!"

Reena nods tightly and briefly grips my arm.

I still feel her touch even after she leaves with the humans.

"She'll never find you!" Paige taunts. "That was a nice trick with the time, but now, you're alone. Do you really think you can fight a thousand demons?"

"Do you really think you can command a thousand demons?" Leaving the question in the air, I magnify my presence a hundredfold, making it look like a flash grenade went off in the night. Most of the demons scatter. They'll return, but I'll be gone by then, one way or the other. "What do you say, Paige? Fancy your chances now?"

Chapter 26:
Spirit's Bane

Trainee Case Report #: MN-110
Case Agent: Master Blaz
Guardian Candidate: Mina Nadir

Since time means little here, I occupy myself by toggling between the various problems and questions I'll eventually have to face. There must be a way to lead Allister here. Our minds have always worked better together. If I could only speak with him, I'm certain we could hatch a viable plan. It'd likely be crazy, but right now, that sounds about right.

To facilitate free thinking, I float back and forth across the cell, drawing near to the bars, walls, or ceiling without actually running into them. When that bores me, I try to stay exactly in the center of the cell. Next, I try resting on the ceiling. Direction really doesn't mean much when in spirit form.

My first clue I have another visitor comes from the spirit cuffs locking themselves together again and yanking me down to the stone floor, facing the door. I expect to see Deimos again, but instead, the Sloth demon glides up to the door. At his wave, the cuffs fly apart and drag me to the back wall, pinning me there with my arms straight out to either side. I test their strength by pulling forward, but nothing happens. I switch to human form and renew the effort. Still nothing. The cold air bothers me, so I shift back to spirit.

"I told him I would hurt you if he kept seeking to find you," says the Sloth demon in his usual unhurried pace.

"So, why are you lecturing me about it?" I demand. "I could have told you he'd disobey that order."

The bars cease shimmering for a second, allowing the Sloth demon to drift into the cell with me.

"Turn human please. You're hurting my eyes."

"Make me."

"As you wish, but first, proper introductions." A gust of hot air blasts through the small cell, blowing away the Sloth demon. In his place stands a very different demon in his human form. His short blond hair has miniature waves sweeping left to right across his head. The lack of a smile emphasizes his high cheekbones and strong jaw. The face appears to belong to a mid-twenties man. Piercing blue eyes search me for a reaction. He's wearing dark pants and a black T-shirt that doesn't do much to hide the muscles in his upper arms and chest.

"Am I supposed to be impressed?" I ask.

"Are you?" The demon's voice is soft and amused.

"A pretty face can still hide a dark heart."

"You're avoiding the question, but no matter. My name is Hadeon. I apologize for not revealing myself during our earlier meetings. I could not reveal my involvement until the plan was far enough along that it could proceed without me for a short while."

"Why pose as a lowly Sloth demon?" I query.

"People ignore them or underestimate them," he explains. "I couldn't very well go around with this face and expect to remain anonymous."

"Are you sure you're not a Pride demon?"

"Quite. I am a member of the Arkanis Brotherhood, roughly the equivalent of one of your archangels, only with a lot more freedom."

"A Royal Guard for old Lucifer himself. Now I *am* impressed."

The comment scores a point and earns a scowl. For a moment, I think he's going to strike me, but he takes a deep breath.

"I'm going to excuse that based on your ignorance, but do

show respect for the Dark Master." Hadeon produces a thick gold chain from his pocket and holds it up for me to see. A heavy-looking pendant hangs from the chain. It's a gold circle with thin bands running to the center where a diamond encases a single grain of dirt. "Do you know what this is?"

I have an idea, but the nearness of the object saps much of my strength. I barely manage to shake my head. The light from my presence dims.

"Isn't it a little soon for gifts?"

"You're special," Hadeon says, looping the necklace over my head.

The cold metal burns my neck and chest. I'm forced to assume my human identity to avoid the searing pain. The light of my presence winks out, but at least the necklace no longer feels like a burden.

The cell's cold hits me anew, making me shiver.

"Much better," he comments, resting a hand on my right shoulder. "This talisman was centuries in the making, but you get to be the first to experience its full effect. I call it Spirit's Bane."

"What's the point of keeping me in human form this way? You could have just opened the bars and invited our friends above to step inside. That would have encouraged me to stick to human form too."

"True, but they have a job to do. Would you like to see your friend Allister?"

"Not if you're happy to show him to me. That means he's in trouble." My human heart beats loudly. I keep my eyes directed upward as the red glowing eyes disappear in alarming numbers. I'm relieved they're leaving me but nervous about where they could be going.

Hadeon snaps his fingers and a scrappy little demon rushes in and delivers a flat object about the size of a book. It's a screen, which Hadeon promptly turns toward me.

"Human technology is wonderful sometimes. You're watching what could be Allister's last stand," he says gravely.

It's hard to really see what's happening on such a tiny screen. Hadeon soon realizes this.

"Shows are always better in person." He's definitely speaking to himself now. "But it'll have to be a quick trip. Can't have the escort distracted for too long."

Before I can unscramble his ramblings, Hadeon summons another little demon. This one delivers thick, gray tape. Hadeon quickly tears off a generous swatch of duct tape and places it over my mouth. Unsatisfied with the job, he tears off a much longer piece and wraps this one around my entire head.

"Can't have you warning your friend, but trust me, you'll have a great view of the action."

At Hadeon's command, the spirit bindings release me from the wall and lock together again in front of me. The dark angel touches my arm and we teleport somewhere high above a desert at night. For a terrifying moment, I plummet to the ground in complete freefall. I haven't tested the limits of my human form. Though I doubt I'd die, I could still break every bone in my body. Screaming into the gag does nothing.

While still about twenty feet from the ground, eight demons grab hold of my arms and legs and bring me to a stop suspended above a fierce battle. I immediately recognize Allister and Paige. They're locked in a frantic duel. I've never seen Allister fight so brilliantly, but I can see what he cannot. Hundreds of demons line the desert sands, waiting for the outcome. Should Paige wish to quit the battle, they could swarm Allister and crush him by the massive weight of numbers.

Allister meets a flurry of quick strikes from Paige. He's getting tired. I can tell by the dip in his shoulders. His presence flickers with fatigue. The light dims, and bold demons fly closer. Soon, they're taking turns diving at him. My friend battles them back with excellent sword skills, but the odds are clearly stacked against him.

I watch in horror as a demon slips around Allister's defenses and strikes him in the left shoulder. I thrash against the demons holding me and scream uselessly into the gag. Another demon lands hard across my friend's shoulders, driving him to his knees. Paige takes a small step back to give them greater access to him.

My vision clouds with tears. I start to shift into spirit until the necklace scalds me. The effect is a bright but brief flash of light.

Hadeon transports me back to the cell and has the spirit

cuffs pin me to the wall again. He rips the tape away.

"That was foolish!"

Exhausted, I let my body sag against the cold stones. A few more tears of worry slip out.

"I have nothing to say to you." I avoid Hadeon's gaze.

He grabs my chin and forces me to look into his icy eyes. The anger fades and cool arrogance returns.

"I would have shown you much more if you'd behaved."

"I saw plenty."

He shakes his head.

"Ah, but you didn't even see the main event."

"What main event?" I realize the question's exactly what he wants from me, but I'm too heartsick to care.

"The Academy."

Hadeon enjoys the effect those two words have upon me.

I gasp. I can't deny that the Academy's a place for training, but it's hardly a place that should be considered a military target. The outrage crystalizes inside me.

"You will regret this."

"I doubt it, but I'll note your concern," Hadeon says. He strokes my chin gently and traces the faint scar across my cheek. "Why did you not have that healed? Surely you know a healer. Perhaps you'll even be a Healer someday."

"Wanted to remember my mistakes," I admit, turning my head. My chin slips free of his grasp.

"You have such a lovely face." He sounds sincere, and his hand still hovers near my face. "It's a shame to leave it marked."

"You could heal it," I say, knowing deep inside that there's truth to the words.

Hadeon looks startled. He withdraws his hand like I'd bitten him.

"How did you know I was once a Healer?" he demands.

"I don't know. It felt right."

The demon retreats a step then recovers the distance and conjures a thin metal weapon. His features twist, and he works himself into a rage in a frightfully short span of time.

"You think you can redeem me?" The question is an accusation. "Think again."

At the press of a button, a short, pointed blade flicks out

of the piece of metal with a soft, sinister sliding noise. With two swipes, Hadeon opens long shallow cuts down both arms from elbow to wrist. Next, he reaches for my left hand and forces the fist open. The blade flicks closed, and he presses it against my palm.

I brace but pain still tears through my hand as the blade sinks into my palm. It feels like I caught an arrow with my bare hand. I long to turn back into spirit, but the stinging at my neck reminds me why I don't.

"Now for the other hand," Hadeon murmurs, reaching for my right hand. "Don't you want wounds like your precious Prince?"

This time, I form a tight fist. I don't bother correcting him on the nature of the wounds.

Hadeon grins as he squeezes my wrist, forcing the fingers to splay wide.

"This is Allister's punishment for being stubborn." Hadeon slowly lifts the blade into place, sharp end pointed toward the soft flesh.

"Lord Hadeon!" cries a frantic little demon.

"What?" he growls, spinning around to point the switchblade at the demon.

"It is done, but there are problems. Lord Than needs your assistance right away."

"Be gone," Hadeon orders the demon. "No, wait. Stay with her." He whirls and looks at me.

I know he's eager to finish delivering "Allister's punishment" but the news has unsettled him, sucking the enjoyment away.

"We'll finish this later." With a flourish, he holds the weapon in front of my face and closes it with another swift sliding noise. His eyes flick up and meet mine. "Let her bleed, but don't let her die just yet. She must meet the Dark Master."

Chapter 27:
Thinking Forward

Apprentice Case Report #: AK-111
Case Agent: Mistress Adira Clarimond
Guardian Candidate: Allister Knight

My fight with Paige goes well until she lets her demon friends in on the fun. I begin to despair. A bright light flashes in the sky off to my right. Two demons latch onto my left arm, but I knock them senseless with Tyre. Hope surges through me, distracting me from the burning pain of demon contact. The light could have many explanations, but I know it was Mina.

"She cannot help you." Paige's taunt only confirms my feeling. "And she will suffer for your disobedience."

Swinging Tyre in a swift circle earns me a little breathing room. My entire being hurts, but Paige's frustration comforts me. She holds up a hand and rises about ten feet off the ground. The obvious bid to feel in control tells me I must be doing something right. At Paige's imperious wave, the demons stop attacking and tighten the circle around me.

"I'd ask you why Mina was taken, but I doubt you could even tell me. Your new master probably doesn't trust you with such important details." The jab's a long shot, but I cling to hope that Paige may rise to the bait and tell me something useful.

"This fight is pointless. Don't make me destroy you." Paige inclines her chin, acting like a put-out princess who's not getting her way.

"You couldn't if you tried," I retort.

Paige tries to give me an icy smile, but it comes closer to a grimace.

"There are many ways to destroy someone, even an immortal." She gestures to her minions. "These demons can each steal a small piece of your soul and carry it to the far ends of the Earth. It'll be centuries before you can gather the fragments again."

"That seems like an awful lot of effort to go to," I muse.

"Last chance, Allister," Paige says, ignoring my latest bid for information. "Surrender or die."

I shake my head.

"You do a lousy job of advertising for surrender. Talk of destroying souls doesn't exactly encourage trust, but thanks for the offer." I'm grateful that Paige seems in a chatty mood. The notion of having demons carry my soul away in pieces isn't very appealing.

"Stall forever if you like, Allister. Nobody is coming to save you."

"I never counted you for such a pessimist."

"You never counted me as anything. That was the point." She gazes around the circle of demons. "He's yours."

The fight descends into a brawl. Every bit of exposed skin gets scalded by the touch of demons. In desperation, I microjump away and land twenty feet outside the circle of demons. They quickly orient themselves and come for me again. I microjump again, but this time, I keep Tyre out in attack position. Many demons turn to smoke and ash. I move to cut another path through the demons, but Paige screeches a challenge and meets me halfway through the crowd. Our swords clash with resounding metallic booms.

Something slams into me and I fly backward. Before I hit the ground, I'm teleported to the Academy in the Heavens.

We land in a heap with Reena on top. I start to laugh but quickly sober when I see her stricken expression. Reena scrambles off of me and summons a pair of small throwing daggers. Tyre thumps on the ground like a fish out of water, trying to get my attention. Snatching up the weapon, I roll to my feet and take in the devastation.

The walls bear scars where demons or their evil weapons struck. Phantom visions float past my mind's eye. It's as if the walls became transparent. I see Paige stabbing Aderes through the back with her spirit sword. In the mortal world, the blow would have been fatal, but here, it merely paralyzes the young angel. She collapses and half a dozen demons scoop her up and carry her off. The details change, but I essentially witness Aderes's fate befall everybody in the Academy. Adelmo and Osmund try to protect each other but they too are overwhelmed. Abdon rushes to their aid and becomes another victim.

My breath catches, and I wonder what happened to Mistress Clarimond. Thinking of Lady A. causes one of the phantom figures to flash and dim like a beacon. Without thinking much about it, I will myself to that spot, which is inside Lady A.'s office. The room floods with smoky memories of demons. Lady A. blasts a wave of demons back with pure energy, but more fill the gap immediately. She holds them at bay for a time, but unlike my fight in the desert, Lady A.'s office doesn't afford much space for movement. Eventually, she's overwhelmed. I blink the visions away before the demons' victory is certain.

"What are you seeing?" Reena inquires. Her tone tells me she knows exactly what I'm seeing.

"Memories. Visions." I shake my head to clear it. "I'm not sure."

"You're a Transporter, Allister." Reena looks around the empty office. "That would explain why leaving a mark on you was so easy." In response to a questioning look, she continues, "That's how I found you even though the battle moved all over that desert." Reena clears her throat. "It also explains what I saw of the battle on my way in."

"What?"

"How long have you had the ability to microjump?"

"A couple of hours," I answer.

"Have you had other visions?"

"Sometimes. Shouldn't we worry about finding the others?"

Reena waves for patience.

"One more question. How's your ability to picture the

future?"

"Spotty, but I've always been decent at thinking forward most situations. Why does that matter?"

"It's a rare ability, but more common among our kind." Reena frowns thoughtfully. "I do not have the ability to think forward, but I do have a plan for finding our people." She pauses for permission to tell me her thoughts.

I imagine the types of plans that would make Reena hesitate. It's probably not a safe plan, whatever it is. Soon, I'm thinking forward the problem. The demons probably left a cleanup crew or rear guard or something. We could confront these beings and trick them into taking us to the others. The plan comes with a whole host of issues, not the least of which is allowing the demons to think they've captured us without that actually happening.

"Should we confront the demons they left behind?" I wonder.

"I was thinking more along the lines of marking them," Reena answers. "They will eventually return to their base of operations."

"We'd have to assume they'd return to the same place our people were taken," I point out. I weigh the idea with instinct and logic. "I don't think that's the case here."

"Do you have a plan?" Reena's question holds no hint of malice, only curiosity.

"Maybe." I indulge in an extended pause to examine my idea from several angles before voicing the plan. "What if we enacted your plan on a larger scale?"

Reena's dark eyes narrow in concentration, but finally, her head bobs in agreement.

"If we can mark enough demons, we'll increase our chances one of them will go to the prison, but are we sure our people were taken to the same place? And what will we do when we find them? And how will we find enough demons to mark?"

I tick the answers off on my fingers to keep track.

"Building a prison for spirits can't be simple. They were likely taken to the same location. When we find the prison, we break the holds over them and escort them to a predetermined safe place. And to find the demons, I say we use humans as bait."

Reena looks worried.

"Allister, we—"

"Prayer warriors," I clarify. "If we get a large enough prayer movement going, demons will be sent to investigate. If those praying know what they're fighting, they should be safe enough."

"I wish we could find our way back to that desert," Reena says. "Some of those demons should know where to go. Perhaps we can corner one and question it."

She might have more to say but I stop listening. Something she said resonates deeply within me.

"What did you say?"

Looking puzzled, Reena repeats her last few statements.

"Some of the demons know where—"

"That's it!" I almost dance with joy. "When you leave a mark, how do you do it? Could part of one's soul become a mark?"

"I … never thought of it like that, but yes, I think that could work." The words come out of Reena painfully slow. "Why do you want to know?"

"Paige wanted the demons to rip away parts of my soul," I explain. My skin still tingles. "I'm still whole—I think—but a few dozen demons broke through my defenses before you arrived."

"Can you locate those pieces?" Reena's expression is cautiously hopeful.

Closing my eyes, I cast my mind outward in search of the soul fragments. It's much like casting a single fishing line into an ocean. However, once I examine how the pieces feel, I can conduct several dozen searches at once.

"I can do it," I report. "But we're still going to need the support of prayer warriors."

"Make a list of everybody you can think of and I'll get to work." Reena appears relieved to have a plan of action. She goes on to explain how I can directly transfer thoughts in much the same way as I can move my body from one place to another via my Transporter Gift. "You can continue concentrating on the search, but we should stay together."

"Should we try to find more help?" I ask. "I mean holy

help."

Reena thinks for a moment. Her grim expression answers before she speaks.

"Right now, we don't know who to trust. We should ask the Glorious King for aid, but we cannot wait for the message to trickle through to him."

"He knows everything, but we should ask anyway," I note.

"There are the treaties to consider," Reena says, trying to prepare me for the possibility of not receiving help.

"I'm pretty sure the rebels just violated a few hundred of those." I struggle to keep my impatience in check.

"The right path is always harder." Reena's sincerity renders the statement innocent rather than mocking.

Our mission to notify the palace takes only a few seconds because they already know. I give Reena my list of humans we should visit and let her take the lead in teleporting us. The list contains everybody with The Sight plus those I remember from my few stints on Prayer Room desk duty.

The first stop is Cheryl Fenster's house. I consider skipping her given the recent troubles she's had with demons, but she'll be stronger while praying. Once I explain the situation to her through her son, Colin, they both settle in to work. After that, I let Reena handle the explanations. Some have to be delivered in dreams while others can be given as direct orders. That depends largely on the listener's skill level.

Time's a tricky thing to keep a handle on when engaged in a task like ours, but I'm sure at least a day passes while we raise an army. Meanwhile, I continue to chase the soul fragments. When I find a piece big enough to function as a mark, I travel there for a split-second to reinforce the connection. I never stay long enough for the demon to suspect anything. When we finish, we'll follow the leads one by one. I do not doubt we will succeed. My only question is if we'll find Mina before she's broken.

Chapter 28:
The Dark Master

Trainee Case Report #: MN-111
Case Agent: Master Blaz
Guardian Candidate: Mina Nadir

While trying to avoid the pain radiating from my wounded left hand, I learn two things. One, I'm a Healer, and two, I have limited control over what part of me turns to spirit and which remains mortal flesh. Unfortunately, I need to concentrate in order to exert any control over switching forms, and my human body is currently exhausted. The placement of Spirit's Bane over my heart prevents me from turning anything above my shoulders into spirit right now.

I'm terrified the demons mean to let my human form perish. They cannot directly harm me due to the unbreakable laws, but if they simply leave me here long enough, that part of me will die. Normally, an angel's human form receives rest and nourishment while one stays in spirit form, but that's not an option for me. I'm not eager to find out what happens if my human form ceases. Humans may seem more flesh than spirit, while angels may seem more spirit than flesh, but we're actually very similar. We need both, like an image in a mirror needs something to reflect.

If I could really control my Gift, my hand wound would close in seconds, but most effort goes into carefully manipulating forms. The task would also be easier if I could use both hands, but my captors embedded the spirit cuffs inside simple metal shackles that hold me fast regardless of form. Many minutes pass while I work at the healing. I manage to knit the bone back together and stop most of the bleeding, but it's still a deep wound.

The little demon left to watch over me while Hadeon is away observes my work with interest. I can tell the idea of healing fascinates him. Realizing this, I start to reason with him and the demons above. I have no way of measuring the impact of the words, but I know they're listening.

"What brought you here?" I address the question to the little demon in my cell. "Do you have a name?" When both attempts to start a conversation fail, I go for a monologue. "It doesn't matter what brought you here. What matters is that you understand that there is a way home again."

At least for some of you. I add silently. Most demonic hearts will already have set their course permanently.

I see a spark of intrigue light in the little demon's eyes at the word "home." I pause and count to ten to let the idea fully sink in.

"Yes, home. Do you remember the Golden City? That was once our home, until the dark times, until the rebellion against the Glorious King. I don't remember it, but I can picture it. Can you?"

At first, silence meets my speech, but then, the little demon bursts into hysterical laughter. The unpleasant sound hits several high notes while still managing to convey mockery and malice.

"I see you're trying to corrupt my help." The soft, vibrant voice cuts through the laughter, stopping it cold.

The little demon dives to the ground.

I fix my gaze on the darkness beyond the cell where the voice came from.

A figure steps up to the bars and the little demon scrambles up and opens them for him. He's an angel in human form, but I can tell it's a projected form, not a true reflection of his identity. The man presented has thick, dark hair trimmed short at the sides but left high and sweeping along the top. He's wearing a perfectly tailored charcoal suit. The scruffy beginning of a beard flows down from his sideburns and covers the lower part of his face, framing his mouth. He's handsome, but I get the feeling he's diminishing his presence on purpose.

"I'm glad I didn't leave you alone longer." He sticks his hands in his pockets and nods toward my hand. "I see you've also discovered your Gift. Congratulations. You would have grown up to be very powerful."

My mind races for something to say, but nothing seems appropriate.

"Do you know why you're here?" The man's casual tone implies I should know by now.

"No, but I assume you'll tell me when you want to."

"What if I don't want to?" He raises one eyebrow to emphasize the question.

"Then you must enjoy wasting your own time. My situation doesn't change either way."

The man rocks back on his heels and smiles.

"I've missed this." Removing his hands from his pockets, the angel steps close, stretches his arms wide, and places his hands gently over mine. His warm breath lands on my right ear. The move is at once intimate and invasive. He drops his voice to a whisper. "They all start like this: brave, defiant, doomed." He draws his head back to add, "But fear not, you're not destined to be a groveling sycophant. You're going to die."

"What does my death gain you?"

"My dear, Mina, I don't think you're hearing me. I said you're going to die." His hands are now warm over mine. "I'm not going to release your soul back to where that magician can send you to a new body. I'm going to end you. The gain is in the deed itself: immortals made mortal. I've made the impossible doable. That beautiful charm you wear is only the first of many. It's taken centuries to perfect. Once I prove it works to my followers, we can make more of them and end this war. You'll be an instrument for bringing peace to my people. Are you ready?"

His fingers press my hands back into the cold stone walls. Next, he presses his thumbs into the center of my palms, directly over the healing gash on my left hand. The pressure gradually increases until I wince. The rest of his fingers slip behind my hands, cupping the wrists like we would begin a formal dance soon.

"I'm going to transfer you to a new place now. Just relax. The spirit cuffs give me that authority, but it will go easier if you don't resist."

A jolt charges through the pit of my stomach. A gust of wind slams into me, blowing away the cell. My eyes clench shut to protect the scant moisture there. For a short time, I feel like something powerful is rearranging me cell by cell. Sharp pain stabs into my head, allowing me to focus. I concentrate on controlling the accompanying nausea. I've never actually thrown up before, and I don't want to start now.

"We're here. You can open your eyes."

"Where is here?" I almost weep at the beauty of the place he's brought me to.

I can tell from the smell of the air that we're on Earth. The spirit cuffs have bound my hands together in front of me again. I'm kneeling in thick, white sand. It's warm to the touch but cooling quickly. Far across the water, the sun puts on a spectacular display of colors as it sinks ever closer to the horizon. Birds chirp and trill to each other, providing proof of life on an otherwise deserted island. Waves throw themselves at the shore, smoothing down rough patches of sand.

A small man with dark hair and deeply tanned skin begins mumbling to himself in Spanish. He's speaking too softly to make out actual words, but I probably couldn't decipher the words if he was shouting them. I understand Spanish perfectly well. Language barriers hold no power over my people. The man mutters gibberish as the demons inside him vie to be heard. He looks frightened. I don't know how he came to be demon possessed, but unlike the man who kidnapped me, I believe this figure is an unwilling host. Sympathy swells in contrast to the realization that he's here to kill me. About six feet of sand separates us.

Hadeon and his Dark Master are also present in their human forms. The rest of the demons stay spirits, hovering over the island and nearby waters. The contrast between Hadeon and his master sharpens when they stand side-by-side. Hadeon's tall, broad-shouldered, blond, and proud, while the Prince of

Darkness chooses the form of a slight, unassuming man.

"Here is a private place where I can run my demonstration properly," says Lucifer.

"Must be a peaceful night around the world," I comment, scanning the thick ranks of demons surrounding the island. I'm not even in spirit and their evil reaches me.

"A few could not make it due to prior commitments." Hadeon sounds unusually grim. "Some fool's running around the United States and Canada stirring up people who pray."

"Some fool" probably means Allister. I allow the hope to comfort me.

"Forget him." Lucifer spreads his arms wide and lets the strong breeze billow his suit jacket. "Feel the wind. Doesn't it make you feel alive?" He directs the question to me.

"Yes, and I intend to stay alive." My voice contains a tremor. I don't know if he's reading my thoughts or my expression. Death's never been much on my mind. Reaching for the unfamiliar fear, I let it motivate me to work fast.

I flip between forms in split-second intervals. Pain pierces me from Spirit's Bane. I build a wall of flesh between me and the evil device. The pain diminishes slightly once I've done this a few dozen times, but it remains pretty intense. Aware my life depends on this work, I continue crafting a shell around the pendant. My shirt hides the progress, but the constant shifts make my body flicker in the fading light.

"What are you doing?" demands Hadeon.

"Kill her!" Lucifer commands, catching onto my plan.

A dozen demons flash into the human. He snatches up a dagger that's been sitting in front of him and staggers to his feet, lurching toward me. His eyes look panicked, and he fights for control of his body. A hundred more demons leap for me. They have little effect while I'm in human form, but those split-seconds when I'm in the spirit burn.

My work continues anyway. The case around the pendant thickens. Slowly, Spirit's Bane becomes a part of me as a new layer of skin forms over it. I wish I had a year or even a minute to contemplate my decision, but I'm very short on time. If I go through with this, I may never be able to go home.

The man reaches me and swings his arm forward to

plunge the knife into me. I flip the lower half of my body to spirit while keeping everything from my heart and up human. At the same moment, I magnify my presence to drive back the demons. The knife slashes through harmlessly. The man stares at me dumbfounded. The demons inside him freeze with indecision. A second later, I'm completely back in the mortal world. Darting forward, I snap the shackles apart, wrench the weapon away from the man, and hurl it into the ocean.

The man screams hysterically. The demons fling him to the ground. Without a weapon, he's no match for me. I may look like a normal teenage girl, but I'm still an angel. Hadeon and Lucifer hadn't counted on me using my human form to fight back, which would be true without my Healing Gift. The brief periods spent in spirit have bound the wounds and restored my strength.

My situation has vastly improved, but I'm still in trouble. Energy-based cuffs still bind me to Lucifer and Hadeon's will. Hadeon looks upset, but Lucifer's calm reasserts itself, intensifying my unease. I prepare to continue the fight, even though I'll likely lose, but Lucifer holds up his hands, causing every demon to fall still. I'm not in the mood to negotiate with the Prince of Darkness.

"Your efforts are admirable but useless," Lucifer says. "Everybody who follows the path of Light has a fatal flaw. Do you know what that is?"

I shake my head.

"You care for others. That makes you weak." Lucifer points to three demon commanders and issues a crisp command. "Show her." Turning to me, he gloats. "I knew this was a possibility, but I admit, your abilities are impressive."

My human heart flutters nervously. The wait is probably about a minute long, yet it seems an eternity.

Twenty-some figures exit a shack several hundred feet down the beach. A large motorboat speeds around the island from the opposite direction, carrying approximately the same number of people. Finally, a third band of people melt onto the beach behind me, rising up from the sand and stepping around trees and out of thick undergrowth. This last group consists entirely of men armed with handguns or rifles. Most of the other people are tied together with dirty ropes, including several small children. Men herd the others along with guns.

Hostages.

I should have known demons would fight dirty.

"I have a point to make, and you will help me make it." Lucifer's voice is back to slow and persuasive. "I offer a simple trade: your life for theirs. Haven't you always wanted to be like your vaunted Prince, the sacrificial lamb?"

"This is different. He chose that path willingly to save the human race. This 'simple trade' hardly qualifies."

"And your answer?" Hadeon presses.

With great ceremony, the captives are led forward and forced to kneel in neat lines. There are forty-three souls present.

"I want a guarantee—"

"And you'll get only a promise," says Lucifer. "If you do not comply very soon, they will die here in front of you."

Full night has fallen, but the men have set up large spotlights to illuminate the beach around us.

Hadeon calls for the last captive in line to be cut from the others. It's a little girl no more than four years old. Her mother screams, grabs hold of the child, and pleads with the men in Spanish. One man hits her with the end of his rifle. She falls backward and the child is dragged to a place equidistant from me and my tormentors.

My mind races, but no answers come.

I need a miracle. My heart prays earnestly for the right answer.

The man who has the child forces her to kneel again, facing me. He steps back and waits. Receiving a nod from Lucifer, he raises a handgun.

If I fight, they'll die.

If I surrender, they'll still die.

I stare into the child's eyes.

Chapter 29:
Reunion

Apprentice Case Report #: AK-112
Case Agent: Mistress Adira Clarimond
Guardian Candidate: Allister Knight
"Something's happening." I don't wait for a response from
Reena.

There's a large gathering of demons to the south, and I
need to be there. I hope Reena will be able to follow me, but I
can't spare the time to explain myself. I feel Mina's presence, but
it's faint and flickering.

When I arrive, I freeze time. Everything in the mortal
world slams to a halt. At first, I think I've misjudged the location
of the demon pack because I'm hovering about twenty-five feet
above a small island in the Caribbean. Outraged cries fly out of
displaced demons, and a pocket of clear air forms around me.
They shy away from the light of my spiritual presence.

Two figures leave their human bodies to deal with my
intrusion. They take on transparent versions of the current
projected human forms. The dark-haired figure glares up at the
taller, blond figure.

"Why is the boy here?" The dark figure keeps his tone
level, but his anger comes through clearly.

The blond spirit, in turn, looks harshly at three lesser
demons standing nearby shaking their heads in disbelief.

"No matter," mutters the dark figure. "I'll deal with him myself. Keep him away from the girl."

I feel like I should know him, but mention of Mina directs my attention to her. She's standing on the beach facing the ocean, flanked by a number of armed men. Four lines of prisoners are arrayed in front of her under the watchful gaze and ready weapons of more men. One child has been culled from the pack and placed in front of my friend. The time-freeze catches Mina's distressed expression. I want to go to her, but rank upon rank of demons line up in the space between us. I can go to her in human form, but if I do that, I'll lose my grip on time. The brief glimpse of the beach scene tells me the man holding a gun on the child will soon fire, if it's not done already.

The dark spirit on the beach changes forms. His presence grows thick, forming a dark cloud and coalescing into a bright red dragon. He shoots a stream of fire at me. I'm almost too shocked to respond, but I let the prayers of the faithful work in me while I concentrate on keeping time stopped in the mortal world. Thick, golden armor encases my body, and a heavy shield appears on my left arm. Tyre answers my summons, landing in my right hand in time to deflect the fire.

"Come, boy. Let us bargain," says the dragon. His voice carries a richer, deeper air to it now. "Your friend is lost. Leave and I will spare the humans."

"Release Mina," I demand.

The huge dragon shakes his head vigorously.

"She has something of mine."

"What could she possibly have that's yours? Who are you?" I recognize him now, but since no plan seems sure, I decide to provoke him into action.

"I am called many things: Satan, Lucifer, Prince of Darkness, but you will know me as Destroyer."

Not much for long speeches, the dragon attacks. His followers form a loose sphere around us, reminding me of my fight with Paige a few days earlier. The main difference is in directionality. Unlike the other conflict, this contest has up, down, and both sides to consider. The dragon is much more maneuverable than I am due to the fact that I need to stay within range of the island to control the time there. I'll need to deal with that shortly. Time will move on without my permission soon enough.

The dragon circles lazily above me, taunting me to come meet him. Instead, I descend closer to the island. His followers close ranks, cutting off that path. If they rush me together, I'll either have to forfeit the island battle or rush through the demons. I'm not sure that path's even possible.

Changing tactics, the dragon dives for me, releasing another stream of fire. My shield holds, but it shakes and shudders much more than before. Thinking forward reveals several unpleasant scenarios. I discard them and try again. These results are similar and sometimes grimmer than the previous ones: the dragon kills me, the demons kill me, the man on the beach kills the child, the man on the beach kills Mina and the child, or the men kill everybody.

Allister, come to me! Mina's voice booms in my mind like she's taken up residence there. It's gone the next instant. She must have switched between human and spirit forms instantly. I've never heard of an angel that could accomplish a transformation that quickly, but I don't question it.

The dragon dives for me, and I fight the instinct to dodge. A crazy idea occurs to me. I need to get to the ground quickly. Spirit forms can follow conventional rules of physics. If I can get the dragon to hit me, he'll save me a lot of effort in trying to bully my way through the thick wall of demons. I just have to keep him from eating me. Devouring me in this form wouldn't be a pleasant experience for either of us, but try telling him that.

He stops short and tries fire one more time. After failing to overcome my shield, the dragon resorts to biting. His head snaps down at me, barely missing. I paste myself to his scaly side. Tyre won't be able to damage him significantly, but I hack away at the tough scales anyway, trying to reach the wings.

I score.

The dragon roars. His wings whip up in protest, smashing me between them. I don't have to fake being stunned. The dragon draws back to observe me, sensing a kill. I roll a few times midair and hover, keeping very still and silently pleading with the dragon to hit me with his tail. The wish turns into a prayer.

The dragon grins at me in triumph.

"Enjoy pulling him apart, my friends," the dragon crows to the lesser demons. Rearing back and twisting away, the dragon swings his tail back and forth.

I curl into a ball. At the last possible moment, I start diving and straighten. The dragon's strike hits my feet like a freight train meeting a small insect. If I were fully in human form, bones would shatter. In the twilight state before spirit form, it still hurts, but I can press through the discomfort. I speed toward the ground, carving a path through the demons. My armor protects me, but a trail of misery forms in my wake until I change to human form.

My hold over time slips as I target the man holding a gun to the child's head. The transformation to human form completes while I'm ten feet above the man. My body plows him into the sand as he pulls the trigger. His curses get lost in the sand filling his mouth. I punch him for good measure.

A dozen guns track my movements. I stand slowly. I'm still a couple of feet away from Mina. Up close, she looks tired but fiercely determined to continue fighting.

"Quite an entrance," she comments.

The wonderful sound of her voice chases away the pesky aches ailing my body from the rough landing. I'm still fully armored, but I'm uncertain of the next best move.

The men shift and nervously eye the dragon. Most of them can't see him, but they feel his presence. It's like liquid dread fouling up the air. The dragon settles down heavily next to the well-dressed blond demon. He shakes from rage at being tricked into helping me. In another moment, the dragon fades, and the demon becomes a suited man again.

"This will not stand!" declares Lucifer. "You will both die today!"

Mina's body shimmers. She shifts to spirit and back in the blink of an eye. Another thought appears in my mind.

Please fetch Kentaro.

The shared thought gives me a further glimpse into her mind. Something called Spirit's Bane consumes much of her attention.

"What's 'Spirit's Bane'?" I wonder, buying time to figure out how to fulfill Mina's request without momentarily abandoning her.

"It's an invention to keep angels mortal long enough to be killed," Mina explains. Her words tumble out swiftly. "I'm keeping it so he can't use it against anybody else." There's a protective, dangerous edge to her voice.

I'm still nowhere near to fully comprehending the situation, but the brevity of Mina's time in spirit form makes sense now.

Lucifer's malevolent eyes stab into Mina.

"Once you're dead, my men will cut the Spirit's Bane free from your corpse. You've accomplished nothing, except bringing destruction down upon these people."

"Please, get me the sword," Mina whispers to me. "We can protect them if I have Kentaro."

Lacking a better plan, I change completely to spirit and split the Veil long enough to call Mina's sword to me. The process takes me several seconds to complete. Knowing the sword won't stay with me long, I toss it to my friend. Mina's hands turn to spirit in time to catch the sword, but the rest of her body remains human. Those without The Sight must think her arms below the elbows have vanished.

A few of the people faint.

"Strike the men with Tyre while in human form," Mina instructs. "The demons won't be able to touch you."

I catch onto her idea as she stabs Kentaro through the man I'd just punched. The spirit sword doesn't faze the slumbering man, but the four demons inside him come out screeching.

Letting the shield return to the Veil, I grip Tyre with two hands and microjump through the men crowding close behind Mina. Demons fly out of them and join the restless horde in the sky above the island. A few more microjumps take me through the men standing guard over the people tied together in rows. The demons flee the assault, and the men look at each other like they wish to awaken from a shared nightmare.

"Surrender or I will break her neck," says the blond demon. His human form is substantial enough to maintain a grip around the little girl's throat.

Mina and I exchange a quick look. It's her call. She has

more to lose here than I do. I won't leave her, but I could escape to the Heavens at any moment.

"Well done, Hadeon." Lucifer faces Mina. "Make your decision quickly, girl."

"All right," Mina says. She lets go of Kentaro, and the spirit sword vanishes. "But let me say goodbye to my friend."

I microjump to her, and she hugs me tightly. She's trembling. Pulling out of the embrace and shifting her back to Hadeon and Lucifer, Mina draws my head down close to her mouth.

"You have to go, Allister." The pain in her voice hits me hard. Mina grips my hands. They turn to spirit and an additional message comes through her hands, which are bound with strong spirit cuffs.

The message is the location of the prison Reena and I had searched for. I don't know how Mina found it, but she tells me to speak with Serrin and Tristam when I reach the Sea of Death and Life.

Duty and loyalty clash within me. I should take this knowledge to the Heavens and mount a rescue for those snatched from the Academy, but that means leaving. Even my teleporting power falls short of allowing me to be in two places simultaneously.

"I can hold them off," Mina's statement is firm with conviction, and she gives me a tight smile. "Come back for me, and we'll break the spirit chains together."

She's not going to give me a choice.

Mina reforms her human hands and squeezes my fingers briefly. Then, she steps away and walks back to face her captors.

Chapter 30:
Kindred Spirits

Trainee Case Report #: MN-112
Case Agent: Master Blaz
Guardian Candidate: Mina Nadir

Allister and I have a Kindred Spirit Bond. The realization strikes me when he appears in the sky above the island. Allister's thoughts and feelings are laid bare to me. The Academy's been attacked, and he's been splitting his time between trying to find them and me. He's frozen time, giving me a moment to think. I can't think forward like he can, but I know the basics. Given our bond, his abilities will eventually be mine and vice versa.

Across great distances our bond will still aid us, but the effect will be weaker. I'm ashamed to admit I didn't pay much attention to the lesson on Kindred Spirit Bonds, though I do remember they are rare and few truly understand them. It's difficult to think of a proper analogy to describe such a connection. It's like living two lives simultaneously.

The bond will make us more powerful if we're near each other, but two major problems must be addressed: the Academy captives and Spirit's Bane. Allister cannot help with the latter problem, and since I am bound to the mortal world for the moment, I cannot help him with the former problem, not directly anyway. I can find the information he seeks. I send out several silent queries to the demons around me. Most are enthralled with the battle between their Dark Master and my friend, but a few hear me out. More importantly, one brave soul answers.

Forsaken Island. I thought it a myth before, but nothing really surprises me today.

When an opportunity presents itself, I give Allister the prison's location. When Allister delivers Kentaro to me, we cast the demons out of the men standing guard over the captives. I dare to believe everything might work out.

Hadeon assumes his human form and seizes the same little girl separated from the others.

Allister stops fighting. He would stay with me and fight the demons arrayed above us, but I cannot allow that. He's the only one who can summon the right help to free our people. I think of Aderes, Adelmo, Osmund, and the other young angels whose fate we now hold. It gives me enough strength to send Allister away and let Kentaro return to the Veil.

I keep my steps slow because I still need to work out several details on a plan I'm forming. I test the theory that communication works with Allister while I'm a spirit. Since it does, I quickly explain what I intend to do. There is no certain way to know if he understands, but the resounding sense of displeasure I'm getting from him tells me he comprehends the plan. My timing will have to be perfect because the element of surprise will only be with me once.

"Take on your spirit form," Lucifer orders.

I hesitate, but follow the directive. There's only one reason for the command to be issued right now. Turning completely to spirit puts my being at war with the pendant. Even in its flesh encasement, Spirit's Bane punishes me for defying it. Allister demands I share the burden, so I do. Still, I struggle to think or move and manage only a few staggering steps toward Lucifer. He grows impatient with my progress and summons me through the spirit bindings. Once I'm directly in front of him, he lets me turn back into my human state and bids the bindings to separate.

My hands fall to my sides, and I kneel on the sand, feeling light-headed. The gentle sea breeze chills me through my damp T-shirt.

Lucifer grins down at me. I can see him weighing the

pleasure of repeating the order with the desire to move things along. The demons around the island press closer.

"Bind her," Hadeon barks to the nearby men. When they move too slowly for his liking, he adds, "Quickly or you will join her."

"If you change to spirit form, Hadeon will crush the child's neck," Lucifer tells me.

The humans rush to obey. Even without the demons dwelling inside them, Lucifer's word is law. One man tentatively offers his superior a pair of metal handcuffs. The leader snatches them from his underling and quickly applies them to my wrists, which have been pulled behind my back. I don't protest. Another man fetches a length of rope from a backpack at the base of a tree. It takes two men working in concert to wrap the long rope around my lower arms and stomach a dozen times.

At Lucifer's order, the men stretch me out on the sand and bind my feet. I twist my head around and try to send the horrified child a reassuring smile, but Lucifer steps between us.

"I told you I would have Spirit's Bane cut from your dead body," he reminds me.

"You won't get that chance."

Working swiftly yet delicately, I set a desperate plan into motion. I coil the chain making up Spirit's Bane around my heart, secure it with new cords of muscle, and transfer it to Allister. If he's misunderstood my message, I'll die. Instead, my body shudders as his heart appears in the space mine just vacated. The transfer's not permanent, nor is it perfect. My healing Gift strains to repair the internal damage of such a disruptive move. I can taste blood in my mouth.

Lucifer loses patience and orders the two men who tied my arms to shoot me. Their guns swing downward.

The child weeps and closes her eyes.

Bullets rip into the ropes that bound my arms and riddle the sand where my head once was, but I am gone. I've changed to spirit and microjumped to where Hadeon holds the little girl. Upon reaching them, I turn solid and knock him back a step before returning to spirit to lay a blessing upon the child. For the next few moments, no demon will come near her, including Hadeon. Satisfied, I microjump a half-dozen more times while in human form, snatching the guns from each of the men.

I deposit the weapons into the ocean and flash back to the beach, landing with a spray of sand.

"Your boat's intact, I suggest you get on it," I inform the men.

There's a mad rush for the small motorboat. Two men have stayed behind, but they do not appear immediately dangerous so I leave them alone.

"Kill them!" Lucifer screams at the remaining two humans.

Though shaking, they refuse.

"Hadeon!" Lucifer barks, but by this time, he can see it's too late.

During the few seconds he rages, I microjump a few more times, laying more blessings upon the captives. They're still tied together, but I can't fix everything now. Besides, keeping together is probably a good idea. The first child I freed sprints to the pack and tackles her mother with a hug.

I move close to the captives and strengthen their spirits, giving them courage. A few of the younger men and women tighten their fists and prepare to battle the two men left.

With the spiritual battle nearly won, I stick to human form and position my body between the crowd of people and the last two main threats: Lucifer and Hadeon. The spiritual bonfire I lit above the captives should keep them safe from the lesser demons.

Allister's heart returns to him and mine comes home to me, complete with Spirit's Bane. Once again, the transfer is mostly successful, but the disturbance weakens my body. It takes much of my remaining strength to stay on my feet, but I refuse to bend a knee to Lucifer this time.

Reena suddenly appears in the sky above us along the water's edge. The demons form a pocket around her and whisper uneasily amongst themselves. To her left, Bali shows up. This time, I hear a small audible pop. Another angel I don't recognize appears to Bali's left with the same slight noise of disturbed air. This time, I catch a glimpse of Allister depositing an angel. Bringing them all together would have been more practical, but this method has the right psychological effect upon our enemies.

My confidence grows in proportion to the number of angels that appear in the sky, breaking up the thick ranks of demons. Most wear full spiritual armor and display their wings prominently. Reena stays in her human form subtly directing them.

As I open my mouth to demand Lucifer retreat, I feel Allister tell me to wait and turn to spirit form.

Bracing for intense pain, I transform. It hurts, but not like before. The angels above us have formed a loose circle around me. Peace floods me from head to toe. The spirit cuffs spark and crackle. I focus my attention on keeping still. The amount of energy coursing through me is dangerous. The process of breaking spirit chains resembles art more than science. It's never the same and one small mistake can be ruinous. Finally, the cuffs shatter and my soul bursts free. Exhausted, I retreat into human form.

"It is not yet time for the final battle, but the choice belongs to you. We will fight you here if you wish, but your ranks are thinning."

My statement draws Lucifer's gaze upward where we can see many demons abandoning their posts. His face pales with anger, but he straightens and offers me a courtly bow.

"I see you've grown attached to Spirit's Bane," he taunts. "Keep it for now. I will come for it in time, and you will suffer for this ... inconvenience." Having secured the last word, Lucifer orders his demons to leave.

Lucifer and Hadeon are the last to disappear. I might have imagined it, but I think there's a grain of respect in the blond demon's eyes. He's not remotely moved by my earlier offer of hope, but he understands the message's appeal and recognizes the threat it represents to his Dark Master's ranks.

I wait until I'm certain they've left for good before letting down my guard. The two men who stayed behind catch me, causing an outcry amongst the captives. A torrent of Spanish flies back and forth like warning shots from both sides. If I don't do something, the former captives will lynch the men who stayed behind.

"Help me stand," I tell the men, rallying my healing Gifts and working furiously. My chest feels like I've got a three-foot arrow sticking out of it.

Allister wants to help diffuse the situation, but his work isn't done yet. He asks if he can at least leave Reena to help, but I refuse. He's going to need every single angel he can muster for the job ahead. Conceding the point, he wishes me well and begins transferring those without teleporting abilities to their new destination, which I'm hoping is the prison on Forsaken Island. I wish I could be a part of the raid, but my work isn't complete either.

I straighten my shoulders before raising a hand for silence. What I tell them sounds more beautiful in Spanish as the lyrical flow to the language lends itself to heartfelt speech.

"We have all done things we will regret for a long time. Certain sins may seem weightier than others, but the physical relief brought to you today holds nothing on the spiritual salvation offered to each and every one of you. Forgive and move on or the hatred will destroy you."

The words don't immediately set everything right, but they help. One of the men slowly pulls out a knife and offers it to a young man who has worked one hand free of his bonds. For a second, I think the kid will turn the knife on the man, but he mutters thanks, cuts the remaining cord, and starts to free the others.

I can worry about how to get everybody off the island later, but right now, I need to sit down. Once I'm reasonably certain the people won't kill each other when I'm not watching, I slowly lower myself to the sand.

The little girl comes over, gives me a hug, and kisses the tears on my cheeks. Her whispered thanks does more good than I can put into words.

Chapter 31:
Forsaken Island

Apprentice Case Report #: AK-113
Case Agent: Mistress Adira Clarimond
Guardian Candidate: Allister Knight

Following Mina's instructions, I stop at the edge of the Sea of Death and Life. I've never been this far into the spiritual lands claimed by the Rebel. Having recently seen him up close, I wonder why the Glorious King tolerates him. He is nothing special.

"Do you come alone?" asks a soft, furtive voice.

"I was told to meet Serrin and Tristam first," I respond.

"And so you have," says a deep voice. "Is it time?"

"It is time," I answer formally.

Two demons appear, hovering over the water a short distance away. The one on the left is a small Guilt demon, and the larger one on the right is a Pride demon. My hand twitches with the urge to summon Tyre.

The demons shudder. Twin bursts of light slam into me. If I had been in human form, I would be blind.

The demons vanish.

In their place stand two angels of Light: Ari and Salmaan.

"Bring the others to this staging ground, and we will see them safely through the Crossing," the bass voiced angel continues. This is Ari, whose name means "the lion of God."

"It will be good to show our true forms," says Salmaan. He flexes the bright white wings that have sprouted from his shoulders. His name means "safety," which is fitting since we're about to trust him with our lives. "You could make the Crossing alone, but some may become lost."

It could be a trap, but I don't believe the Rebel planned that far ahead. Little information exists about the prison on Forsaken Island, known simply as The Fortress. It's supposed to be impossible to get to unless you know the way. Trap or not, I am prepared to fight.

Bowing to our prospective guides, I summon the others. They appear in one group with Reena at the center. I turn and face them. We were only able to gather three dozen angels on such short notice, but they still require a portal to transport that many beings. Two stayed behind to continue spreading the call for aid. If we wait, the Rebel will learn of our plans and move the prisoners. Still, we can't rush in waving our swords about and making demands. I study the gathered angels. A sense of pride sweeps through me, causing me to glance at Ari. He nods solemnly, acknowledging that I've noticed his touch.

"I forgot what it was to use my Gift that way," he murmurs.

We certainly make an interesting invading force.

"We'll go in pairs. Ari, Salmaan, and I will take turns shuttling pairs over to the island. Reena and two others will stay here to guard the portal." I look to Reena, half-fearing she'll protest her role. "Once you reach The Fortress, find our people and escort them to the beach. Either Ari or Salmaan will be there to guide the captives here. In every pair, I want one fighter and one seeker. We need to be fast because once the element of surprise is lost, we're going to have quite a fight on our hands. Any questions?"

"Should I take them home one by one or wait for a group?" Reena inquires.

"Take them as they come," I instruct. "The angels guarding the portal can watch over those that arrive when you're not here."

"Shall we pray before we begin?" asks Ari.

"Certainly," I answer.

Ari's prayer is short and heartfelt.

"Great Glorious King, hear our plea. Strengthen our hearts and sharpen our swords. Let your protection rest upon these warriors."

There's not much left to say. We quickly divide up into pairs. Annie, a Healer, and Kadie, a Minder with the Gift of Intelligence volunteer to stay behind. Annie will tend the wounded, and Kadie will coordinate the rescue efforts.

Salmaan explains that teleporting directly across is possible, but not advisable due to the many traps laid out.

"If you teleport through a trap, you could end up on one of the other islands or deep inside the prison." He watches us carefully to make sure we understand the warning. "In either case, you won't be able to help with the rescue, and you could end up lost forever. Some traps are looped portals to dead worlds, and others lead to the Lake of Fire. Ari and I have done guard duty countless times. We can show you where most of the traps are located."

For the first trip out and back, I don't take anyone with me. Instead, I note the places Ari and Salmaan avoid. The sea lives up to its name. The waters sustain plant life on the scattered Black Isles, yet the sea's whims are hard to predict. At times, it's calm as glass, but then, it turns into a roiling cauldron of deadly waves the very next instant. Being careful to follow our guides, we manage to get every pair safely across the Sea of Death and Life.

By the time I enter The Fortress, the battle's in full swing. The fighters engage the demons while the seekers search the cells. Most of the young angels are held in normal cells like you would find in any human prison because they've not manifested Gifts that could free them.

Assuming the important prisoners will be held in the lower dungeons, I head there. Opposition's fierce, but I microjump past most guards until I reach the more complicated cells. These have a variety of tricks to keep angels from changing forms.

Four Destroyer demons rush me when I enter the lower level. Their faces are flickering black masks, and their obsidian swords flash menacingly. Two teleport behind me while the other two stay in front of me. The move startles me, but I recover in time to avoid being sliced in half. They move through the space where I was standing. I can't fight off both pairs alone, but before despair settles in, I experience a surge of confidence. I'm not alone.

They pause to savor the moment, thinking the dread will cripple me. I use the time to call Mina's sword, Kentaro, from the Veil. The katana's a two-handed weapon I've barely touched during my life, yet when it lands in my hands, it feels like I've practiced with it for years. I release Tyre and bid the weapon to guard my back. The broadsword hovers behind me to ward off the Destroyers approaching from that direction.

With loud snarls, the Destroyer demons in front of me take on the form of black wolves. Their swords turn into a thousand shards that would have sliced me to pieces, but I teleport to the nearest wolf and swing Kentaro down at his head. The shards return to him and form a shield for his head, but the blow still knocks him down. I swing sideways from left to right to force one of the other Destroyer demons into a cell wall. He yelps. Energy courses through his whole body, and he bursts into a fine black mist.

I turn to deal with the last two. Tyre's done an excellent job of keeping them at bay, but it can only do so much on its own. Under my direction, the spirit sword whips back and forth across the hallway, blocking the shards the Destroyer demons send my way. The demon at my feet stirs, and I hit him again with Kentaro. The two demons tire of fighting my sword and teleport past Tyre. The mistake costs them the fight. I switch Kentaro to one hand and stretch my other toward Tyre. The spirit sword comes to me through the left Destroyer demon then sails away again through the right demon. They dissipate with angry cries. They'll reform later, but I'll be long gone by then. The demon at my feet takes on his human form and raises his hands in surrender.

Trust being in short supply, I instruct Tyre to watch him closely.

"Open the cells," I order.

"I can't," says my prisoner.

"Can't or won't?" I demand.

When he hesitates, I seize his shirt and fling him into the closest set of cell bars. This second surge of energy overloads whatever's been keeping the door locked and the bars charged with energy. The bars lose their bright golden color, turning a dull gray. I can now see through the bars. Inside this first cell, I find Master Blaz. He's bound to the far wall with thick chains. From the haggard look he wears, his stay here has not been pleasant.

"Spirit cuffs," he manages to say. His eyes flutter and drift shut.

"Not a problem," I assure him.

I rush forward and stretch my hands over both shackles. I'm not sure what I intend to do, but I end up transplanting Master Blaz. Essentially, I switch places with him, teleporting him to where I stand and using Mina's Gift for rapidly changing forms to trick the spirit cuffs into believing it still holds Master Blaz. Once I'm certain he's truly free, I teleport out of them. They drop to the ground harmlessly, and I slice them in half with Kentaro.

"Can you come with me?" I don't want to leave him here, but I need to search the other cells.

"Leave me here," Master Blaz says hoarsely. "Adira's one cell over." He shakes his head slowly and points right, trying to rally his strength. "Valen's near too."

There are six cells on this level, and each one of them possesses the same security measures Master Blaz's cell had. Having no more Destroyer demons to sacrifice to the locks, I tap another of Mina's Gifts: Healing. Lacking a better plan, I overload the shock system on each door through simple touch. The contact makes my hands feel like they've been dipped in a strong acid, but I repair the damage instantly.

Lady A.'s actually two cells over from Master Blaz, but I can hardly fault him for the small mistake. He's lucky he can stand. I suspect they've kept him in human form his entire prison stint, probably to keep him weak and susceptible to whatever evils they had in mind for him. By the time I free Lady A. from her spirit cuffs using the same trick as before, Master Blaz has switched to spirit. In this form, his strength is full.

"Let me take her," he offers.

I don't want to relinquish my hold, but I have three remaining cells to check. Now that I'm practiced, I make short work of the locks. Master Blaz looks eager to be gone from this prison, but he understands my need to be thorough. In the last cell, I find Valen in much the same state as Lady A. and Master Blaz. I carry him out, bidding Kentaro and Tyre to safeguard us until Valen can gain enough strength to change to spirit form.

Shortly after ascending to the main level, we pick up an escort of four angels. One of them takes charge of Valen. I grip Kentaro and watch for more trouble. I'm torn between staying behind and searching for more prisoners.

"Do we have everybody?" I ask Kadie, speaking directly to her mind.

"Yes," she answers. "Plus some. Come home."

The simple response is all I need to order everybody to return to the portal. The transfer process takes longer than I'd like, but eventually, it's done. The operation winds to a close, but I feel uneasy. I'm not opposed to freeing other prisoners from The Fortress, but what if we liberate something not meant to be free?

Chapter 32:
Slight Setback

Dear Than,

Do not be discouraged. You've done well to keep your cover intact. Daeva's role as Paige is complete. She has been reassigned. I'm considering placing her in charge of the plot against Allister since revenge consumes her. If she needs your aid, consider the request. If help can be given carefully, do so, but do not endanger your primary objectives in preparing for another strike against the Academy.

Protecting the youngest angels during the siege was an excellent touch. I believe the Dark Master's ultimate desires were fulfilled, even if the method of their deliverance wasn't planned for. We came close to ending this war early, but we've always been prepared for a lengthy conflict. The rescue happened before the true trap could be laid, but no matter. At least we had the foresight to move the most important prisoner to a different location before the attack.

The Kindred Spirit pair is formidable. Divide and conquer might be easier than we could hope for in this case. Give me regular updates on the girl.

Do you wish to take up the campaign against Mina?

I do not ask that question lightly. I need to know if you feel any sympathy for the girl. Yours is a dangerous role. It's natural to deceive yourself into believing the way of Light is right.

The Dark Master has offered dominion over the entire Western Continent on Earth to whoever captures the girl. That might generate opportunistic interest, but they will likely fail. The Council of Light is on high alert. Now is a waiting time. The girl will no doubt be confined to the mortal realm for the foreseeable future.

If it can be accomplished subtly, offer your services as an intermediate. Allister will want the role, but he's far too valuable to be wasted on such a menial task. You, on the other hand, are the perfect blend of hero and ordinary angel right now. We will let things settle. The Council may have several Guardians posted over the girl for a while. In time, they'll grow complacent, or the girl will become impatient with the protection. I'll send several of the best, most discrete Guilt demons to work on her. By that time, I expect every agent to offer up their best plan for dealing with her.

Outright killing the girl will be more difficult given the Gifts she shares with the boy. From every report of the desert battle and the island confrontation, I can safely say this pair possesses the most unique set of abilities I've ever seen. When fully trained, their power could rival that of our bitter enemies, the archangels. Your ignorant questions tell me you don't grasp the significance of this. Allow me to enlighten you.

Alone, Allister's Gifts of Teleportation and Transportation and Mina's Gift of Healing would hardly be worth mentioning. Hundreds of angels have these Gifts. However, the boy can manipulate time in the mortal world, and the girl can switch between human and spirit forms swiftly. Both side abilities magnify the main Gifts. More disturbing is that unnatural balance the girl can strike between the forms. This pair is even more dangerous because the Kindred Spirit Bond means that the boy's Gifts belong to the girl and vice versa. Also, it should be noted that their Gifts manifested at near master status. That level of control over such Gifts ought to take years of practice and study, yet these two were born to it.

We should have given Spirit's Bane to the boy. He's more impulsive. I see that now, but it's far too late. The girl may be one of the few beings ever created to be able to resist Spirit's Bane. Even with access to the Healing, I'm not certain the boy would have made the same choice Mina did. Impatience cost us this round, which is why I'm urging more planning and caution moving forward.

Do not mistake my analysis for awe. I respect them, but they can be beaten. Moreover, I believe this will be an important victory for us. These young ones have become symbols, a rallying point. Breaking them will hit the enemy's morale hard.

The Dark Master's pride suffered a blow, but he will turn it into fuel for his wrath. That is what we too must do. This is a setback, not a defeat.

Mina may have to be provoked into action. Contemplate the matter. She's already proven a weakness for this tactic. There are many wonderful opportunities, but they require emotional attachments and those take time to grow. Help her find friends if she needs it, but do not seem overly interested in her.

I do not know enough about Allister to predict his vulnerability to being manipulated through threats to humans, but the girl is his weakness. If we can capture her, he will be ours to command.

Keep up with your reports. I will insert another agent soon, but right now, you are our only eyes and ears there.

Heed these words.
Hadeon, Servant of the Dark Master,
Director of Operations

Part 5:
Graduation

Chapter 33:
Council of Light

Trainee Case Report #: MN-113
Case Agent: Master Blaz
Guardian Candidate: Mina Nadir

A delicate truce exists between the men who stayed behind and their former captives. I reluctantly play peacekeeper. Most of my thoughts remain with Allister, and I add my prayers to the many being raised on behalf of the rescue mission.

Eager to win acceptance, the men show the people where the stockpiles of provisions are hidden. Food and water ease the initial tension, but inevitably, new fights break out over who gets how much and how quickly. Since my voice is the only one heeded evenly by both sides, it falls to me to work out a system. I set the strongest people to carrying out the boxes and delegate food preparation and distribution to several older women. I have those who wish to help lay out blankets and gather firewood from the dry brush on the island. Hopefully, we won't be here too much longer, but the tasks keep the people busy and productive. It also gives them less time to bicker.

The floodlights add warmth, but the fires provide comfort and light. Discussion over the evening meal soon turns to ways to escape the island. I try to stay out of it, but they demand an answer. I could probably return them home, but that's not good enough for them either. They want me to get them to the United

States. That's what they paid the smugglers to do.

Although I sympathize with them, it's not my place to make such a decision. I'd have to ask Mitchell—the angel in charge of that region—for permission to break the law for the good of the people. The Council of Light could hand down a ruling that supersedes the angel's wishes if he's not willing, but I think Mitchell is pretty fair-minded. I have a difficult time articulating that to these people. My mind's a scattered mess tonight. I barely keep the tempers in check.

Relief fills me when Allister appears at my side and the questions shift to him. Rosa, the little girl Hadeon tried to kill, has hardly left my side. She squeezes me hard and buries her face in my side to avoid looking at Allister. Most of the people murmur prayers and cross themselves to express their fear and awe.

"It's time to go," Allister says, ignoring the people.

"We need to help them," I tell him. Although only a couple of hours have passed in the mortal world, I'm not sure how much has transpired in the spirit world.

"Reena and Jordan will see to that," Allister promises. "They're discussing the matter with Master Thomas as we speak. He will present the petition to Master Mitchell. The Council of Light has been called, and you and I have been summoned."

"Don't go," pleads the child clutching my side. The Spanish words are filled with familiar heartache that tells me this is not the first parting she's experienced.

Kneeling, I hug the child close and whisper into her ear. I speak the words in the holy language, knowing they will reach the girl in her native tongue.

"Dear Rosa, I need to answer questions for my people. I hope to find you again someday, but if not in this world, find me in the next one. Follow the Way. Follow the Son. He will lead you to a place where I will be." Taking her shoulders in my hands, I seal the blessing upon her forehead with a kiss and stand. "Farewell."

I step away from the girl, mentally brace, and turn to spirit. A burning sensation spreads throughout my chest, but I manage to keep a thin shield of flesh around it by rapidly changing from spirit to human over and over. The solution's not perfect, but it will suffice to let me attend the Council meeting for a short time. Allister wraps his arms around me and teleports us directly to the meeting. He could have simply taken my hand, but the hug provides more moral support. Despite my thoughts not exactly being coherent, I can guess what this meeting will be about.

Allister releases me when we appear in the chamber. I'm surprised to see that it's a large cavern somewhere on Earth. I allow my body to reform so Spirit's Bane will stop tormenting me.

The Council members are already in full swing by the time we arrive. It quickly becomes clear who stands on which side of the debate.

"Why are they here?" demands Master Josiah Delshad. "This is to be a free discussion!"

"Precisely," responds Mistress Adira Clarimond. "This matter concerns them. They have every right to be here."

"You have a conflict of interest, Adira," says Master Josiah. "I suggest you tread lightly."

It does my heart good to see Master Blaz—the newest Council member—and Master Titus glare at Master Josiah. On the other hand, Master Korin, Master Micah, and Lady Deliah nod agreement.

"My connection to Allister gives me more reason to be here, not less," Mistress Clarimond argues.

"They are dangerous," Master Korin declares.

"They have the *potential* to be dangerous," corrects Master Blaz. "There's a huge difference."

Everybody has the potential to be dangerous. I'm not sure if the thought belongs to me or Allister, but I agree with it regardless of the source.

"What would you have us do with them?" Mistress Clarimond challenges.

"They need monitoring," persists Master Josiah.

"They need more training," says Master Blaz, at the same time.

"Can't both be accomplished?" Mistress Clarimond wonders. "Let us give them missions but monitor them more closely as we would with apprentices."

My ears hone in on the words and my mind reels with the implication. If we're no longer to be considered apprentices, they've either decided to fail us or to graduate us. At this point, I'm not sure which path they've chosen, since they seem evenly split.

"Their powers are beyond you," Master Josiah mutters. "They're beyond all of us. That's the problem. If they join the rebellion, they—"

"They won't!" Master Blaz's response is echoed in Mistress Clarimond's expression.

"We won't!" Allister shouts.

"Allister—" Mistress Clarimond begins.

She's cut off by Master Josiah.

"You are not permitted to speak unless answering a direct question."

Allister bows his head, but I can feel hot anger rising in waves off of him. Anger burns in me too. They should be strategizing on how best to use our Gifts to further the kingdom, not wallowing in the fear we might turn against them. Did they not just witness everything? The enemy tried to destroy us, yet we survived.

A different, more painful ache rips me apart and my illusions shatter. We may claim to be enlightened beings, but we're prone to the same failings as humanity. We fear what we can't control, and hate what we fear. If I truly have Allister's Gifts, I can teleport. Though I've never tried it, I'm more than ready to experiment. I suddenly need to be elsewhere.

Sensing my intentions, Allister grabs my left arm and shakes his head. His eyes beg me to stay, but he releases his grip.

"Do you see how quick to anger he is?" Master Josiah crows.

"I see you provoking him," Mistress Clarimond answers. "And he's doing an admirable job of controlling himself."

"Let the King decide," says Master Titus.

"Confine them to the Academy until the Glorious King gives us a ruling concerning them." This suggestion comes from Master Korin, but it rings with a sense of Master Josiah.

"They cannot stay here," Mistress Clarimond says. Her tone holds genuine regret, and her eyes reach out to hold me.

She really means me. Allister can go wherever he wants, but the location of this meeting is yet another reminder that everything's changed for me.

"The Rebel has targeted them. Their presence would endanger the Academy," Mistress Clarimond explains. "They need to be somewhere we can better protect them until we can come up with an answer for that abomination Mina wears."

"What if he can control her through the necklace?" Master Josiah's look reeks of suspicion.

Heavy silence falls.

"Was that a question directed at me?" I ask, returning Master Josiah's stare. I don't wait for an answer. "If he could control me through Spirit's Bane, he would have done so already."

"How do we know he doesn't control you now?" Master Josiah's expression tries for neutral and fails. "Perhaps you're a spy sent to learn our strategies."

And perhaps you're an idiot.

"Perhaps we should turn the discussion to how to defeat what is in me," I say, speaking slowly to better control my rising anger. "I probably want this gone more than any of you, but I will not release it until I'm certain we can destroy it. Hadeon indicated it was the only one that existed for now. He wanted to use it as a model to create more. We need to study it because if they made it once, they will make it again."

"I agree," Master Josiah says.

That is not what I want to hear.

"Let us take you to a secure location to safely study its effects," he continues.

"No." Allister's a hair's breadth away from growling at Master Josiah. "You will not torture her to get your answers."

"What if it's the only way?" I ask, catching his hand in mine.

"There's always another way," Allister retorts.

"Yes, but how much longer will 'other ways' take? How many will die while we search for answers?"

Master Josiah's questions twist a knife of guilt within me. I really don't like him, but his logic is sound.

I tip my head forward in a bow.

"Do what you think is right, but we should not emulate our enemy in an effort to defeat him."

"We should take a break," Mistress Clarimond suggests. "It's clear the discussion will not conclude quickly."

"What's to discuss?" demands Master Blaz. "These angels and their Gifts should be celebrated. A Kindred Spirit Bond has not happened for a few thousand years! We should embrace them and start thinking of ways to turn them loose against Satan and his ilk."

"'Turning loose' something we do not understand is foolish," Master Josiah argues.

I know in my heart they will rehash the same arguments for many more hours, but I do not have to wait for them. I turn my back to their debate.

"Where are you going?" Master Josiah's question is definitely directed at me this time. He's offended that I've turned away, reading more into the symbolism than he ought.

I only turn my head toward him.

"You can argue my fate without me."

"But will you submit to our ruling without question?" Master Josiah presses.

I face Master Josiah fully.

"I will always have questions, but if I deem your ruling just and in the interest of defeating the Rebel, yes, I will submit."

The words do not quite mollify Master Josiah, but he waves dismissively. After a final look at Mistress Clarimond and Master Blaz, I teleport away from the meeting. Because I don't have a specific destination in mind, I end up only a short distance away. Allister would call it a microjump. It's not much, but it is enough for now.

For the first time ever, I truly feel alone. Then, I get the sense that I'm being watched.

Chapter 34:
The Commission

Apprentice Case Report #: AK-114
Case Agent: Mistress Adira Clarimond
Guardian Candidate: Allister Knight

I can sense that Mina hasn't gone far. Our connection means that I can join her if I wish, but she needs some space. Besides, I have something crazy to try. If I'm wrong, the insult will forever put me on the wrong side of the Council of Light, but I don't think I'm wrong. Being right here carries its own brand of horror, but I need irrefutable proof.

Master Josiah's still blustering about Mina's abrupt exit.

I freeze time and teleport directly through Master Josiah.

That wouldn't work if we were in the Heavens, but the meeting is on Earth to accommodate Mina. The action involves two tests. First, the time freeze gives me one way to test my theory. To full mortals, such an action would keep them in place indefinitely. Angels are only affected for a fraction of a second. Demons take about two or three seconds to fight through the effect. Second, the touch gives me an additional, more definitive way to test my theory.

By the time Master Josiah comes out of the time freeze, I'm behind him. I place a hand through the center of his back. He springs away from me with a pained cry. The accompanying burning sensation coursing through my hand is proof enough for me. Realizing what I've done, the demon transforms into a shadowy, horned creature that shrieks and scrambles away.

Tyre's in my hands the next instant, but it's too late. The creature's gone.

The entire Council looks shaken. To their credit, they each have spirit weapons drawn and ready.

"Where is the real Master Josiah?" Lady A. voices the question on everybody's mind.

"Never mind that, we need to find Mina," says Master Blaz. His concern comes through plainly, but he sends his spirit sword away.

The others follow suit.

"She's fine," I assure him, letting Tyre return to the Veil. "How long do you think Master Josiah's been … gone." I avoid using the word "replaced," but they know what I mean.

"Allister, please go get Mina," Master Blaz orders.

"Why?" I'm not trying to be defiant, but if there's going to be more of the same discussion, Mina won't willingly return.

Master Blaz looks to the other Council members, seeking approval before returning his attention to me.

"I think our path is inevitable now. We give you your commissions."

"Just like that?" The question shows my suspicions.

"This is difficult for everybody, Allister," Lady A. says. "You've proven your point and revealed a serious breach in our security. It will take some time to sort through every implication, but it casts doubt upon his reservations about you and Mina."

"We should not doubt his logic simply because he may have had an ulterior motive for his opinions," argues Master Korin. "We should examine it more closely. What game was he playing?"

"We can't avoid the issue of Spirit's Bane for long," warns Lady Deliah. "The problem remains. We don't know how to disarm it, and we can't afford to have Mina wandering around Earth with a weapon that powerful that we don't understand."

"We can't hold her prisoner either," Master Blaz notes.

As the argument looks like it'll circle around again, Lady A. holds up her hands to halt the discussion.

"Each of us wants the same thing. We want to know about Spirit's Bane, and we want Mina to be safe. Holding her in the Heavens would be painful. It's out of the question." Lady A. pauses to let Master Korin and Lady Deliah know she won't budge on that point. "And she will not tolerate overt guards."

I agree with that assessment.

"What choice do we have?" Master Korin demands.

"I believe Master Blaz is right." Lady A. speaks slowly, almost absently. "We complete the commission and give her meaningful tasks to do that can be accomplished without traveling to the Heavens. If we pick the right tasks, we may even have an excuse to send others to help her." Her gaze fixes upon me. "Do you think she'll find the plan acceptable?"

"Yes, ma'am," I answer, knowing Mina would come around to the idea after a long argument. "May I work with her?"

Lady A.'s answer is contained in her sad smile. She knew that question would come. Every Council member is shaking his or her head.

"You will have your own missions," Master Blaz promises. "But we cannot allow you to work closely with Mina until we know more. You're both valuable targets for demons right now."

"But we're more powerful together," I protest, trying not to whine.

"It's only temporary," Lady A. says, attempting to soothe me. "Many angels will be assigned to the investigation into the pendant's origins and limitations. We will have answers soon."

Mina appears by my side.

"You're back!" I exclaim. I ask a few questions silently and receive a plea for patience.

She must have been keeping track of the conversation through me, for she jumps right in without missing a beat.

"I find your plan acceptable," Mina informs Lady A. and the rest of the Council of Light. She seems calmer and more confident than before. "But I do not want other Guardians shifted away from their normal duties on my account. I will check in often, but I am more capable of defending myself than most humans. Let them keep their protection."

"Your concerns are noted, Mina," Lady A. begins. She pauses to gather her thoughts before going on. "However, we must face the prospect that this thing you wear holds wider implications."

Master Blaz picks up the explanation.

"If it lives up to its potential, Spirit's Bane could decimate our ranks. I don't have to tell you what that would do to our ability to protect the human race from the Rebel's forces."

I'm glad the message is delivered by Master Blaz.

Mina weighs her master's words carefully. She holds his gaze for several long seconds before lowering her eyes to the cavern floor.

"What do you require of me?" The formality in her question acknowledges the change in their relationship. Her voice is soft and steady, though I sense she's pained by this new distance between herself and Master Blaz.

"Nothing for now," he answers. "But there may be tests to run in the future. We must find a way to safely free you from the weapon."

Mina's mouth opens to respond, but she shuts her lips and nods curtly. A subtle shift in her emotions tells me she's holding something back. Spirit's Bane flares within her, protesting its imprisonment. A slight warming in the center of my chest echoes what must feel like a hot knife buried inside Mina. She covers for the pain well, but it tells me a powerful truth.

She's choosing this.

Master Blaz must pick up on something in her, for understanding suddenly enters his expression.

"You don't have to do this," he tells Mina.

Lady A., Master Korin, Master Micah, and Lady Deliah bounce their gazes between my friend and Master Blaz. Master Titus studies the cavern floor.

"I'm missing something," Lady A. mutters.

Master Blaz looks at Lady A. coolly.

"We were mistaken in assuming Spirit's Bane must remain in Mina."

"Is this true?" Lady A.'s eyes find Mina's and hold.

"It is," Mina answers reluctantly.

"Why would you hold on to something that pains you?" Lady Deliah wonders, sounding genuinely mystified.

"I don't know who I can trust," Mina answers.

The honesty humbles everyone in the room, including me.

"Give us the medallion." Master Korin sounds absolutely serious. "We can protect it better than you can."

Lady A. chuckles at the statement.

"Kor, we're not on steady ground where judgments are concerned today. Who knows how long that demon walked among us?" Lady A. addresses her colleague but keeps her attention on Mina. "No, she is right. We can't be trusted with this task."

"She has no experience!" exclaims Lady Deliah. "She's barely more than a child."

"She has more raw power than most," Master Blaz counters.

"*She's* also standing right here," Mina says with a sigh. "I am no more special than any being created by our Glorious King, but I am willing to walk this path wherever it may lead."

"Are you frightened?" asks Lady Deliah, picking up on the tremor in Mina's voice.

I almost burst out laughing at the ridiculousness of the question. Of course, she's scared. She'd be a fool not to fear. For no fault of her own—or mine for that matter—the Rebel chose to act against us. One could not make a more powerful enemy.

"I am afraid of many things, but the recent events have revealed much about the Rebel," Mina says. "He grows increasingly desperate. I want to be there when he falls, and in the meantime, my efforts will go to thwarting him at every turn. If that involves bearing Spirit's Bane for a while longer, I will do it." She shrugs like it's not a big deal.

"Your bravery is noteworthy, but unnecessary," Lady Deliah insists. "If you don't trust us, we'll find an independent party appointed by the King to oversee the studies into the medallion."

"How do you know it's a medallion?" I ask, focusing exclusively on Lady Deliah.

She waves off my suspicions.

"It was in Mina's report," she answers.

I look to my friend for confirmation and get it in the form of a quick half-smile and a nod.

"Are we in agreement?" Lady A.'s attention rests for two seconds on each Council member.

She receives several murmurs of assent.

"Good. Master Blaz, would you like to do the honors?" Lady A. summons her spirit sword, raises it high, and levels it at Mina and me.

Master Blaz and the rest of the Council repeat her motions.

"Please kneel," instructs Master Blaz.

Mina and I drop to our knees, essentially sitting on our heels, backs held straight and eyes facing forward.

"Allister Knight and Mina Nadir, we the members of this Council of Light recognize you as Guardians with all the rights, privileges, duties, and obligations that such a position entails. From this day forward, you are called to honor the Glorious King through your service to the Chosen among his people, both human and angelic in nature. If you accept these commissions, say 'we do.'"

"We do."

"Congratulations and welcome to the Order," says Master Blaz. "You may rise. There is much work to do. Prepare your hearts and minds for the trials to come."

Epilogue:
Ambassador

Case Report #: MN-114
Case Agent: Master Blaz
Guardian: Mina Nadir

After our commission, the discussion turns to more practical details, but I have difficulty concentrating. Allister does not ask what brought me back, but I know he's curious. When I left, I had no intention of returning for days or even weeks, but just outside the cave system, I met our Glorious King. I did not recognize him at first because he disguised himself as a man. However, no normal person would be this far from civilization. He told me there would be time for questions later but I should return to the meeting. I obeyed. One does not ignore a request from the King lightly.

At the earliest opportunity, I ask permission to be excused. When the Council members grant me leave, I wave to Allister and microjump to the same spot I ended up at before. A new day has dawned and the sun hangs high in the sky, telling me much time has passed.

The King stands almost exactly where I left him. I look around, expecting to find guards or attendants, but we are alone. I stay still, unsure of the protocol here. Knowing of my discomfort, he smiles and waves me forward.

"Come." The word is an invitation, not an order. "You have many questions for me. I am here now, and I will answer what I can. But not all mysteries are meant to be revealed in this present age."

I close the space between us and kneel before my King, yet the questions I long to voice get stuck somewhere between my heart and my head. I consider turning to spirit so I can sense more of his presence, but I wish to avoid the distraction of pain right now. Deep peace sweeps over me, pushing back fears and opening a way for tears. I struggle to hold them back, but the King comes to me and wipes the tears away with his thumbs. His warm hazel eyes embrace me.

"You wish to know why you were chosen to carry this burden."

I nod, then shake my head, and shrug. Heat floods my face.

"Why does it exist?" I ask. "Why do you allow it?"

His smile widens.

"You really mean 'why do I allow the Rebel to roam about at will.'"

The statement rings true.

"He mocks you and seeks to destroy the things you hold dear, yet he lives only by the grace of your patience. Why don't you end him?"

My knees begin to ache. He draws me up to a standing position, hands still resting on my shoulders.

"Dear child, have you ever seen a gardener tending to weeds among her flowers?" Even as the Glorious King asks the question, he shows me a vivid mental picture of someone carefully plucking weeds out one by one.

"I have now," I answer.

"There are harsh chemical sprays the gardener could use, but she chooses not to because they cannot distinguish between flower and weed. Do you understand why I tell you these things?"

"The Rebel is the weed," I say, "but who are the flowers?"

"You must search for them." There's a new, passion sparkling in his eyes. "Find my people, nurture them, and guide them home." His expression turns serious, pained even. "I do not wish any of them to perish, but the choice is still yours. I can remove Spirit's Bane from you and restore every part it damaged, but I cannot destroy it without also harming you."

"What will become of it once it's removed?" I wonder.

"It will eventually fall to another either now or in the future, and that person, whoever they are, will face the same decision you do now. Thus, the cycle continues."

"Is there a way to safely destroy Spirit's Bane?" I ask, hoping for a straightforward answer.

"Everything that has been made can be unmade, but the price must first be established and then paid," the King explains. His grip tightens slightly. "Mina, I have chosen you for this task because your Gifts are perfectly suited for dealing with the ill effects of the weapon. I can pass the responsibility on to another if you wish, but I believe you can do this."

Having the Council of Light say similar things could hardly compare to the King telling me to bear up under the burden. I could not begin to fathom His reasons for running the universe as he does, but I could at least agree to do my part in saving the lost.

"I am who I am because you have made me this way. I am your servant." I don't know why I can't give him a simple word of agreement. The statement feels cold and distant.

The King pulls me into a tight hug, cradling my head with a hand.

"You were always more than a servant. You are my beloved daughter and honored ambassador to the people you'll meet in this land. I love you not because of what you can do for me but simply because you are you." The King kisses the top of my head and pulls me out to arm's length. "Remember these words in good times and in bad. When you feel your strength fading, think of me and let my strength renew you."

I close my eyes to absorb the blessing. The warmth of his hands upon my arms lingers, but I know he is gone.

When I finally open my eyes, I see Allister standing a respectful distance away. He looks nervous. I wave him over, and after a brief hesitation, he microjumps to my side.

"The Council doesn't think we should be alone together." Allister's trying to explain the hesitation.

"What do they think's going to happen?" I ask, just to

watch him squirm.

"Mina." He fills my name with frustration. This is far worse than the awkwardness that sprang up when we started our training along different paths. Grabbing my hand, Allister cradles it between his palms. "This isn't fair."

"We were never promised fair," I remind my friend. My throat feels raw.

"Where will you go?" Allister asks.

"I'm sure I'll be shown the way when I need to know," I answer, infusing more confidence into my tone than I'm actually feeling.

"I should go with you!" he declares.

"It's a little early in your career to be defying the Council," I remark. "Wait at least a week."

He glares, hurt by my terrible attempt at levity.

I sigh and pull him into a hug.

"Don't make this harder than it needs to be," I plead. "We'll find a way to beat this thing."

At first, Allister stands rigid like a stone statue, but slowly, the life returns.

"The Kindred Spirit Bond will always connect us, no matter what distance lays between us. If you need me, use it, and I'll find you." Allister forces a smile. "I expect to hear from you often. I want regular updates on human life."

"You'll be too busy playing hero to listen to what I ate for dinner," I say. A small pang of jealousy springs up, but it dies quickly. His life won't exactly be as normal as we'd planned growing up. The Rebel targeted him as well and would not let him rest for long. "Be careful."

"What could possibly go wrong?" Allister laughs as I punch him in the arm.

"Everything."

A cleared throat draws our attention to the small gathering approaching from behind me. It's the Council members plus Reena.

"Allister, it's time to go," Mistress Clarimond calls. "Reena will see her to the next destination. It's best you don't know what that is."

He shoots me a panicked look. His thoughts are too

jumbled to follow.

I hug him one more time before backing up a step.

"Go rescue cats or something. I'll just be here contemplating world domination."

"Channeling me doesn't suit you," he complains.

"Now you know how I've felt for the last few years." My throat tries to close as a sudden sob gets stuck there.

"Not even close, but we'll have lots more years to make up for that," Allister says optimistically. He steps close and lowers his voice. "If you forget me, I'll come back to haunt you."

"Please do," I say, surprised at how much I mean that. I don't want to get him into trouble with the Council, but the loneliness is already creeping in.

The Heavens feel so far away, and the person who most reminds me of home is about to disappear for an untold time.

Am I an exile or an ambassador? Either way, I cannot dwell in the past. The only way home is through the destruction of Satan's cruel invention. Spirit's Bane flares painfully within me as if it knows I mean it harm. Earth is not my true country, but I must stay here for a while. I might as well make the best of it.

"Are you ready?" asks Reena.

"Not right now, but I will be," I say, choosing to interpret her question with a deeper meaning.

THE END

Thank You for Reading

Each book is a labor of love that I enjoy sharing with people.

Please visit my website: **www.juliecgilbert.com** to find a link to the current free works. It's my goal to set individual ebooks free, but if you still wish to show support, there are combination books and other formats to purchase. The audiobooks have fantastic narrators, and there is something special about paperbacks.

Join the Facebook group "Julie C. Gilbert's Special Agents" for monthly book discussions and giveaways.
I would love to connect via email:
devyaschildren@gmail.com
juliecgilbert5steps@gmail.com

Other Contacts:
www.facebook.com/JulieCGilbert2013
www.instagram.com/juliecgilbert_writer/
https://twitter.com/authorgilbert
www.bookbub.com/authors/julie-c-gilbert

Love Science Fiction or Mystery?

Choose your adventure!

Visit: **http://www.juliecgilbert.com/**

For details on getting
Ashlynn's Dreams and The Kiverson Case
absolutely free